PRAISE FOR NANCY THAYER

"In this touching summer read, forgiveness benefits both the person bestowing it and the recipient."
—*Kirkus Reviews*, on *Island Girls*

"Nancy Thayer is the queen of beach books. . . . All [these characters] are involved in life-changing choices, with all the heart-wrenching decisions such moments demand." —*The Star-Ledger*, on *Summer Breeze*

"Readers will delight in these women's struggles to reconcile their desires and dreams with the cards they've been dealt." —*Publishers Weekly*, on *Summer Breeze*

"Filled with intrigue and romance, this novel shows how women's unique bonds can survive even the most tempestuous times." —*Woman's Day*, on *Summer Breeze*

"This beautifully written novel examines the lives of three women who have recently become neighbors. With unflinching honesty and perspective, the story delves into life-changing decisions that most women can relate to. The characters are wonderful, and the voice and pace of the story pull the reader in right from the start." —*Romantic Times*, on *Summer Breeze*

ISLAND GIRLS

BY NANCY THAYER

A Nantucket Wedding
Secrets in Summer
The Island House
A Very Nantucket Christmas
The Guest Cottage
An Island Christmas
Nantucket Sisters
A Nantucket Christmas
Island Girls
Summer Breeze
Heat Wave
Beachcombers
Summer House
Moon Shell Beach
The Hot Flash Club Chills Out
Hot Flash Holidays
The Hot Flash Club Strikes Again
The Hot Flash Club
Custody
Between Husbands and Friends
An Act of Love
Belonging
Family Secrets
Everlasting
My Dearest Friend
Spirit Lost
Morning
Nell
Bodies and Souls
Three Women at the Water's Edge
Stepping

ISLAND GIRLS

a novel

Nancy Thayer

Ballantine Books • New York

2018 Ballantine Books Mass Market Edition

Copyright © 2013 by Nancy Thayer
Excerpt from *A Nantucket Wedding* by Nancy Thayer copyright © 2018 by Nancy Thayer

Published in the United States by Ballantine Books, an imprint of Random House, a division of Penguin Random House LLC, New York.

BALLANTINE and the HOUSE colophon are registered trademarks of Penguin Random House LLC.

Originally published in hardcover in the United States by Ballantine Books, an imprint of Random House, a division of Penguin Random House LLC, in 2013.

ISBN 978-0-525-61835-5
Ebook ISBN 978-0-345-53883-3

Cover design: Eileen Carey
Cover images: Ralf Schultheiss/Corbis/Getty Images (girls), Alex Bramwell/Getty Images (umbrella)

Printed in the United States of America

randomhousebooks.com

9 8 7 6 5 4 3 2 1

Ballantine Books mass market edition: July 2018

For Linda Marrow

ACKNOWLEDGMENTS

I am fortunate and extremely grateful to work with the superlative team at Ballantine. I send my sincere thanks to my editor, the peerless Linda Marrow, and to Libby McGuire, Gina Centrello, Junessa Viloria, Dana Isaacson, Kim Hovey, Quinne Rogers, Alison Masciovecchio, Mark LaFlaur, and Penelope Haynes.

My gratitude once again goes out to the true blue island girl Meg Ruley, my excellent agent. Also I thank Peggy Gordijn, Christina Hogrebe, and everyone at the Jane Rotrosen Agency.

Finally, a brief explanation: I realize that in my novels women meet wonderful men on Nantucket. Honestly, this is simply a matter of fiction imitating fact. Thirty years ago I came to Nantucket to visit a friend. She introduced me to Charley Walters. We've been married for more than twenty-eight years, some of them relatively challenging, pun intended. Charley is my constant inspiration for all good men. He is my companion, my champion, my cavalier, and the steady center of my soul. Thank you, Charley.

Maybe everyone should be an island girl, at least once.

ISLAND GIRLS

ONE

Arden's half-hour television show for Channel Six, a local Boston station, was called *Simplify This*, which Arden privately knew was a ridiculous title because, really, nothing in life was simple.

She couldn't remember when she'd last had a vacation, and even when she had a weekend off, she worked, tapping away at her laptop or considering DVDs prospective entrants had sent her, or reviewing call sheets or expenses. Even watching television was work because she recorded and savagely studied competing shows, comparing theirs to hers, searching for what she was missing, what she could improve. Reading books and magazines: same thing. Even exercise was work for Arden because she had to keep her thirty-four-year-old body in shape for the merciless cameras that made everyone's butt look ten inches wider and ten pounds heavier. Same with having her nails and her hair done. She was fairly certain she worked when she slept.

Simplify This expressed her hard-won life's motto: to simplify your life, to stuff useless old family heirlooms like grandmothers' tea sets and framed photos of relatives so distant you couldn't remember their names into neat cardboard boxes, tidily labeled and piled in the attic or basement, or given away to the secondhand shops so you could claim a tax deduction. As you did this, you vanquished the ghosts of the past, the should-haves and could-haves, the expectations of parents, the dreams of childhood. Then your present life was clear and spacious, facing forward, not back.

Arden had spent her adult years simplifying. She had created a television show and her own life's battle cry out of the desire to simplify her odd, complicated family (if you could even call it that), which was like a jigsaw puzzle with the pieces scattered by the winds.

Today she parked her posh little Saab convertible in her reserved spot in the station's lot, whipped through the glass doors, nodded to the security guard, and strode down the corridor to her private lair. She unlocked it, stepped inside, leaned against the door, and kicked off her high heels.

It was a hot day for early May. Arden stripped off her suit jacket and unzipped her tight skirt. She collapsed in the wonderfully padded chair behind her desk, put her feet up, and listened to her voice mails.

Messages: The dry cleaner said the stain wouldn't come out of the lavender silk dress. The masseuse reminded her she'd changed the time of her appointment. Marion Cleveland understood that all entries to Arden's *wonderful* show should be sent by mail with a DVD, but

Marion was a *close personal friend* of Ernest Hilton, the program director of Channel Six, and so Marion thought Arden wouldn't mind Marion phoning directly because Marion's house would be *perfect* for *Simplify This*.

Four forceful thuds sounded at her door, and before she could speak, Ernest Hilton barged in, followed by a tiny wide-eyed brunette.

"Ernest." Arden swung her legs off her desk and straightened in her chair, yanking her shirt down over the undone zipper of her skirt.

"Arden." Ernest hauled a chair from the corner of the room, moved the stack of folders off it onto the only empty space on Arden's desk, and set it next to the visitor's chair facing Arden. He gestured to the size zero to sit.

I'm not going to like this, Arden thought. She knew Ernest well enough after six years of working with him. He was fifty, jovial, and fat, and he never appeared in front of a camera.

"I'd like you to meet Zoey Anderson."

Arden smiled. "Hi, Zoey." The young woman was dazzling, with enormous dark eyes and long dark hair clipped loosely to the back of her head. Her dress was a simple sleeveless sheath of linen, at least two sizes smaller than what Arden wore, and Arden was slim.

"So here's the deal," Ernest continued, after Zoey gave a brief smile. "Channel Six has been bought out. New management. Now new show." He held up his hands and spread them in a banner. "*Simplify This from A to Z.* Get it? From Arden to Zoey."

Arden's heart turned to ice.

"What the numbers are telling us, see, Arden, is that we're not getting any of the younger demographic. You've captured the marrieds, the empty nesters, the first new homes in the suburbs, but no one under thirty watches *ST*."

"I wouldn't say *no one*," Arden objected.

"Time to move on, any old hoo." Ernest slapped his hands on his mammoth thighs. "Things get old fast. Gotta change."

"*ST* has excellent ratings," Arden reminded him. "The ratings show—"

"Of course, of course," Ernest interrupted. "But they could be even better, and they will be once we've got Zoey on board. She can work with the under thirties. Who needs help simplifying more than they do? They live in lofts, share apartments, don't know how to do their taxes or keep records, trip over all the wires for adapters for their thousands of devices. . . ."

Zoey spoke up for the first time. Her voice was high pitched and girly girl. "One week I'll do the youngies, and the next week you can do the oldies." Arden was surprised Zoey didn't put her finger in her dimpled chin.

The youngies, Arden thought, inwardly moaning. *The oldies.*

Another tap at the door. Once again it opened before Arden could speak. Sandra, her secretary, stuck her head in.

"Sorry, Arden, but you've got an emergency phone call."

Arden stared. She had no husband, no children. She

didn't even own a pet. "Thanks, Sandra." She nodded toward Ernest. "Excuse me, I'd better take this."

Her mother spoke. "Arden? Honey?" Her voice sounded different. It didn't crack with its usual take-charge, *You know I've found the perfect house for you*, Boston real estate agent's pizzazz.

"Mom? Are you okay?"

"I'm fine, darling. But, Arden, . . . your father died."

"My father died," Arden repeated in robot tones, trying to make the words compute.

"Oh, that's so sad." Across from her, Zoey's enormous eyes filled with real tears.

"He died on the island," Nora continued. "I've spoken with Cyndi and Justine. The funeral will be on Monday."

"Mom, can I call you back?" Arden asked. "I've got people in the office. I need just a minute. . . ."

Her mother clicked off.

"I have to go to Nantucket," Arden reported in a stunned monotone. "My father died. The funeral is Monday."

Ernest nodded lugubriously and got to his feet. "Terrible thing, terrible thing," he intoned, although for all he knew, Arden's father could have been an ax murderer. "Take all the time you want, Arden. In fact, you've got a lot of vacation due you. Why not take a month. Or two. Or three? I'm sure Zoey can handle it. The timing is just right; she can start her part of the series, and then in the fall we can segue you back in."

Arden sat dumbfounded, staring at her boss and his new, *young*, discovery. She knew how Ernest worked. With some degree of accuracy, she could interpret his every mouth crimp or eyebrow lift. Terror struck: Was she losing control of her own show?

That would be a horrible thing, a betrayal of her and the years she'd put into *Simplify This*, and into this station, but as Arden sat quietly smoldering, there stood little Zoey with her eyes full of tears.

Lucky little Zoey, who wept when someone's father died. Obviously, Zoey's father had never abandoned her and her mother.

Arden could imagine Zoey's life clearly: parents who adored each other and never divorced, brothers and sisters who were *real* siblings, a father who was a strong disciplinarian but fair, a mother who attended the school plays where Zoey had the leading role.

Nothing like Arden's mess of a life. Or like Arden's oh-so-charming disaster of a father.

She had always assumed she would somehow get more of him later. My God, Rory Randall was only sixty and in good health. He golfed, he played tennis, he swam! How could he be dead? Arden still had so much to say to him, so many difficulties needed to be discussed and settled—*he* had so much to say to her, she knew he did, she knew! She was his *first* daughter, his first child. Because of that, she was special! Her mother had made a mistake, someone had gotten their information tangled; Rory Randall might be ill, perhaps in the hospital with a minor heart attack, but not dead.

Emotions shifted within her like fractures in the earth, warning of a tidal wave surging her way. Arden reminded herself she was a pro. Some people in the station considered her practically a goddess; she was gorgeous, clever, energetic, invincible. If she allowed herself to display anything except expertise bordering on disdain, everyone in the station from the janitor to the CEO would think she'd broken down because of Zoey's arrival. It wouldn't matter that Arden's father had died. Everyone knew Arden's only love was her work.

She would not humiliate herself.

"I'll pencil in another meeting for next Wednesday," Arden said decisively. "I've got to leave now."

"Of course." Ernest and Zoey went out, closing the door respectfully behind them.

Arden zipped up her skirt, then grabbed her purse and jacket. She slipped her feet back into her murderous high heels and trotted out of her office to her secretary's desk.

"Sandra, I've got to go to Nantucket for a week. My father died. You can reach me by cell."

"Oh," Sandra began, "I'm so sorry—"

But Arden didn't trust Sandra. She knew the moment she was out of the building, Sandra would be gossiping about her with the other employees and interns. Really, there was no one you could trust.

Atop those impossible heels, she stalked, head high, out of the station. She got into her car, fastened her seat belt, and drove away. She didn't allow herself to cry.

TWO

Meg Randall sat in her ancient Volvo tapping her fingers impatiently on the steering wheel as she waited for the car ferry to bump into its place in the pier so the vehicles could be unloaded. She considered herself one of the most moderate, gentle, easygoing women she knew, but at this moment she felt as impatient as Secretariat stalled behind the starting gate.

The steamship *Eagle* rumbled, shuddered, and groaned into its berth. Chains clanked as the dockworkers raised the ramp into place, jumped aboard, and waved the cars off. With a flash of triumph, Meg drove onto Nantucket.

She was here before Arden!

It had been years since she'd been on the island. She'd never been old enough to drive here before, but her car carried her with perfect assurance down Steamboat Wharf, through the cobblestone grid of town, and along the winding narrow lane of Lily Street, into the driveway of her father's house.

She stepped out into the sunshine and looked around. The street, with its houses clustered closely together, its narrow brick sidewalk, and tidy trimmed privet hedges, lay in timeless peace beneath the morning sun. It was very quiet.

Meg stretched. She had actually arrived before Arden, and she passionately wanted to have first choice of bedroom. That was why she'd hardly slept last night, and had left Boston before six a.m. to make the nine thirty ferry from Hyannis. Meg was going to claim the back bedroom overlooking the yards, lawns, and rooftops of the other houses in the village.

She beeped her station wagon locked, reached into her pocket, and took out the small key to the front door. It lay in her hand like an icon, like a treasure. It *was* a treasure. She had never had a key to this house before. Even though she had lived here, she had never belonged.

White clapboard, three stories high, with a blue front door sporting a bronze mermaid door knocker, the house was similar to the others in the neighborhood. The driveway next to the house was short, ending at a privet hedge centered by a rose-covered arbor. Already some of the pale roses were blooming. On either side of the front door, blue hydrangeas blossomed, and pink impatiens spilled from the white window boxes.

A storybook house. A house with many stories.

Meg went up the eight steps to the small porch, took a deep breath, and opened the door.

Cleaners had been in; she smelled lemon polish and soap. Ignoring the first floor, she took the stairs to the second floor two at a time. Like all old Nantucket houses, this one rambled oddly around, with rooms that had fire-places or closets built in at odd angles. But the path to the bedroom, *her* bedroom, was embroidered into her memory like silk thread on muslin.

Here it was, at the back, with the morning glory wallpaper and two walls of windows gleaming with light. An old-fashioned three-quarter mattress lay on a spool bed, covered with soft old cotton sheets and a patchwork quilt in shades of rose, lemon, and azure, echoing the colors in the hand-hooked rug covering most of the satiny old pine floor. An enormous pine dresser stood against one wall, still adorned with the posy-dotted dresser scarf that had been there when Meg was a child. This room had no closets, only hooks for clothes, but that had never mattered to Meg. She had cherished the room because of the slightly warped, ink-stained wooden desk and creaking cane-bottom chair placed against the back window, where she could sit and write or contemplate the starry sky and dream.

When she was a girl, for a year this had been her bedroom. Then Arden got into one of her jealous snits, claiming that since she was the oldest, she got first dibs. Meg had to take the side bedroom, which should have delighted her. It was twice as large as the odd back bedroom, and actually decorated. The theme was mermaids, and Meg's mother, Cyndi, who at the time had been the current Mrs. Randall, had gone a bit wild, draping the windows with mermaid curtains, covering the twin beds with mermaid sheets and comforters, softening the floor with a thick Claire Murray mermaid rug. Even the bedside lamps were held up by mermaids. It should have been a young girl's paradise.

It just made Meg cranky. She wouldn't give her older, snotty half sister Arden the satisfaction of showing she preferred the back room, and she *really* wouldn't beseech Arden to exchange rooms with her. She just accepted it. She was used to acceptance as a way of life.

Then their father married Justine and adopted Jenny, and Meg got to spend one blissful summer there. The next summer was when what Arden and Meg called The Exile began. After Justine took over, Meg and Arden didn't get invited to spend any time at all at their father's house, not one summer month, not one summer day.

But that was then, and this was now, a new stage in life, a new day. Years had passed.

Meg would pretend to be selfless, thoughtful, taking the small back bedroom, allowing Arden one of the big front rooms. Jenny had the other front bedroom, years ago done up in pinks and greens.

She needed to unpack quickly, before anyone else got here. She needed to spread her belongings out all over the room, claiming her territory.

She clattered down the stairs and out the front door to the car. She regarded the number of cardboard boxes filling the open hatch, took a deep breath, reached in, and hefted the first heavy box.

Most of what she'd brought to the island was either books or notes or steno pads filled with research. In spite of the terrifying fact that she'd have to spend three months living with the two women who disliked her most in the world, Meg was thrilled to be here, because at last she'd be able to focus completely and solely on writing her book.

Because it was the last day of May, the humid heat of island summers had not yet arrived. Still, after Meg made a few trips up and down the steps carrying the boxes, her clothes were damp with sweat. She sank down on the top step of the stoop to catch her breath and gather her long, wild strawberry-blonde curls into a clump high on her head. The cool air on her neck felt sensational.

A soft breeze drifted over her skin, tickling her slightly, making her senses stir in the most pleasurable way. Leaning back on her elbows, she sighed deeply, closed her eyes, and breathed in the salty island air.

And allowed herself to think of Liam.

She'd been in her cramped office in the liberal arts building of Sudbury Community College, bowed over her desk with a pile of English composition exams. Occasionally she tilted her head to face the ceiling and relieve her neck and shoulders. She sometimes stood up and loosened her stiff back with some light exercises, knee bends, waist bends, arm swings. But mostly she worked steadily, not allowing herself to look out her window at the green lawn where students lolled in the warm sunshine.

Meg had been happy. Okay, if not exactly *happy*, she'd been content. She enjoyed her work; was amused, challenged, and annoyed by her students; and spent a lot of time wondering whether the semicolon and colon would fairly soon disappear from common usage, or at least blur and blend. In the Twitter age, punctuation was an endangered species.

So, she prized her work. But she missed having a love life. She was afraid she'd end up like the head of the department, Eleanor Littleton, PhD, a charming if rather homely single woman whose entire world revolved around the English department and her two Yorkshire terriers.

Meg's desk was of battered metal with three drawers down each side and a shallow drawer in the middle where she kept pens, rubber bands, scissors, breath mints, and Scotch tape. Its top was layered with blue books, exams, and e-mails she'd printed out because she got tired of staring at her computer screen. She sat on a basic government-issue secretary's chair with a squeaking back that provided little support. She kept calling maintenance about it; they kept promising to bring her a better chair.

"Big fat liars," she muttered.

"Who?"

Meg didn't have to look up to identify the man standing in her open office door. She knew Liam's voice all too well. That was a pleasure and a problem.

Liam Larson. Liam Larson, PhD. Professor Larson, full professor of English, author of the well-received *Nineteenth-Century American Poets*, a poet himself, published in several online and university reviews. Liam Larson, tall, fair, Camelot handsome, and five years younger than Meg. The first time she'd seen him walk down the hall, she'd said under her breath, "Oh, come on. *Really?*"

Probably five pounds lighter than Meg, too. At twenty-six, Liam was six three and as slender as a marathon runner. At thirty-one, Meg was five four, and while no one would call her fat, they might say—men had said—that she had a fine full figure. A big bust, wide hips, all of it highlighted by her white skin. She let her pale red hair grow past her shoulders and often wore it loose, trying to make her hair seem equal in volume to the rest of her body. She camouflaged her shape with khaki slacks and baggy skirts, corduroy jackets, tailored shirts buttoned to the neck. In the summer, she wore shapeless tunics. If she was ever going to get tenure at this college, she had to appear professional. Academic.

Liam looked academic and sexy at the same time. Chinos, white shirt with the sleeves rolled up, blue tie to set off his blue eyes.

Meg smiled at him. Leaning back in her chair, she stretched her arms and yawned. "The maintenance men," she explained. "They've been promising to bring me a decent chair for two weeks."

"Let me take a look."

Before she could object, Liam was in her space, filling up her incredibly small office. He squatted behind her chair and fiddled with the knob, trying to tighten it. His breath stirred her hair. His knuckles brushed her shoulders.

Please don't say I'm too big for this chair, Meg prayed silently. She knew the chair was too small for her; it was too small for almost anyone. She guessed the college ordered these chairs because they were cheap or had been discarded by some other university system.

"This thing is hopeless," Liam decided. Standing up,

he leaned over Meg and picked up her phone. He hit a few numbers. "Maintenance? Professor Liam Larson here in LB20. I need a new desk chair. This one's broken. Immediately. Thank you."

Hanging up the phone, he grinned at Meg. "The word *professor* has got to be good for something."

"You could have said Dr. Larson," Meg told him.

"Nah. Then I'd have to take out his appendix." Liam pushed a stack of papers out of the way and slid his slender butt onto Meg's desk. His long legs dangled down in front of her three drawers.

Meg shoved her chair away from the desk. And Liam. "Thank you."

"We'll see if anything happens." Liam looked down at her piles of work. "Exams?"

"Always."

"Only three more weeks till end of semester. What are you doing this summer?"

Meg rubbed the back of her neck. "I'm going to work on my Alcott book. I'm determined to finish it."

"Seriously? You're not teaching summer school? But you're the best teacher we've got. The students will be devastated."

Meg rolled her eyes in reaction to his compliment, but she knew he meant what he said. She was a favorite of the students, and Liam admired her for it. "Liam, I've scrimped for a year to save enough money to live on for three months. I'll subsist on cereal and water. No movies. No frills. No clothes. Just work."

A lopsided smile crossed his face. "No clothes? How about letting me come be your editorial assistant?"

Meg felt herself blush. "I mean I won't buy any new clothes. Austerity is the rule for the summer."

Liam lowered his eyelids into a bedroom eyes stare. She hated when he did it; it made her all shivery and silly feeling. "I'd better plan to take you out to dinner at least once a week. For the sake of the college. We don't want our professors dying of starvation."

Her resolve almost melted in the warmth of his smile. She reminded herself that Liam was five years younger than she was—significant years, impetuous, impulsive, romantic years, when you were allowed to make mistakes. That Liam was intellectually, academically mature was obvious. He'd skipped grades in elementary school and high school, sped through his BA and MA, won his PhD, and published his book of poems to great acclaim by the tender age of twenty-six. But emotional maturity was different, and brilliant scholars were often emotionally stunted.

She could tell he had a crush on her. True, they were the best of friends and they both were dedicated teachers. They read each other's essays in draft form and expertly critiqued each other. But Meg couldn't allow it to go any further. Liam was so handsome—he was almost beautiful. It would be easy to allow herself to respond to him. That would lead her, she was certain, to heartbreak.

Her phone rang. Literally saved by the bell. She snatched it up.

"Meg? Sweetheart, it's Mommy."

Meg straightened in her chair, alerted by her mother's voice. "Are you okay, Mom?"

"Meggie, I'm fine. Listen, though, I have to tell you

something. It's a hard thing to say. Meggie, your father died."

Seated on the front steps of the house on Lily Street, Meg blinked away the memory of her mother's phone call. Since that day, time had accordioned into a blur of action: Packing for the island. The funeral. The reading of the will in Frank Boyd's office and her father's bizarre and manipulative last letter, so typical of Rory Randall, a lightning bolt from the hand of the all-powerful Zeus who even after his death arranged the lives of his daughters, without, as usual, asking their opinions, and especially without, *as usual*, being there to respond to the emotional fallout.

All right, Meg couldn't control it, but she could contain it. She could use it. She needed three months to work on her book. Now she had them, and in a historic house on a magical island. That her half sister and stepsister were going to share the house did not mean this would be hell on earth. She would be polite but aloof. She would be poised, dignified, restrained. So would Arden and Jenny. The three of them were adults, after all.

THREE

As a child, Jenny had been sad not to have a father. She hadn't been embarrassed, because several other kids at school didn't have fathers, or had fathers who lived far away and never visited. But she minded not having even a photograph of her father. Her mother would say only that she didn't know who Jenny's father was, and that was that. For years as a little girl, Jenny daydreamed about meeting her father someday. Her mother had such glossy black hair, and Jenny's was dramatically black, too. She wondered if her father's hair was also black, like a pirate's or a Gypsy's.

When she was ten, her mother married Rory Randall. He legally adopted Jenny, and he loved her as much, he promised, as he loved his biological daughters, Meg and Arden. He made her mother happy at last, which relieved and thrilled Jenny, and as the years went by, she didn't wonder about her "real" father so much. For long stretches of time, she never thought about him at all.

She did mind that Rory Randall had red hair and so did his first two daughters, while Jenny's was black. So when the three were together with their father, everyone assumed that Arden and Meg were Rory's daughters, which, of course, they were. Jenny was his daughter, too, his *chosen* daughter. If she could have worn a sign on her chest stating that she was Rory Randall's daughter, she would have. It was wonderful to have a father.

Having sisters had been wonderful, too—for a while. Jenny was exactly Meg's age, three years younger than Arden. The first year of their life together was chaotic, with Arden and Meg living mostly at their mothers' but staying at the Nantucket house for the summer.

The second year had been the year of The Exile, and since then, although they saw one another, Arden and Meg had not accepted Jenny as a real sister.

Well, they would have to now.

They had to live with her for three entire months in the same house. As if they were family.

Jenny had seen Arden's and Meg's faces when the lawyer read their father's letter. Meg had gone white. Arden's lips had thinned in anger. Then Arden and Meg looked at each other and something passed between the two of them, an unspoken message they did not even think to share with Jenny.

It was partly her mother's fault, Jenny knew. She could understand why Justine told Rory the other two girls were not allowed to come to the summer house anymore, and back then, when she was eleven years old, she'd been smugly, foolishly glad. That made Rory all hers. He had chosen her, he had adopted her, and then, as if in a fairy tale, the stepsisters had been whisked out of sight, out of mind. She hadn't cared about Meg and Arden's feelings.

Well, Jenny had paid for her mother's decision and for her own childish sense of triumph. Twenty years had passed, and she'd been raised as an only child. During those years, their father did "get his girls all together" from time to time in Boston, taking the three of them out to lavish meals in la-di-da restaurants or treating them to *The Nutcracker* ballet at Christmas. But even though, in front of their father or any of their mothers, the three behaved politely, Jenny had no doubt Arden and Meg hated her.

Jenny was hoping they'd do better this summer. Since their father's letter had decreed they spend three months together, it wasn't unreasonable for her to expect that slowly, gradually, Arden and Meg would get used to Jenny's presence, and start to like her just a little, and then accept her a little more, and then, eventually, welcome her into their sisterhood, for they were all, one way or another, daughters of Rory Randall.

Jenny had e-mailed the other two to inform them she had a Jeep Cherokee, so they wouldn't need to bring a car to the island. The house was in town, an easy walk to the post office, library, even to Grand Union. They could share the Jeep. But Meg had insisted on bringing her Volvo over because she had so many boxes of books. Arden had, through e-mail, sided with Meg, stating that having two vehicles at their disposal would prevent any awkwardness if more than one person absolutely needed a car at the same time. So fine. The short drive next to the house had just enough room for two cars.

As for bedrooms, Jenny had already staked her claim. One of the two spacious front bedrooms had been her bedroom for more than twenty years. After college, when she first had started up her computer business on the island, Rory and Justine still came down from Boston for summers and holidays. Jenny had installed her bank of computers, printers, and monitors at one end of her bedroom in order not to invade her parents' space.

Jenny had informed Meg and Arden of her possession of the front bedroom in her last e-mail. In a moment of guilty private gloating, she'd Express Mailed them newly copied keys in case she wasn't there when they arrived.

Because she had keys to the house and they didn't.

It was like being schizophrenic! Half the time Jenny longed for her sisters' affection; the other half of the time she battled to one-up them. And she was thirty-one years old. When did a person ever outgrow childish behavior?

Today she'd certainly stormed the citadel of selflessness. She'd gone to all the markets and stocked up on baskets of fresh vegetables, bags of staples, and wine. By the time she'd finished the shopping, it was past noon, and she arrived back at the house to discover a Volvo in the drive.

Her heart thumped. Meg was here.

"Hello!" Jenny called as she elbowed the back door open and humped the bags of groceries through the mudroom and into the kitchen.

Footsteps clattered down the back stairs. Meg appeared. She looked younger than she had at the funeral—well, of course she would, they all would, they had all been so formal and somber at the funeral and the reading of the will.

Meg had her amazing golden-red hair pulled back in a bushy ponytail. She wore a pale lime sundress that set off her blue-green eyes. Her skin held the pallor of an academic who never did sports, or in Meg's parlance, the radiance of a virtuous maiden. Whatever, she was dazzling.

Jenny wore jeans and a white cotton shirt. She thought she looked practical, capable, independent, adult, all that.

Meg skidded to a halt at the bottom of the stairs. "Oh. Jenny. Hi." Her smile was anxious.

Jenny had warned herself it would be this way; it would be weird if their first interactions weren't lukewarm at best. She was certain Meg was hoping it was Arden she'd see first, that Arden would be here so the two of them could gang up on Jenny just like always. Jenny had steeled her heart.

No chance of any sort of sisterly hug. With considerable effort, Jenny tried for a light, friendly tone. "Meg. You're here! Hi! Come in. Well, of course you can come in whenever you want to, I mean, because . . ." She was already tongue-tied. "I bought groceries. Stuff for breakfast and bread. Sandwich and salad makings. Some wine. To get us started."

"What a good idea." Meg hesitated. "Um, any more in the car that I could bring in?"

"Yeah, that would be great."

The screen door banged as Meg slipped outside, and banged again as she returned, arms loaded. "You got a lot of food," Meg said, setting the groceries on the counter. "I'll have to reimburse you for my share."

"Yeah, let's wait till Arden's here and we can sit down and draw up a weekly meal menu and shopping list."

Again, a pause. "Oh, okay. Although I plan to take care of my own meals. I need to watch my weight. I intend to get in shape."

Progress, Jenny thought. Meg was sharing something personal. Turning around, she said, "Please. You already have a shape like Marilyn Monroe's."

Meg snorted. "I wish. No, I need to lose weight. But mostly I'll focus on my work."

"Don't you teach at a college?"

"I do, but I've got the summer off. I'm going to write a book about May Alcott."

"Oh, Louisa May Alcott. I read her—"

"No, *May* Alcott. Her younger sister. She was a brilliant artist and no one knows about her." Meg came alive as she spoke, her cheeks pinking, her eyes sparkling. "She was so talented, her work was chosen over Mary Cassatt's to be exhibited in the 1877 Paris Salon."

Jenny arched her eyebrows, trying to express her interest in this, although really she had no idea what Meg was going on about. Realizing that Meg wanted some kind of response, she racked her brain. "Um, isn't there a Meg in *Little Women?*"

"Yes, there is, Jenny. But I'm not at all like Meg. And

Louisa May Alcott's real sister, May Alcott, the youngest sister, had an *amazing* life!"

Jenny bristled. "My life isn't so very *un*amazing."

"W-what?" Meg sputtered. "Oh, I didn't mean to imply that . . ." She frowned. "I'd better get these groceries put away."

"Right," Jenny agreed. "It's not really hot yet, but I did buy some ice cream and some yogurt. I don't know which bag it's in. Also some fruit, watermelon and grapes that need to be cold." She was babbling now, kicking herself for reacting so defensively to Meg's remarks instead of just keeping her mouth shut and listening.

For a few minutes they worked side by side in something like companionship, wordlessly dividing the task so that Meg put away refrigerated items and Jenny put away everything else because, understandably, Jenny knew what each cupboard held and Meg didn't.

"Now!" Jenny set her hands on her hips and looked around the room. "I think we should make some iced tea and enjoy a nice cool glass in the backyard."

"Oh." Pause. Meg looked at her watch. "Okay."

Jenny set about putting the kettle on to boil and filling the old brown teapot with Lipton bags. "Have you unpacked?" she asked over her shoulder.

"I have. I took the back bedroom."

Jenny paused. "The back bedroom? For heaven's sake, why? It's the smallest room and the furniture is so shabby."

"I think it's adorable. I want to sit at the desk by the window and work on my book."

"The desk is awfully rickety. I'm not even sure the air-conditioning reaches back that far. . . ." Jenny poured the boiling water into the pot to steep the tea.

Meg got out the ice tray and two glasses. "I won't mind the heat. I prefer that little room."

"I think you should take the other front bedroom," Jenny told her. "It's much bigger and brighter. Or take the mermaid room. It's so cheerful. That back bedroom's like a nun's cell. Do you want sugar or artificial sweetener? I put Sweet'n Low in this little china bowl. Spoons are in this drawer."

"I've already unpacked," Meg said firmly. She watched Jenny lift the hot teapot. "If you put a knife in the glass, the glass won't break when you pour the hot tea over the ice. It's a trick I learned—"

"These glasses won't break. They've lasted forever."

"Really." Meg's voice was cool. "I've never seen them before. You must have got them after I was banned from the island." She went out the screen door, letting it slam behind her.

FOUR

Arden took a taxi from the airport to the house. She'd considered calling to ask for a ride, but neither Meg nor Jenny had bothered to let her know their plans, so Arden thought *Fine*, she'd keep her information private, too.

Two cars were parked in the driveway. Hefting her purse, duffel, and computer over one shoulder, Arden pulled her rolling suitcase up the walk to the front door. It was unlocked. She let herself in.

"Hello?"

No answer.

Dumping her luggage by the stairs, she went through the house to the kitchen at the back. The window over the sink neatly framed the backyard, where Meg and Jenny sat sipping iced tea and talking.

How cozy.

Be nice, Arden told herself. *You need this gig.*

First of all, she couldn't return to her Boston apartment because, with her mother's help, she'd rented it for

the summer to a French couple, and the money was superlative.

Second and much more important, she'd come up
with a strategy for juicing up her part of *Simplify This*.
She'd do second-home segments, starting with Nantucket! She'd spend the summer making contacts and
scouting out sexy locations, fab old mansions that needed
face-lifts, family summer homes bought by corporate en-
trepreneurs and techy trailblazers. Perhaps by August she
could start shooting, get some of the cameramen down
here. . . .

First things first. Arden scanned the kitchen, found
the necessities, made herself a glass of iced tea, and carried it outside.

"Hello, ladies." She sauntered toward them in the
yellow linen Fiandaca suit that she could never have af-
forded. Designers often gave her clothes to wear on the
show. She chose this for her first appearance with the sisters. She was the oldest, the most successful, the most
polished.

"Good, Arden, you're here!" Trust Meg to act as if
this summer were some kind of sorority camp. Meg
jumped up and lightly kissed Arden's cheek.

"Hi, Arden." Jenny greeted her cheerfully enough but
ruined it by adding, "Would you mind removing your
shoes? The heels are digging divots in the lawn."

Arden bit back a sarcastic response. "Sure." She took
a wicker chair, sipped her tea, sighed, and looked around
the yard. Only after a few moments did she remove her
heels. She had to admit it felt good to take them off.

"I didn't hear you arrive," Meg said.

"I came in a taxi just now. Dropped my luggage in the front hall."

"I saved the front bedroom for you," Meg announced.

"Oh, I don't want the front bedroom. I want the little bedroom at the back, the one I always had."

"Well, actually," Meg said, "I had it, too. I had it first. Then you wanted it. . . ."

Arden waved a careless hand dismissively. "That was years ago. Who can remember? Anyway, I'll take the back bedroom."

"I've already unpacked." Meg looked just slightly pleased with herself.

"The front bedroom is the master bedroom!" Jenny cut in, obviously trying to make peace.

"Meg." Arden leaned forward. "I really want the back bedroom."

Once upon a time, long ago, Meg had been in awe of Arden, who was three whole years older and sassed her mother and knew how to wear nail polish and needed a bra long before Meg did. In the earliest years, Meg's mother still felt guilty for stealing Rory away from Nora, leaving three-year-old Arden without a daddy in the house, so she worked hard to encourage Meg to be kind to Arden. To let Arden have what she wanted.

A lot had changed since then.

"Arden." Meg smiled over her glass of iced tea. "So do I."

Jenny shifted uneasily in her chair. She bore the largest burden of guilt because it was *her* mother, Justine, the third and longest-lasting wife, who had instigated The Exile, banning Arden and Meg from the Nantucket house.

"The front bedroom has an en suite bathroom," Jenny reminded the others.

Before she could enumerate its qualities, Arden cast a hooded-eye glance her way. "Yes, and it's where *my* father slept with *your* mother." She shuddered.

Jenny's breath caught in her throat. So they were going to continue to punish her for their father's behavior. . . . Well, and Jenny's mother's, too. They did have a point.

Meg leaned past Jenny. "So you want *me* to sleep there? Thanks, Ard."

Arden glared at Meg.

Meg glared, chin lifted defiantly, back at Arden.

"Fine." Arden capitulated. "I'll take the mermaid bedroom."

"Oh, Arden," Jenny protested. "That's so much smaller than the front bedroom."

Arden relented, softening her tone. "Enough. I can't sleep in their bed. It's just too grisly to think about. I'll take the mermaid bedroom, but I've got work to do, too, so I'll use the front bedroom to work in. I'm sure there's some table I can use for a desk."

"Good. That's settled, then." Jenny relaxed, but only for a moment. "Now. About food. I thought we might make a plan about meals. I bought a ton of food to get us started, all the staples and some wine, too, but I don't know what you all like to eat—"

"I'll eat out mostly," Arden said. "I hate to cook. I never cook at home. I'm too busy, and I go out a lot to meet people for work."

"I told her I'd take care of myself, too," Meg agreed, nodding. "I'm going to diet."

"Oh, come on." Jenny shook her head. "Don't tell me you want to live like grad students with food divided into different shelves of the refrigerator. That's ridiculous. Plus, we need to talk about keeping the kitchen clean. I'm not going to do it all."

"I thought Justine had a housekeeper," Arden countered.

"She does. Clementine Gordon. She'll come once a week for the heavy stuff, but we have to do our own dishes. For heaven's sake," Jenny continued, "let's be adults about this. Do we have to buy three coffeemakers and each make our own coffee in the morning? That's just silly."

Arden studied Jenny for a long moment. Jenny the Enemy. Jenny who stole their father's love and ripped away all the Nantucket summers just when Arden would have enjoyed them most. Although, to be fair, it had been Jenny's mother, Justine, who had banned Arden and Meg from the house.

"I can understand," Arden said in her soft, calm-the-client-down voice, "why you feel as if this house is yours and that you have the right to tell me and Meg what to do, and how to live our lives here. But this house was left to the three of us equally. Isn't that right?" When Jenny didn't answer immediately, she persisted: "Don't you agree?"

Jenny flushed, which made her look like Snow White, with her dramatic dark hair and eyes and her pale skin. "I certainly wasn't trying to tell anyone what to do." She blinked several times—was she blinking back tears? "I apologize if that's what you think. I was only offering to devise some organization for the three of us."

Arden wasn't surprised when softhearted Meg chimed in.

"Jenny, I'm not sure I know what kind of work you do. Do you work on the island? I mean, will you have to keep to a schedule, like nine to five or something?"

Jenny smiled gratefully at Meg. "I own a computer tech company. My clients are both on- and off-island, but I usually work from home, troubleshooting on my computer. My workstation is in my bedroom. I've got three screens up and going all the time. May Alcott would probably faint."

Meg and Jenny laughed.

Arden thought: Huh? What were they laughing about? Who was May Alcott? Some neighbor who'd stopped by before Arden arrived? It unnerved her that Meg and Jenny were allies.

"So, food," Arden said, bringing them back to the topic. "I suppose Jenny's idea has merit. It sounds like we're all going to be working here, and it's not like I'll be able to send my assistant for some takeout—"

"You have an assistant?" Meg was impressed. "How glamorous, Arden."

"Yes, well, a lot of it is glamorous," Arden agreed casually. "And a lot of it is boring, repetitive slog. Anyway, here we're a good two or three blocks from the nearest café or restaurant, and in the summer everything's jammed. So, yeah, I think it would be more efficient to organize some kind of food buying and meal cooking."

"What if we took turns?" Jenny suggested. "Each of

us take a day to be in charge of buying groceries and preparing dinner and cleaning the kitchen."

"Only dinner," Meg put in. "I think we can handle breakfast and lunch ourselves."

"As long as someone makes a big pot of coffee," Arden added.

"Great!" Jenny clapped her hands, pleased with herself. Arden thought Jenny looked like a damned Girl Scout; she might as well have a kerchief around her neck and badges on her shirt.

"Look, Jenny," Arden said, "most of the time I'll probably take my food up to my room to eat while I work."

Jenny tossed her head. "Fine with me. I'll probably be out most nights myself, at cocktail parties."

Arden's eyes widened. "Cocktail parties? What kinds of cocktail parties?"

Sensing Arden's interest, Jenny was arch. "Oh, you know, the kind where people drink cosmopolitans and martinis and the caterers pass munchies."

Arden leaned forward. "Jenny, you know I have a TV show. *Simplify This*." No point mentioning the dreadful Zoey. "I want to do a Nantucket version. I need to meet people with fabulous homes who might like to be on the show."

Jenny nodded thoughtfully. "A lot of the richest people wouldn't dream of having their intimate space broadcast all over the air," she said, and then, realizing too late that she'd insulted Arden, she hurried to add, "But I'm sure some of them would glory in the publicity."

"Well, I'm not going to get right in their faces first

thing," Arden began defensively. "I'll talk to them, get to know them, see what they're like. . . ."

Jenny's smile was very cat/canary. "I get that. Hey, I'm going to a party tonight, Arden, a fund-raiser for a local artists' coalition. Do you want to come with me?"

"Yes," Arden replied. After a moment, she added, "Please."

FIVE

The Nantucket parties Arden remembered from when she was fourteen, and for a while when she was fifteen, when her hormones were on red alert, had been beach parties. In shorts and a bikini top, she'd danced barefoot in the sand with girlfriends, giggling idiotically and stealing sips from abandoned beer bottles. Princess Diana had still been alive, and Arden had been young.

The party Jenny took her to tonight was different. Well, of course, it would be; they were all grown-up now, even if the salty ocean breeze made her feel fresh, sassy, and eager for all that summer could bring. It was held at a house on the cliff. Bars were set up both inside the house and out on the lawn overlooking Nantucket Sound. Waiters passed trays of canapés and a bluegrass band played.

Jenny wore a simple red dress that set off her striking dark hair and eyes. She wore a sleek pair of red sandals, too, with stones glittering across the straps as she easily

crossed the lawn, *not* making divots in the grass. In the
car on the way over, Jenny told Arden she'd broken up
recently with a hunk named Bjorn. Jenny was ready for a
new romance. When they arrived at the party, Jenny
spotted someone and, with a careless "I'll be right back"
to Arden, hurried away through the crowd, leaving Arden
alone.

Arden had only her basic everyday beige sandals—she
had brought all her four-inch heels for parties, but had
decided not to wear them tonight because Jenny told her
they'd be mostly outside. She wore a simple sea-green
shift that accentuated the green of her eyes. Not many
people had true green eyes; Arden did. She knew she
looked good, and she was comfortable in large groups,
not afraid to be alone. Anyway, it was the house itself she
was interested in.

She took a glass of wine off a tray and wandered
through the open French doors to the living room. It was
a true old summer house with wide-board floors slanting
unevenly and faded curtains and sofas that had appar-
ently been there forever. Framed photographs cluttered
the bookshelves, crammed in with golf and tennis trophies and dozens of ordinary shells, no doubt treasures
discovered by grandchildren. She peeked into the kitchen,
where the caterers were working hard and fast, and
grinned. Ah, what a find. An original kitchen, no doubt
a horror to work in, the only new appliances a microwave set on an antique walnut table and a roll-away dishwasher with an adapter at the end of its electric plug. Fire
hazard waiting.

"I know who you are, and I bet I know just what you're thinking." The voice was low, sensual, deeply masculine.

Arden turned. Early thirties, tall and elegant in an expensive pink Brooks Brothers shirt and a Rolex watch.

Arden asked, "We've met?"

"No, we haven't met, but I've seen you plenty of times on your TV show. *Simplify This.*" Humor brightened his brown eyes, as if he knew exactly what her reaction was and found it amusing.

"Ah. So that explains why you know what I'm thinking."

He leaned forward, ostensibly to survey the kitchen, touching her shoulder with his. "You want to get in there and modernize that kitchen. Am I right?"

A waiter swung toward them with a giant tray. Arden moved back into the dining room.

"You're right," she admitted reluctantly. He was arrogant, another self-satisfied conquistador. Yet she found him oddly compelling.

He held out his hand. "Palmer White."

His name was familiar. She put her hand in his. "Arden Randall."

He took his time about releasing her hand. "How do you know the Beaudreaus?"

"I don't. My, um, sister Jenny does. She brought me along." They slowly strolled through the house toward wide doors opening to the lawn. "How do you know them?"

"Oh, Ivan's been a partner of mine in crime for a long time." A glint of complacence edged his voice.

"What do you do?"

"I'm in television. I own air space and so on."

Arden's interest flared. "Do you own Channel Six?"

"I do now. Among others." He slid his hand through her arm and bent close to her, whispering in her ear. "I'll give you a hint. Don't waste your time on the Beaudreaus. Genevieve Marie is emotionally attached to every dust bunny and paper clip in this house. Plus, they wouldn't dream of having their home exposed to the public on a show like yours."

Arden bridled at his insult and yanked her arm away. "A show like mine?"

"Aimed at the upper-middle section of the demographic span—and understandably so, that's your audience. But people like to dream. More than that, they like to see how the rich live. We all do. It's human nature. Your ratings are beginning to fall—"

Insulted and frankly shocked that this stranger was so brash about what was intimate professional information, Arden took a step back. "Don't bother worrying about my television show. I know what I'm doing."

"Do you?" Palmer White inquired.

All Arden's professional life, she'd been plagued with men who thought because she was good-looking and relatively young, they could tell her what to do. They were wrong. "Excuse me," she said, and blindly strode away.

She wove through the crowd, jaw clenched. She didn't see Jenny anywhere in the crowd. She thought she might just walk home. She didn't know anyone here, she was tired from packing and making the trip to the island, and Palmer White had started her summer off with a blast of bad juju.

Somehow she managed to get stuck in the crowd. She turned sideways, trying to squeeze her way through.

Someone stepped, crushingly, on her foot.

"Ouch! Holy damn!" Instinctively, she hopped on her good foot, holding the injured one off the ground. Not the most elegant pose.

"Oh, excuse me," a man said. "I stepped on your foot. I'm so sorry. Are you all right?"

She looked up. And up. The man had to be six four, his blue blazer marvelously delineating a slim, muscular torso while accentuating his blond hair and blue eyes. He wore a red tie with sailboats on it. She liked men in ties.

"I'm fine," she replied politely. "If I could just get over to a bench . . ."

"Let me help."

She allowed herself to be ushered gently, his hand on her elbow, through the crowd to a wrought iron bench by the lily pond. She sank onto the seat. To her amazement, the man knelt down, taking her foot in his hand.

"I think it's swelling," he said. "You may even get a nasty bruise."

His blond hair was thick. His hands were long and elegant. His Nantucket red trousers were faded from age in a way that would impress even Ralph Lauren.

He eased her sandal off and gently touched her toes.

In spite of herself, Arden flinched. "Ouch."

"Yep," the man said. "I did a thorough job." He looked up at her ruefully. "I am awfully sorry."

"Don't worry about it," she babbled. "Happens all the time in mobs like this. Really, it's fine."

"I'll get some ice." Before she could object, he disappeared.

Arden inspected her foot. It *was* swelling. What a way to start the summer! Laughter and snippets of conversation drifted her way through the warm evening to where she sat, alone and in pain. She knocked back the rest of her wine—for medicinal purposes.

"Here we go." Suddenly he'd returned, with ice wrapped in one of the caterer's white napkins. "Can you hold it against your foot? That should keep the swelling down."

She felt like an idiot, sitting in such an unalluring position, with one leg up, knee to her chin, as she held the ice on her foot, trying to keep her dress tucked tidily beneath her thigh.

He sat next to her. "I'm Tim Robinson, and my clumsy feet are the bane of my existence."

She laughed. "Arden Randall."

Companionably, they eyed his feet, neatly shod in tasseled leather loafers.

"You do have big feet," she remarked gently.

"Size twelve. You'd think by now I'd be used to them. I've had them all my life."

Arden laughed. It seemed natural to ask, "What do you do?"

"Computers," he told her. "I'm 'the computer guy.' That's the name of my store here on the island: The Computer Guy. I sell computers, printers, accessories, and I repair computers. I make house calls to help people when their computers are being obstinate."

"You must be the most popular guy on the island."

"I'm not sure *popular* is precisely the right word," Tim joked. "By the time people call me, they've worked themselves up into a state of four-letter fury that makes them completely inarticulate. It usually takes me more time to understand what the problem is than to fix it."

Arden laughed. "Oh, I know. *Nothing* makes me as angry as my computer." For some reason, she thought of Palmer White. "Well, almost nothing."

"When computers do work, things happen so quickly that it makes everyone short tempered when a problem isn't fixed instantaneously." He looked at her ice-covered toes. "How's your foot?"

"I think it will be okay," she told him. "Nothing broken."

"That's good. I hope you don't have to lead a hiking tour tomorrow."

"I'm on vacation," she assured him. "I'll lie in the sun and recuperate from my terrible injury."

"Where do you live when you're not here?"

"Boston. But I'll be on the island for the entire summer."

"Three months vacationing on the island? Nice."

She shifted to face him. He was a handsome man to face. "It's a bit more complicated than that," she said. "I'm actually drawing a salary while I'm vacationing, plus I'll be doing some research for the television show I host in Boston."

"You host a TV show? Impressive. What is it?" Before she could reply, he hurriedly explained, "I don't watch television much anymore. I get my news on the computer and play DVDs when I have the time."

"No problem, though I believe I have a universal message. My show's called *Simplify This*."

He burst out into a full-bodied laugh. "Man, if only!"

Their conversation was interrupted by a tapping at the
microphone.

"Hello, y'all. I'm Genevieve Beaudreau, and I'm the
hostess of this li'l ol' get-together."

Genevieve had back-combed white hair, a silver sequined dress draped over a tall, voluptuous yet shapely
body, and everything about her glittered. Even though
she was at least in her fifties and of more than generous
proportions, she still wore bling covered with bling. She
was like a 1930s movie star, lacking only the white fox
stole.

"I'm just so happy to see all of you, and I want to
thank you for coming to help support this new organization, the Arts Coalition of Nantucket. Now I know I'm
just a li'l old summer person from Texas, but I've been
comin' to this adorable island for years and years, and if
there's one thing I know in my life, it's that this island
breeds super artists like a raccoon breeds fleas. Now that
we've entered the new age of technology, I believe we
owe it to the world to let everyone know all about the
artistic excellence of Nantucket, and that's why I founded
the arts coalition, and that's why I'm asking you charming people for your help."

Arden looked around the crowd to gauge their reaction. Some of the women were exchanging looks of
skepticism and amusement, but every man there had his
eyes glued to their hostess's sparkling form. As she continued to talk, the audience warmed up, smiling, then

chuckling, then outright laughing at Genevieve's southern charm. Arden decided the savvy Texan hostess knew exactly what she was doing. She knew how to get attention, and how to keep it.

After a few more minutes, Genevieve stepped off the platform and the band started up again. A gentleman in a tux handed Genevieve a glass of wine, and a flock of other men surrounded her.

"I believe she's going to make a success of her cause," Arden remarked.

Tim agreed. "Who could turn her down? She reminds me of Jean Harlow."

"I should have known you two would find each other."

Arden looked up from her bench to see Jenny standing above her, hand on cocked hip, eyes narrowed dangerously.

Jenny said, "I should have known that out of all this crowd, you'd find my sister."

Tim almost leapt from the bench. He stood just inches in front of Jenny, glaring down at her. "You told me you don't have any sisters!"

"Well," Jenny sputtered, "I only sort of do—"

Tim pounced. "You *lied*!"

Arden watched, fascinated. Tim and Jenny faced each other with such passionate intensity, Arden couldn't decide whether they were going to murder each other or throw themselves into a torrid embrace.

"I did not lie!" Jenny insisted. "Arden isn't my sister—"

"You just said she was!" Tim reminded Jenny triumphantly. "You are a proven liar."

Jenny went purple. "Arden is my *step*sister. I haven't even seen her in years."

Tim tore his gaze away from Jenny's face and aimed it at Arden. "Is this true?"

Arden knew she had the opportunity to get Jenny in trouble. It was just too delicious to resist. Sweetly, she replied, "It's true that we're stepsisters. But we *have* seen each other every year. Our father would take the three of us out on the town for a special dinner, so we'd all be together."

"Oh, turkey breast," snapped Jenny, in her turmoil reverting to her childhood swear. "One night doesn't count."

"Yes it does," Arden insisted, surprised to find herself becoming emotionally involved. "What Jenny probably means is that we never met on *Nantucket* because she got me and my real sister exiled."

"That was not *my* fault!" Jenny hissed.

Before Arden could respond, she noticed their hostess, Genevieve, coming toward them, all smiles and glitter.

"Darlin's!" Genevieve swooped down to gather Jenny and Tim against her like baby chicks. "I'm so glad to find you here together like this. I just knew it was the right idea, and look here, I'm right again."

Jenny and Tim both smiled nervously.

"Now, we need to have a meetin' soon because I want the two of you to design, build, and run the arts coalition website," Genevieve declared.

Arden bit back a smile as she watched Jenny and Tim exchange a meaningful glance.

"Of course you know I'll pay you, and top rate, too," Genevieve cooed. "You're only young'uns, and I wouldn't expect kids like you just starting out to donate your time, so don't even think about it. Bill me like you're both lawyers." She chuckled at her own wit. "Okay, Monday morning, my office, eleven?" She bent to peck a kiss on Jenny's forehead and stood on tiptoe to kiss Tim's chin, then whirled away, leaving a mist of perfume as sweet as a Taylor Swift song.

Jenny's smile disappeared. Her face grew stormy. "I'm going to kill myself," she muttered.

"Grow up," Tim told her. "We can do this."

"I'm sys admin," Jenny snapped.

"That is so wrong. You should be site designer and the graphic artist—that's the stuff you do well," Tim retorted.

Arden's head turned back and forth as if she were watching a tennis match. *Okay*, Arden thought, *Tim gave Jenny a compliment. Now Jenny will be nice back.*

Jenny only bristled. "I do *everything* well."

Tim stepped closer to Jenny, hands on his hips, mouth tense, glaring down at her with the ferocity of some futuristic death-ray machine. Arden thought he might zap her with a toxic glow and Jenny would disappear. *Serve her right*, Arden thought with a wicked inner smile.

Instead, Tim spoke with obvious patience. "Let's just make the meeting and go from there, okay? This could be important to both of us."

Mouth tightened into a thin line, Jenny nodded. Then she spun on her heel and stalked away.

Tim took a long, deep breath. After a moment, he realized Arden was standing there. "So she's your sister?"

Arden made a helpless shoulder shrug. "As she said, she's a stepsister. We're not exactly close. Our relationship is neutral at the best of times. It's complicated."

Tim smiled at her. "I'd like to hear about it."

Wow, did this guy have a dangerous smile. Arden narrowed her eyes suspiciously. "Why? So you can learn more about Jenny?"

"Believe me, I know all I need to about her," he answered. "No, so I can learn more about you. I don't believe I've started off on my best foot, so to speak. Let me take you out to dinner. Or better yet, out on my boat."

"It would be heavenly to get out on the water," Arden said.

"Next Saturday?"

She thought for a moment. She wasn't used to having free time, but for three months, she had all the time in the world.

"Next Saturday," she agreed.

SIX

Meg kept looking at the clock.

Arden had assured Jenny they didn't have to eat before the party because there would be so many catered goodies on offer. They'd hurried into the house to shower and dress, leaving Meg alone in the garden.

Meg had tried to relax in her chair. Tried to enjoy the soft summer air. But she was hurt that Jenny hadn't invited Meg to the party, too. She felt left out. She *was* left out. Restless and annoyed with herself, she went back into the house and up to her room, trying not to notice the fragrance of Arden's and Jenny's bath salts and perfumes. She shut her door and seated herself at her desk. She organized her papers, laying her research notes, computer, books, and notebooks on the rickety wooden table. She almost didn't hear Arden calling out "Bye!"

After they left, Meg went down to the kitchen and made a sandwich—from the food that Jenny had bought. She scribbled a note in her little book of days so she could keep track of what she owed Jenny. God forbid she'd ever be indebted to her, even for five cents. Jenny's mother, Justine, would take Meg to court.

She could have walked into town and enjoyed a meal at any number of restaurants, but she didn't like eating alone, and she didn't need to gain any more weight. She wasn't in the mood to go out. It had been so long since she'd been on the island. She wanted to see the town again in the daylight, to take her time observing what remained from her childhood and what had changed.

Returning to her room, she leaned on her desk and watched the light play over the little town. Really, it was enchanting, and probably almost exactly what the town looked like over a hundred and twenty-five years ago when May Alcott was living with her brilliant older sister Louisa in Boston. Birds were singing and rustling in the trees and bushes outside—and then a strange, modern ring interrupted her thoughts.

Her cell phone. She checked the number: Liam.

They'd gotten into the habit of calling each other every day to talk, some days more than once, mostly about college matters such as students, deadlines, committees, conferences, but lately their conversations had taken a more personal tone. She had gotten too relaxed, genuine, comfortable with him, assuming he saw her as a kind of big sister. *Big* being the operative term. She knew she was good-looking in her full-figured way, with a pretty enough face; rather striking, even she would admit, strawberry-blonde hair; and her curvaceous body, but she wasn't enough of a babe to attract someone as downright gorgeous as Liam. Over the school term, she'd flirted with him in a lighthearted, frivolous fashion, but when he'd asked her out to dinner, she'd been surprised, even suspicious.

They'd been in his office on campus at the end of the first semester. She'd brought in a chunk of her Alcott outline for him to critique over the Christmas holiday. He'd asked her out to dinner. She'd laughed. "You mean, like on a date?"

Liam had crossed his office to stand close to her. With a slight smile on his handsome face, he'd said, in a low voice that gave her shivers, "I mean absolutely like on a date."

She'd backed off so fast she'd bumped into the bookcase. "Don't be silly. We can't date."

"Why not?" He took a step closer. She could feel his breath. She smelled cinnamon.

She thought: *Because you'll sleep with me, make me fall in love with you, and drop me for the first Gisele Bündchen look-alike you see.* She said, "Liam, you and I are such good *friends.*"

"I know. Why can't we be more than that?"

She shook her head. "No. Somehow one of us would do something stupid and we'd ruin our friendship. I don't want to do that."

"Meg—"

She slid sideways, out of his reach, and pulled open the office door. "Happy holidays, Liam. I'll see you in January."

"Wait, Meg." He'd looked perplexed, and no wonder, she thought. She was probably the first woman who'd ever turned him down in his life. "Not until January?"

"The holidays are always so busy," she gabbled, knowing she should run for her life.

"Can we at least talk on the phone?"

"Of course, just like we always do." Relieved, she threw him a big smile over her shoulder as she hurried away.

Sometimes on the phone they talked about the books they were reading, and the Alcott book Meg was gathering notes for, and about the freshman syllabus she'd designed and used to great success in the fall semester. About the poems he was writing . . . He read them to her over the phone while she lay in bed, trying to react intellectually, nearly swooning over the sweetness of his voice. She was the only one he shared his first drafts with. That was an honor for her and a gift of intimacy she couldn't bear to lose. Perhaps he had a schoolboy crush on her, but she had to be strong. She *was* strong. She made light of any amorous comment he made. She evaded his touch. She was sure she'd managed to safeguard their friendship.

In the solitude of her small room, she lay back on her bed and answered the phone.

"Hey, Meg. Just calling to see if you got there okay."

Liam's low, masculine voice flowed through Meg's body like a warm balm. "Oh, Liam, hi. Yes, I'm here. I'm looking out my window at the town. It's like looking back in time."

"How was your trip?"

As they talked, Meg could just see him, probably on the back deck of the little ranch house he rented in Sudbury, his long legs stretched out as he lazed on a lounge chair. He told her he was looking at the stars, enjoying an early June night that was as mild as deep summer.

His blond hair would gleam in the starlight.

"How are you getting on with Drusilla and Anastasia?" Liam knew enough about Meg's life to use the Disney names for her step- and half sister.

"So far, so good," she told him. "We're all tiptoeing around on hot coals, trying to be pleasant and not offend each other. They're at a party now—"

"And you're not?"

Meg tried to sound offhand, even witty. "Didn't get asked to go along."

"What little witches."

Liam's indignation on Meg's behalf made her laugh. "It's not like that. I think it's a business kind of thing for Arden, although we haven't had a chance to talk seriously."

"Want me to come down and give them a piece of my mind?" Liam suggested hopefully.

"Save it. But I do want you to come sometime to enjoy the island," Meg answered gently. "Just not quite yet."

"I miss you," Liam told her.

Meg took a deep breath. Aiming for the voice of a sexless Girl Scout leader, she replied flippantly, "I haven't even been gone for one day." Before he could disarm her with any more sweetness, she rushed on, "You know I'm determined to dig into this book."

"Good for you." Liam hesitated. "Okay, then, well, if you ever need me . . ."

"I want you to come visit, and soon," Meg promised. "I need to get settled and accomplish some work first."

But after she said good-bye to Liam, Meg went to her desk. Rather than reading, she observed the night sky and pondered life's mysteries. Louisa May Alcott had financially supported her philosophical but impractical father and the rest of the family. She'd worked incessantly, scribbling away by hand, not only her *Little Women* books but, under a pseudonym, a series of wild thrillers starring dangerous hypnotic villains. She never had a suitor of her own, never married.

Gales of laughter interrupted her thoughts. Arden and Jenny were home.

For a fraction of a moment, Meg considered keeping her dignity and staying in her room, but instead she went out into the hall and leaned over the railing, looking down at the two women bent over with laughter. "You must have had a good time."

"We got stopped by a policeman on—on—on—" Jenny sputtered.

"On *what?*" Meg demanded, so curious she hurried down the stairs.

"A *bicycle!*" Arden burst out. "He was ten years old!"

Meg arched an eyebrow. "You were arrested by a ten-year-old policeman on a bike?"

Jenny leaned against the wall in the front hall, pulling off her sparkling sandals. "It's a new arrangement here in the summer, bike cops to help with all the traffic violations."

Arden added, "He wasn't really ten, he just looked it." She wandered into the kitchen. "I've got to drink some water."

"God, me, too." Jenny followed.

"Are you drunk?" Meg demanded, entering the kitchen.

"Jeez, Meg, don't be such a prig," Jenny carped.

"We're not drunk," Arden informed Meg in a nicer tone of voice. "We hardly drank at all."

"Then why did you get arrested?"

"We didn't say *arrested*," Jenny corrected her. "We got stopped. I didn't have my lights on."

"So you *were* drunk!" Meg argued.

"No," Jenny said with patience. "It was just turning dark. This nature thing called twilight? It stays light here late in the summer. We'd only gone one block when the child in black biker shorts and yellow shirt with POLICE on it stopped us. He just reminded me to turn on my headlights. We were very law abiding and respectful, okay?"

"But then," Arden added, "we had to watch him pedal away over the cobblestones. It's extremely hard to appear dignified and tough when your butt's bouncing on a bike."

"So did you make some contacts?" Meg asked Arden.

Arden waggled her eyebrows. "I'll say."

"Arden, I'm warning you, don't trust that guy," Jenny reminded her.

"*What* guy?" Meg demanded.

Arden smiled smugly. "His name is Tim Robinson," she told Meg. "He's a computer techie and a dreamboat."

"He's an idiot," Jenny snorted.

"I've got a date with him next Saturday," Arden told Meg. "Wait till you check him out."

"You'd be much better off going out with Palmer White," Jenny told Arden. "I thought you went to the

party to make contacts, not to hit on good-looking morons."

In a flash, Arden flicked from lighthearted to cranky.
"Well, you know what, Jenny? If I'd been able to spend
some time here every summer when I was a teenager instead of your mother imposing The Exile, I could have
had my fill of good-looking morons. But I missed out
then and I'm all in now."

"Arden, stop it," Jenny said, her voice soft. "It's not
my fault my mother kicked you two out. That's unfair."

"I don't think so," Arden responded. She stormed
out of the room and up the stairs. Her bedroom door
slammed.

"We have got to talk about this," Jenny said. "Or it
will fester."

"I know," Meg agreed. She sat down at the table,
thinking Jenny would join her.

"We have to do it with the three of us together," Jenny
said. "Maybe tomorrow." She left the kitchen, saying
over her shoulder, "Turn off the lights when you're done,
okay?"

After a moment, Meg turned off the lights and went
upstairs to her room.

The next morning, Jenny returned from her early-
morning run to find Arden and Meg sitting at the kitchen
table.

"Hey!" Jenny let the screen door slam and stood pant-
ing away with a big smile on her face. Running shot good

endorphins through her. "What are you two doing here on this excellent day, still in your PJ's?"

Arden gave Jenny a sullen glare. "Jenny. It. Is. Eight. O'clock."

Meg added, "On a Saturday morning. But you know, I guess that since Arden and I have been working our butts off for the past few months to pay the rent instead of lounging around in our father's house working whenever we feel like it, Arden and I deserve a little Saturday laziness."

"You guys." Jenny threw herself into a kitchen chair, folded her arms on the table, and scowled, her happy mood vanished. "Give me a break here. The past is over and done. We all want a slice of the sale of this house. The only way we're going to get it is to do what our father stipulated. We've got to be here for three months, together. No way out. Why can't we three act like civilized adults and behave with a little courtesy toward each other?"

"Easy for you to say," Arden grumbled. "You are the winner and still champion of our father's affections, even though you aren't even his blood."

"Thanks for reminding me," Jenny replied.

Her voice quiet but firm, Meg asked, "Do you expect us to forget that you got us kicked out of this house?"

Jenny shook her head in frustration. "But *I* didn't. It was my mother who made you two leave because one of you stole her emerald necklace."

Arden shoved back her chair and stood up, all one hundred ten pounds quivering. "I did *not* steal your mother's damned necklace!"

Meg shook her head stubbornly. "I didn't, either."

Jenny shut her eyes and took a deep breath. Her endorphins were fading, but she still felt the results of a great run on a sunny day by the ocean. "Let's start again, please. Let's agree that none of us stole it, okay? Let's forget about that."

"Forget about it?" Meg's fighting spirit rose. "That would be fine with you, wouldn't it, Jenny? You got to spend every summer of your life here in this fabulous house on an island with golden beaches and gorgeous boys, while Arden and I were in exile. You've been living rent-free in Dad's house for at least the past ten years, while Arden and I have had to work to pay our rent. And you would like us to forget about it? I don't think so."

"What do you expect me to do?" Jenny demanded. "Turn back time?"

Arden and Meg were silent, arms folded over their chests. Arden wore pink silk boxer short pajamas that brought out the red accents in her auburn hair. Meg was wrapped in a cotton robe like Joseph's Technicolor coat and her glorious strawberry-blonde hair was loose.

"You guys are stunning," Jenny observed quietly. "You both have Dad's red hair."

Arden rolled her eyes.

Through the screen door came the trill of a bird.

Impulsively, Meg shifted in her chair. "I want to walk on the beach."

"Wait," Arden told her. "Jenny's right. Let's finish this first. We can't turn back the clock. We have to live here for three months. We don't need the atmosphere to be toxic."

"True." Encouraged by Arden's words, Jenny proposed, "I think we should make a list of rules."

"Oh, Jenny, grow up. We're adults. Let's just agree to be civil to each other, as if we're, oh, I don't know, three strangers renting the house for the summer. We can be helpful, we can even have fun, we can let go of the past."

"For three months," Meg specified.

"For three months," Arden agreed. She looked at Jenny. "And I don't want to hear anything about Tim Robinson, okay?"

Jenny bit back a few choice words. "Okay."

Meg shifted in her chair, rewrapping her colorful robe around her. "I was just thinking. You know what? None of the three of us has been married yet, and we're all in our thirties."

"Well, duh, Meg," Arden snorted. "Why do you guess that is?"

"I know." Jenny jumped in before the others could say it. "You were both too busy working to meet men. So it's my fault." She sat back in her chair, satisfied.

Arden squinted at Jenny. "Actually, for me, it's true. I've been too busy working to settle down!"

Meg asked, "But what about you, Jenny?"

"I was kind of with a guy for the past two years." She gave the thought a moment's regret, then shrugged. "But, you know, I've been working, too. Maybe Dad paid my college tuition, but I had my nose to the grindstone making those grades. Understanding computer code and algorithms isn't that easy, either—"

"Enough." Arden put her hands to her head. "You're

hurting my brain. Fine, we believe you. You've worked hard."

"Who was the guy you were with for two years?" Meg asked.

Jenny paused. "Bjorn," she said.

"Bjorn?" Meg echoed.

"He's Swedish. Once you see him, you'll know why I went with him for two years. He's like California Ken except he lived here. He's crazy about Nantucket. Crazy about swimming, surfing when he can. He worked as a bartender at High Winds. Everyone knows him. He's a truly sweet guy."

"Why did you break up?" Meg asked.

Jenny pulled her shoulders up to her ears. "The truth? Bjorn's adorable, like a yellow lab puppy. But he's . . . maybe not the brightest guy in the world."

"Well, not everyone can talk about algorithms," Arden pointed out.

"I realize that. We're just on different planes, we have fun doing different things—listen, why doesn't one of you go out with him and you'll see what I mean."

Arden grinned. "You take him, Meg. I've got Tim Robinson."

Jenny snorted.

Meg said, "I can arrange my own love life, thank you very much. And Bjorn doesn't sound like my type, anyway." She stood up, gathering her flashy wrapper around her. "You two might not be aware that I'm working on an important—no, a *significant* book." Meg coiled her finger in a long fiery red curl, and her blue-green eyes grew luminous. "Do you know that Louisa May Alcott paid for

May's art lessons, made her gowns, took May with her to Europe to study art, and when May's painting was accepted by the Paris Salon, May wrote in her journal . . ." Meg paused before quoting the passage verbatim: " 'Who would have imagined such good fortune and so strong proof that Lu does not monopolize the Alcott talent. Ha! Ha! Sister, this is the first feather plucked from your cap!' "

The kitchen was quiet.

"I don't know what you're talking about," Jenny said at last, gawking at her sister like she was a nutcase. "I've got work to do, too." She left the room and jogged upstairs.

SEVEN

Monday morning, Arden pulled on white capris, a black tee, and black sandals. She slung a straw bag over her shoulder and set out to renew her acquaintance with the town.

The big brick edifice of the Jared Coffin House rose on the corner of Centre and Broad Streets, a touchstone for Arden. From here she could turn left and stroll past Bookworks, the Brotherhood—yum, cheeseburgers!—and down to the Whaling Museum, or turn right and walk down Centre Street, past all sorts of glorious boutiques. She turned right. She window-shopped, thinking about what she needed to buy for a casual summer.

Main Street was charming, as always, with brick sidewalks edging the cobblestone street and more stores filled with enticing goods. She walked down to the water, today rippled by a light wind, back up to Easy Street, and over to the library. She renewed her library card, checked out a mystery, then returned to the fresh air and sunshine.

She needed sunblock. She needed a new swimsuit. She needed a sun hat.

Two hours later, happily lugging several bags from various shops, she collapsed, exhausted, at a table at the Boarding House's patio. After ordering a salad, she leaned back in her chair and surrendered to the pleasure of people watching.

How soon would she be able to gracefully contact Genevieve Beaudreau about the possibility of appearing on *Simplify This?* Even though Palmer White had warned her that Genevieve wouldn't ever want any advice about her summer house, the kitchen could definitely use an update. She took her notebook out of her bag and jotted down some ideas.

"May I join you?"

Arden looked up. Palmer White stood by her table, tall, confident, splendidly dressed in white ducks and a blue polo shirt.

She hesitated. She needed to get to know people on this island, and he probably knew a lot of people she'd like to meet.

"All right," she answered indifferently.

Palmer had scarcely pulled out his chair when the waitress arrived, all smiles and flapping eyelashes. "Mr. White, how wonderful to see you again. Would you like your usual?"

"That would be great, Andrea."

After the waitress went off, Arden said softly, "You know her?"

Palmer looked pleased with himself. "I know lots of

people." He lounged in his chair. "That's why you should be very, very nice to me."

Arden took a deep breath. "And I'm supposed to be nice to you *how*?"

"Don't look so indignant. I'm not asking you to crawl toward me in harem pants."

Her mouth quirked with amusement at the thought. She couldn't help but admire his persistence. She'd been accused of being too assertive herself.

"I'm suggesting," he continued, "that you accompany me to a few parties. You'd be making some crucial connections."

"What would you get out of it?"

"I'd have a beautiful and moderately famous woman on my arm. Most important, an intelligent woman. I get tired of good-looking airheads."

The waitress appeared with his beverage—iced tea. Arden narrowed her eyes and coolly observed him. She'd Googled him when she got home from the party, naturally, and was impressed. He'd gone to St. Mark's boarding school, Harvard, and the London School of Economics. He owned several technology and media companies. He'd been married and divorced, without children. Not that it mattered to Arden.

"Fine, then," Arden conceded. "When's the first event?"

"Now, see," Palmer complained, "I don't consider that to be pleasant or even nice. Couldn't you at least pretend to be feminine?"

"I *am* feminine!"

"No, you're controlling and abrasive. You want to make it crystal clear that you would only go out with me as long as I'm aware that it's a kind of business deal. Let's just make that understood, okay? I get it. So when we're in front of other people, you don't treat me like some kind of snake. You'll act as if we're on a date."

Arden bristled. She found the man irritating—and tantalizing. She needed to keep her balance here. "All right, then, but you've got to stop taking the way I am personally. I talk to everyone the way I talk to you. It's how I get things done. I have a chance to rejuvenate *Simplify This*, and that's my priority. I'm not interested in flirting with you so you'll marry me, make me rich, and allow me to lie around having my toenails painted. I can already afford that myself. I'll go out with you because you'll introduce me to some people I need to meet, and I'll be pleasant, but it's agreed at the beginning that there's no kind of sexual *niceties* involved, okay?"

Palmer narrowed his eyes and lowered his voice. "Of course I'd like to take you to bed. You're bewitching. But I'm thirty-eight years old and quite a bit more complicated than the men you've obviously been seeing."

"You know nothing about the men I've been seeing," Arden shot back. Truth was, she hadn't seen *any* men for quite a while.

Palmer sipped his iced tea. He waited.

The waitress brought Arden's salad. It did not skip Arden's notice that her salad came much later than Palmer's iced tea. Of course, a salad took more time to prepare than . . . *Oh*, she ordered herself, *stop it!*

"Palmer," Arden said in an amiable voice, "I would be pleased to be your companion at any events you might wish to invite me to attend with you."

"How about next Friday night, then? Black tie, at the Forbeses'. I'll pick you up at eight."

"That sounds nice," Arden replied, thinking, *Which Forbes?* But she wouldn't give Palmer the satisfaction of asking. She'd find out online when she got home.

"Good." Palmer stood up. "Enjoy your lunch."

At eleven on Monday morning, Jenny sat in Genevieve's office, located in what had once been the front parlor of the historic old home. Tim Robinson sat in a chair next to her as they waited for Genevieve to make an appearance. Genevieve's maid had ushered them into the room, asked if they wanted coffee, and promised that Ms. Beaudreau would join them soon.

Jenny usually wore tank tops, jeans, and flip-flops, but in deference to her southern hostess and temporary client, she'd pulled on a blue dress, sandals, and earrings. She wanted to tell Tim that she hadn't dressed up because she was seeing *him*. She understood that Genevieve was an authentically considerate benefactress who wanted both island computer experts to be on board with her arts project. Genevieve was all about cooperation and harmony. It would upset her if Jenny and Tim couldn't appear to be friendly. Genevieve had no idea of the personal history between them.

Tim wore khakis and a white button-down shirt with the sleeves rolled up. His sandy hair was, as usual, sort of sticking up all over, not for style's sake but because each strand seemed to have a mind of its own.

"Look," Tim whispered to Jenny now. "Let's agree before she gets here that you'll design the logo for the arts coalition, and the home page of the website."

Jenny shook her head. "I think Genevieve should hold a contest among the artists for the design of the logo and the general overall appearance. We'll take it from there."

Tim didn't flinch. "Hey, great idea. I should have thought of that. Okay. You take the lead when Genevieve gets in here. She doesn't need to know every detail of what you and I are going to do; she couldn't understand the whole code-writing business."

"We'll say we're going to share the work and the pay, right?" Jenny asked. "Half and half, equally?"

"Right," Tim agreed, just as their client entered the room.

Genevieve was frothed in turquoise silk from shoulders to ankles. "I am so sorry I'm not dressed yet," she apologized, although she could have worn the garment to a party. "But you can just ignore that, okay? Now, what do you have for me?"

Jenny explained the idea of a contest for a logo and the overall look of the site.

Genevieve's brow puckered. "But won't that just take forevah?"

"Not if we put a deadline on it," Tim told her. "We'll e-mail the artists on your list today, tell them we need the idea by Thursday, and the three of us can decide on Friday."

Her lily-white brow crinkled even more. "The *three* of us will decide?"

Jenny leaned forward. "You'll have the final say, of

course, but Tim and I will have to weigh in on feasibility and efficiency."

"Efficiency?" Genevieve looked as if the word hurt.

"Some designs might be simpler, and offer more versatility for our purposes. We can get the site live faster. Also, what might be striking on paper might be impossible to reproduce on a website."

"I see." Genevieve tapped her lip with a long, perfectly filed silver fingernail.

Jenny and Tim waited.

"No." Genevieve shook her head. "No, I don't like this idea. Someone's feelings are gonna get hurt. I don't like having to choose one person over the others. Those artist types are already sensitive enough. No. You two design a prototype and e-mail it to me by the end of this week. We've got to get the site up and running before August."

Jenny glanced over at Tim. They both took a deep breath, then smiled at Genevieve.

"You got it," Jenny said.

Genevieve stood up in a ripple of turquoise. "All right, then. I think we can do most of this by e-mail, okay? You have my e-mail address?" Reaching in a drawer, she took out two cards and handed them over.

Jenny and Tim stood up. Genevieve sashayed out of the room.

Jenny looked at Tim. "So. How are we going to do this?"

"Let's go to my office," Tim suggested.

Jenny started to object, then remembered that her office was in her bedroom.

It was all too complicated to explain right now, how she couldn't put an office downstairs because the house wasn't wholly hers and her stepsisters were living there this summer. She didn't want to spend the money to rent a space on Nantucket yet. Besides, most of her clients contacted her online and she'd meet them at their place of business. She seldom needed a face-to-face meeting. Tim's office was in a building in a minimall on Airport Road. "Fine," she agreed.

Tim held the door open for her as they walked outside into the sunshine. "I'll meet you there."

She nodded. In her car, she gave herself a moment to compose her roiling emotions. Why did that man get her so revved up? She'd have a heart attack and die someday arguing with him over something like the size of a font.

Meg lay on her towel in the sand, listening to the gentle lapping of the waves against Jetties Beach. She'd been waiting almost twenty years for this moment. Next to her was her beach bag, stocked with bottled water, sunblock, and a book that so far, surprisingly, she had no interest in reading. It was just too sweet to lie here feeling the sun on her skin.

Because it was early June, the air was a perfect temperature, in the high seventies and cooled by an occasional sea breeze. Other people had their own spots established up and down the beach, but it wasn't as crowded as it would be in July and August.

Perhaps by then she would have managed to lose

enough weight so that her bust wouldn't bulge out of her suit like too many pillows in a case.

Perhaps not.

Did she eat as sublimation for sex? She'd talked with friends about this enough. She hadn't been a chubby teenager. Well, she hadn't been thin, either. She'd just been nicely rounded. She'd been that way in college, too, and when she was working on her master's.

Of course she'd dated. She'd even had flings. Kind of. In her deepest heart, she knew that for years, perhaps most of her twenties, she'd been obsessed with literature, poetry, and women writers. Her two best friends, both graduate students, got married; Meg was a bridesmaid for both of them. Kyla married another grad student who was working toward his PhD and expected Kyla to be his cook, housekeeper, and general gofer. Winnie married a studly mechanic who looked like sex in tight jeans and didn't know who Edgar Allan Poe was. Winnie now had two adorable children, and her dreams of her own PhD and a career teaching English literature had evaporated.

Meg didn't want either one of their lives. As Louisa May Alcott had said, "I'd rather be a free spinster and paddle my own canoe."

But Meg wanted children. And she had to admit she wanted them with a husband, a man she admired and desired, who would cherish his children, and all she asked was that he be *intelligent*. Well, *kind* would also be a good quality.

Would she give up teaching to be a wife and mother? Why should she have to? If only she could meet an insurance agent, or the manager of a Home Depot, or a mail-man. A good guy with a steady job and a steady, kind, reliable heart. Was that too much to ask?

It was some comfort that Arden and Jenny weren't married or engaged, either. Back in the old, old days, when the three of them were on the island for that first summer after their father married Justine, it was already clear that Arden was the man magnet. Of course, she was fourteen, with boobs and curves, while Jenny was the stick she still remained and Meg had looked like a plump little kid.

Now that Meg allowed herself to sink back into the memory, she marveled at how much fun that long-ago summer had been.

After breakfast, the three girls would gather up their beach bags and hurry along the narrow lanes to Jetties Beach. They'd toss down their stuff—beach umbrella, sunblock, and cooler of cold drinks—and dash into the surf. They'd have swimming races, contests to see who could stay under the longest; they'd build extravagant sand castles; they'd beachcomb; they'd fall asleep on their towels, returning home red as lobsters. They were always giggling at something, anything, a woman's jiggling bosom, a boy's smile—everything seemed hysterically funny.

After lunch, they'd walk into town to check out books from the library or buy fashion magazines and ice cream. In the heat of the afternoon, they'd sprawl in the back-yard, reading and snoozing, or if it was raining, they'd play games. Monopoly. Scrabble. Clue. In the evening, they might go back into town to see a movie or just to hang around Main Street, people watching, listening to the street musicians, giggling at how cute the guitarist was.

Meg didn't remember them fighting, not that first year.

It was the next year, when Arden was fifteen and she and Jenny were twelve, that everything changed.

Arden had cut her long red ponytail into a short asymmetrical mess that fell in her eyes. She had three holes in her left ear, two in her right. She wore heavy eye makeup, black fingernail polish, and slutty clothes. While Jenny and Meg were still singing songs from the Disney movie *Beauty and the Beast*, Arden was blasting the house with Nirvana and Pearl Jam.

The three girls had seen each other about once a month over the winter, when their father took them all out to dinner and a play or a movie, so Meg was aware of how Arden was changing, but living with her in the Nantucket house was a whole new experience. Meg expected Arden to favor her over Jenny; after all, Meg and Arden were half sisters, not stepsisters. But Arden treated Meg with the same disdain as she treated Jenny. It was confusing, and it hurt.

When they first arrived on the island, as they lugged their duffel bags up the stairs, Arden said to Meg, "I'm taking the back bedroom this year."

"But I choose the back bedroom," Meg protested. "I can pretend I'm a writer there."

"Tough. I'm taking it."

Meg changed tack. "Your bedroom is so much prettier, with all the mermaids. You've got so much more space."

Arden had whipped around and hissed at Meg, "Yeah, and I can lie there and hear Dad and Justine talking and laughing. The happy married couple. They always make me turn down my music." She stormed past Meg, dragging her luggage, down the hall, into the back bedroom, and slammed the door.

Unhappily, Meg had moved into the mermaid bedroom, which was pleasant, she had to admit. She didn't know why Arden had been so upset, but she didn't have a portable CD player, and she didn't listen to Nirvana. She was twelve, but a young, unformed twelve, continuing her lifelong obsession with reading. More and more aware of her weight, she didn't want to go to the beach as often, or out for an ice cream cone. Jenny got cranky because Meg was always reading. Arden was either out of the house or locked in her room, and she refused to play any board games, ever, which limited what Meg and Jenny could play. Meg could overhear her father and Justine arguing about the girls: Justine wanted Rory to make Arden be polite and Meg stop being such an introvert. Rory reminded Justine she was talking about teenagers.

By July, the atmosphere in the house was radioactive. Arguments erupted. Doors were slammed.

Since Justine cooked for all five in the family, she insisted that the three girls take turns cleaning the kitchen after dinner. One night Arden wandered into the house shortly after seven, when the others had just finished their evening meal and were still sitting around the dining room table.

"Where have you been?" Rory demanded.

"Walking." Arden shrugged, reaching over to pick up a carrot from Meg's plate.

Justine said, "We've finished dinner."

Arden tossed her head. "Fine. I'm not hungry."

"It's your night to do the dishes," Jenny reminded her.

"Since I didn't eat, I shouldn't have to do the dishes," Arden countered.

A silence fell, the calm before the storm.

"I cooked enough food for you. I set a place for you. It is your turn to do the dishes." Justine spoke calmly, but anger made her voice tremble.

"I don't agree," Arden responded, cool as ice.

Justine made a small gasp. She shot Rory a black look. When he didn't speak, Justine shoved back her chair, rose from the table, and approached Arden. "While you're living in this house, you'll do as you're told."

Meg rushed to intervene. "I'll do the dishes tonight. Really, I don't mind."

Arden gave a fake bitter snorting laugh. "Oh, Christ, Meg, you're such a pussy!"

Justine slapped Arden's face. "Don't you use that language in my house."

Arden went white, tears shimmering at the edges of her eyes, lips trembling. Meg jumped up from the table and rushed to put her arms around her.

"Don't you hit my sister!" she spat at Justine.

Eventually, Rory had resolved the argument by laying down the law: Whether or not Arden ate with them, she had to do the dishes on her night.

From then on, Arden's presence in the house created tension. Meg went to the library more or hid in her room, reading. She began to sneak candy bars into her room to nibble. She felt a void deep inside she couldn't seem to fill.

Meg lay on the beach in the sunshine, a grown woman shaken to her core by memories. She warned herself: *Stop right there.*

Years had passed since that horrible summer. At boarding school and college, Meg had met girls whose families made her own look enviable. World literature had shown her families who killed one another for land, money, or power. What she'd gone through was nothing to cry about. It was only complicated and it had been unfair, but life was complicated and unfair. *God*, she said to herself, *stop whining.*

Suddenly the sun was too hot, and her back hurt from lying in the sand. She began to gather up her stuff.

As she did, a blonde woman, fortyish, spread out her towel next to Meg and slathered sunblock on her arms.

"Hi," she chirped pleasantly to Meg.

Preoccupied, Meg replied briefly, "Hello."

"Oh, am I disturbing you?" the blonde asked.

"What? Oh no, not at all. I just remembered something I've got to do."

Meg rose, picked up her beach bag, and tracked up through the hot sand, wondering why the other woman had seemed disappointed at her departure.

EIGHT

Justine had always been a beauty. She'd nurtured this quality with careful nutrition, yoga, exercise, spa treatments, manicures, pedicures, and, in the past five or so years, weekly visits to the hairdresser. Clothes shopping had been a serious occupation for her, and she'd utilized great taste, not to mention money, in decorating their large, historic Belmont house to perfection.

Now she wandered around the perfect house in a stained robe, her hair lank, tipped with split ends. Makeup hadn't touched her face since she returned from Rory's funeral, and as far as nutrition—well, she was getting most of that from wine.

How would she get through the rest of her life without Rory?

How was she going to get through the next *hour* without Rory? He was the love of her life.

They'd met at the perfume counter in the Natick Mall Lord & Taylor. Rory was looking for a present for a client, he told her, an older woman who had just purchased a posh town house. He wanted something classy, and his glance at her let her understand he knew she was all about classy.

Tall, wide-shouldered, blue-eyed, and red-haired, Rory exuded confidence, joie de vivre, and sexuality. He laughed easily, his eyes twinkled, and when they touched— so Justine could spray perfume on his wrist—angels sang.

He took a long time selecting his gift—Chanel No. 5— and returned the next day saying he needed to buy perfume for his secretary's birthday.

The third time he came, he told her with an honest nervousness that he was buying a present for his wife. Perhaps they could talk? He'd like to talk. Rory took her to lunch.

She was thirty. She'd had a child out of wedlock, little Jenny, who was now nine and had never had a father. Nothing tragic, Justine confessed, only foolish. She'd made a mistake when she was in college and became a single mother at twenty. She'd married once when she was twenty-five. Her husband had been not exactly mean to his stepdaughter but cold. Cold to five-year-old Jenny. That marriage hadn't lasted a year. After that, Justine had sworn she'd never marry again.

Rory told Justine he was thirty-nine, a successful real estate broker, and husband to a nice woman named Cyndi. Together they had a little girl, Meg, just nine years old.

"We each have a daughter nine years old," they said to each other in a kind of awe, as if this formed an unbreakable bond between them.

Rory had been married once before, briefly, to a woman named Nora, and they had a daughter, too, twelve-year-old Arden.

"Classy name," Justine told him.

"She's a classy kid. Smart as a whip, too. I don't see her as often as I'd like, but every other week and most of the summer Arden stays with Cyndi, Meg, and me."

"You all get along?" Justine asked.

"As well as any family, I suppose." Rory had hesitated, then sat back in his chair and regarded her helplessly. "What are we going to do?"

Heart aching, Justine aimed for lightheartedness. "We're going to finish our lunch and go our separate ways. You'll start buying your perfume elsewhere."

They were married a year later, after Rory's no-fault divorce from Meg's mother, during which he agreed to let Cyndi have the Boston house, her Lexus, and a whopping pile of money. He kept the Nantucket house, the house he'd first bought with Cyndi.

They introduced the three girls to one another gradually, starting off on fun social occasions where their attention was sidetracked and they could perceive the reality in a kind of sideways fashion. Movies, theme parks, museums, aquariums were all visited before they brought the three girls into their Nantucket house for the first sleepover.

Although, of course, Jenny was already in the house.

A quiet, shy little girl, Jenny was considered something of a puzzle by her caregivers and teachers. At day care, she ignored the other children, finding a corner for herself where she built tiny intricate worlds out of all the broken bits of toys the other children ignored. When she started kindergarten, she was assessed and deemed to be quite intelligent. She could talk; she just didn't. She learned to read and do math early. She colored between the lines. She never acted out. She wasn't a problem, so she was overlooked at school. While Justine didn't ignore her daughter, by the time she returned home from standing on her feet behind a counter all day, she was too exhausted to do much more than microwave Kraft mac and cheese for Jenny and collapse on the sofa with a glass of wine.

Rory Randall was like the sun shining on a plant that had lived struggling in the shade. With his booming voice, easy laugh, and entertaining manner, he lit up their lives. He was a generous, loving, intuitive man. The first year of their marriage, he took much of the summer off so he could stay at his Nantucket house and help Jenny learn to swim and sail. Jenny blossomed like a rose in June.

Justine had never known that people could be so happy. Jenny was smiling, laughing, making friends at school, getting invited to birthday parties, bringing girls home! Justine realized her own heart had been trapped in a cage of anxiety and caution: She had hardly done anything for fear of doing something wrong. Justine *adored* Rory. He was her hero, her champion, her prince.

In her happiness, Justine secretly vowed to be loving to Rory's other two daughters, even if Arden, the older, bratty one, was a challenge. The first summer on Nantucket, they invited Arden and Meg to come stay for most of the summer. This length of time would give them a chance to know one another, Rory decided, and Justine wanted to make Rory happy.

The first year wasn't so bad. Rory kept them on a madcap schedule of swimming, sailing, and tennis lessons. He enrolled them in art and science courses. He set up jigsaw puzzles on the dining room table. He brought home videos and took them to movies at the Gaslight. The girls squabbled sometimes, but they laughed together, too. Rory was happy, and Justine was happy for him even though she was overwhelmed with buying groceries at the crowded stores and feeding all five of them three meals a day.

Then it all changed. During the school year, Arden transformed from a sullen girl into a rebellious slut.

Every time Arden came over to spend the night with Meg and Jenny, who still played with their American Girl dolls and took riding lessons, the difference increased. Arden's skirts got shorter. Her shirts plunged lower. Suddenly her auburn hair had purple streaks in it. She tossed around curse words like confetti in spite of Justine's admonitions. She made jokes about condoms and blow jobs.

Justine was horrified. She'd been a rather racy little teenager herself, back in the day, but nothing like this, and she hadn't even had sex until she was nineteen, at which point she got herself knocked up. She tried having private counseling sessions with Arden, talking with her about the pressures of adolescence, but Arden only stared at Justine with shark eyes.

During the school term, it was tolerable. Arden ignored the younger girls to tap away on her computer or watch videos while Jenny and Meg hung out together, and when Rory came home from the real estate office, they all sat together at the table, eating dinner like the books said to, one big happy blended family. Justine talked to Rory about Arden, but he dismissed what Justine interpreted as serious signs of a personality disorder as the normal teenage desire to be different.

Then came the second summer on Nantucket.

Justine thought that perhaps she'd made a mistake, back then, when she did what she did. Certainly it had driven a stake into the possibility of Jenny having a close relationship with her stepsisters. Justine had been younger in those days, and caught up in a family happiness she'd never dreamed she'd have and was terrified of losing.

Now, with her precious Rory gone, she kept revisiting those early days. She could only hope this summer would provide an opportunity for Rory's daughters to become friends—and, more than friends, sisters. Then perhaps Justine's guilt would not lie so heavily on her spirit.

NINE

Palmer White was as good as his word. He escorted Arden to the Forbeses' black-tie party and introduced her to dozens of the glittering wealthy and chic, some of whom were quite pleased at the idea of being on her show.

"Call me, darling. We'll have lunch." Three women had said that to her, and Arden had their phone numbers punched into her cell. Score! It actually made her feel, if not fond of Jenny, less resentful of her. They were all in their thirties now, the past was over and done, here they were on the island, so why not have a wonderful summer?

Thursday was her night to cook, and buoyed by her high spirits, she decided to serve lobster for dinner. Lobsters, Bartlett's tomatoes, corn on the cob, and tiny new red-skinned potatoes. A chocolate cake from the Bake Shop. A tart white wine. She bought daisies for the center of the table.

"What's all this?" Meg came into the house through the kitchen door, her arms full of books.

"Oh, I'm feeling hungry for lobster," Arden told her blithely. "I mean, what's summer on Nantucket without an occasional lobster dinner?"

"Gosh, Arden, this is fabulous. Can I help you do anything?"

"No, thanks. As soon as Jenny shows up, I'll drop the lobsters and the corn in their pots. Until then, let's have some wine."

Meg's eyes narrowed. "Arden. Tell the truth. Something happened."

"Nothing happened. I'm just in a generous mood. Don't worry, I'm sure it will all balance out over the summer. Some nights I'll give you bologna sandwiches."

Meg laughed. "I'll get rid of these books." When she came back down, she'd brushed her glorious hair and put on dangling shimmery earrings. Blushing, she explained, "I thought I should look nice for the lobsters."

"Oh, wow!" Jenny stood in the doorway, surprised. "What happened?"

"Arden's in a good mood for once," Meg jested, grinning at Arden as she spoke.

"That's true," Arden agreed. "I felt like making a perfect Nantucket summer meal. I haven't had a lobster dinner in ages."

Jenny's countenance softened from suspicious to hopeful. "I haven't, either. Lobster's so expensive."

It was the perfect thing to hear. Arden shrugged carelessly. "I can afford it."

Jenny accepted a glass of wine and joined Meg at the

kitchen table while Arden lifted the lids on the pots to see if the water was ready.

"A few more minutes," she said, and sat down with them at the table. "To be honest, Jenny, I'm kind of celebrating because Palmer White introduced me to some people I can use on my show. Ariadne Silverstone, for one."

"Very cool," Jenny said.

"I wouldn't have met Palmer if you hadn't taken me to that party. So, thank you." She lifted her glass to Jenny.

Jenny blinked shyly. "I'm glad it's working out for you."

Meg, not wanting to be left out, chimed in. "Plus, Arden met Tim Robinson at the party."

Arden looked smug. "That's true. So thanks again, Jenny."

Jenny hid her face as she chugged a long drink of wine, then went into a coughing fit. When she could speak again, she said, "Just remember, Arden, I warned you about Tim."

"Why don't you like him?" Arden asked. "He strikes me as one of the few decent men I've met recently."

Jenny shifted uncomfortably. "I met him when I met Bjorn. I could tell Tim didn't like me dating him, though I never understood why. A gang of us used to go out in Tim's boat with a cooler of beer. We had fun, but Tim always gave me the cold shoulder. After Bjorn and I broke up, Tim stopped talking to me except about work, like this arts coalition site. I just think he's unreliable. Maybe bipolar."

"Oh, for heaven's sake, everyone's bipolar," Arden said.

"Or bisexual," Meg added, giggling, her cheeks rosy.

Arden laughed to see sweet little Meg getting tipsy. "At least bicoastal," she added, and rose. "The water's bubbling. I'm putting the lobsters in."

While the corn and lobsters boiled, Arden melted butter in the microwave and set bowls of it in front of the three place mats. She'd already put out the plates, silverware, and shell crackers, and she added bowls to toss the shells into. Jenny and Meg offered to help, but Arden insisted that tonight was her night to cook.

"Tell me about your day, Meg," Arden invited as she moved around the kitchen.

Meg lit up. "Heavenly. I've been reading about women artists in the late 1800s. Did you realize that back then women weren't allowed to draw the male figure nude because women were considered too delicate? In Boston, they were so prudish. Women were allowed to take classes in male drawing, but they had to wear veils, so if the model ever passed them on the streets, he wouldn't recognize them."

Arden and Jenny broke into peals of laughter.

"The man sat there naked and the women wore veils?" Jenny asked.

"Kinky," Arden said.

The kitchen filled with steam, and Jenny and Meg jumped up to help. When everything was done, they gathered around the table, dipping the sweet fresh lobster flesh into the salty melted butter, crunching into the corn on the cob, their fingers and lips shiny with butter.

When they were done, the shells of tails, claws, and legs towered in the bowls. They licked their fingers. Arden got up from the table and returned with a roll of paper towels. They wiped their hands and leaned back in their chairs and groaned with pleasure.

"Dad used to get all excited about lobster dinners," Arden mused. "He fancied the *event* of it all, getting out the shell crackers and picks."

"I remember," Meg chimed in. "We had special bibs."

"Right, and Mom gave him an apron and chef's hat because she couldn't bring herself to drop the lobsters into the boiling water," Jenny added.

A momentary silence fell. Arden broke it, saying truthfully, "I never saw the apron and hat. But I'm sure he treasured it. He was mad for dressing up."

Grateful to Arden for smoothing over what could have been an awkward patch, Jenny agreed. "He *was* a bit of a peacock. I always thought he took the three of us out to the ballet and dinner so he'd have an occasion to wear a suit and that swanky coat of his with the velvet collar and cuffs."

"We got to dress up, too," Meg said. "I always looked forward to that."

Arden stretched her arms lazily. "Did Dad ever take either of you out by yourself? I mean after we were all grown up."

"Not me," Meg answered.

"Nor me," Jenny added. "I think Dad favored the idea of family."

Arden snorted. "That's why he married three different women."

"Well, yes," Jenny argued thoughtfully. "He was kind of a philanderer, going from Arden's mom to Meg's mom to my mom, but he wasn't a cad."

Arden quietly said, "I don't think my mother would agree with you." She ran her fingers around the rim of her glass. "But he did keep us nicely financially supported. And when he was with us, he was really *with* us. Not thinking of something else, not in a hurry to get away from us."

"He loved us," Meg said. "In his own flawed, charming way, he loved us."

"He was so handsome," Jenny mused. "I suppose it's hard for a man that handsome to stick with one woman."

"It wasn't just his looks," Meg pointed out. "It was his personality. He was vibrant. (Can a man be *vibrant*?) He loved life. Whenever I was around him, it was like the world went brighter, more vivid." Suddenly she buried her face in her hands. "Oh man, I miss him."

"I know." Arden had tears in her eyes. "The bastard, dying like that."

"I can't believe he'll never hug me again." Jenny wrapped her arms around herself and lowered her head, swallowing her grief.

"He could always make me laugh," Arden said.

"He always made me feel beautiful," Meg said.

"You *are* beautiful," Jenny told her.

"I'm fat," Meg choked out.

"Oh, get over yourself," Arden ordered. "You're not fat. You're stacked."

"Plus, your hair. Your skin. Sorry, no sympathy for you at this table."

"He made us all feel beautiful, I think," Meg decided.

"It's true." Jenny pulled a tissue from her pocket and wiped her eyes, yet continued crying. "I don't want him to be gone. I really don't."

"I know," Meg agreed. "I'm so sad."

After a few moments, Arden blew her nose noisily. Lifting her head, she announced, "Ladies. I also bought a chocolate cake."

"I'm supposed to be dieting," Meg complained.

"Fine," Arden teased. "Don't eat any."

"Temptation, thy name is Arden." Meg shook her head, smiling helplessly.

Jenny said, "Arden, thank you. You gave us a wonderful meal."

"You're welcome," Arden told her. "I know what else we need. TV. A movie—something with Sandra Bullock and a speeding bus."

"Oh, absolutely."

Their sorrow drifted away as they rose from the table. Hurriedly, they cleared the dishes and cleaned up the kitchen, working in silent accord. They headed into the den. Jenny searched for a movie with the remote, and found *Speed*. They plopped down on the leather sofa together, laid their feet on the coffee table, and watched.

After a while, they paused the movie and went into the kitchen for huge slabs of chocolate cake.

TEN

Late Saturday morning, Arden met Tim at the yacht club. They took the launch out to his daysailer, and while Arden lounged in the stern, rubbing sunblock over her face and limbs, Tim readied the boat.

The day was warm, the wind gentle, just brisk enough to skip them over the waves to Coatue, a long strip of sand at the east end of the island. Tim didn't talk while he steered, but contentedly observed the harbor waters, blue sky, and long stretch of golden beach.

Arden observed Tim. Almost movie-star handsome, so tall, lean, and muscular, with long tanned limbs, he was not the kind of guy she usually dated. For one thing, the men she went out with talked. Incessantly. Like Arden, they were ambitious, creative, on their way up the ladder of success, with ideas, strategies, plots, and projects cascading out of their overactive brains. They were definitely not Nature Boys, although if they had to woo a client, they could play a decent game of golf or tennis.

Tim steered the boat into the shallows. "I'll anchor here."

Arden nodded. "What can I carry?"

"Grab the beach blanket and towels."

She did. He hefted the cooler and they waded in to shore. The water was cool but inviting.

They dropped their burdens on the sand. Tim glanced at Arden questioningly.

"Oh yeah," she said. "Let's have a swim."

The water enveloped her, turquoise silk, azure satin, radiant with sunlight. Tim struck off in an easy crawl, steadily heading for the other side of the world, or so it seemed, as he effortlessly sent his long, slim body through the water. Arden swam a bit, but mostly floated on her back, letting the water support her, closing her eyes, drifting.

Later, they came dripping up from the water, dried off, and put on sun hats to protect their faces. Together they unfolded the blanket and spread it over the sand to sit on. They doled out the treats they'd bought at Something Natural: sandwiches, chips, cookies. Tim had brought beer and soda, too. They sat cross-legged on the sand, gazing out at the sparkling water, eating, chatting. Sun sparked his blond hair into gold and illuminated the rather wondrous lines of his torso. *This guy must work out*, Arden thought.

Aware that he noticed her studying him, she said, "You seem at home here."

"I grew up here," Tim told her. "My father's a contractor; my mother works for the chamber of commerce. My older brother is the superachiever, lucky for me. He's in

New York, working for a law firm. I get to be the mellow one."

Arden laughed. "Mellow?"

"When I went to MIT, my father had high hopes I'd go on to Silicon Valley and invent a new computer, or at least gaming software. But I always knew I'd return to the island, and the timing was perfect for what I wanted to do. I came back two years ago and started The Computer Guy, and I have more work than I can handle." He took a swig of beer. "What about you?"

Arden was about to answer when Tim continued, "You're Jenny's half sister, right?"

She refrained from sharply pointing out that she wouldn't say that was the most significant fact about her. Instead, she said, "Stepsister."

"Right. The famous one."

Arden aimed a flirtatious smile at him. "I do a show on Channel Six in Boston. I don't think it makes me famous, but some people recognize me."

"How did you get into that?"

"I always wanted to be on television, but not as an actress. For a while," she admitted, "I wanted to be a weather girl on the Weather Channel." Arden rose to her knees and waved her arm toward an imaginary screen. "And the highs today in the Ohio River Valley will rise to an unprecedented eighty-three degrees, while down here in Tucson, my goodness, folks, they're expecting snow!" She realized her green bikini set off her lean, fit figure as she moved. She was vain, and knew it. She enjoyed his frank appraisal of her as she posed.

Tim laughed. "Seems like a natural for you."

Arden shrugged and sank back into the sand, wrapping her arms around her knees. "A girl has her dreams," she joked. "I actually took a course in meteorology in college, but it wasn't for me. Plus, the whole time I was at BU, I thought I might end up selling real estate. Mom and Dad both were real estate agents. After college, I worked in Mom's office in Boston for a while. Then I started helping a friend of Mom's who's a professional house stager."

"A what?"

"There's a whole industry of people who help you sell your house by getting it ready for prospective buyers to see. Buyers don't want to see your baby photos or your high school basketball trophies or even your historic silver. They need to envision a house as it would be with *their* stuff in it. Most people can't strip it down themselves. They're too attached to their possessions, and they think what they have is just right. So stagers come in, remove the clutter, rearrange the furniture, and get it ready for showing."

"Sort of like my mom going through my room when I was a kid."

Arden laughed. "Sort of. Anyway, I was so amazed at the crap people hang on to and how it hampers their lives, even their vision of what their future might hold. So I came up with a plan for a television show about that, and Mom just happened to be dating the general manager of Channel Six at that time. . . ."

"Aha," Tim said.

"Hey, it's all about who you know, right? Bud liked the

idea, I put the show together, and it's run for four years now."

"Think you'll move on? To New York or LA or Atlanta?"

Arden drew a curvy design in the sand with her forefinger as she contemplated the question. "I don't know. I like Boston. And I like being close to my mom."

"And your sisters."

Arden hesitated. This was officially a first date, and she didn't want to let loose all her pent-up sarcasm about Jenny, Justine, and even Meg and Cyndi. She knew it made her sound sour. "I don't know how much I'll see Jenny," she replied at last. "Since she lives on Nantucket and I don't get here very often."

"Do you think Jenny will stay on the island?" Tim asked.

"I have no idea. You know about our father's last controlling-from-the-grave deal about the house, right?"

"No, actually, I don't."

"The three of us will inherit the Lily Street house only if we spend three months of this summer together in the house. Then we can keep it or sell it and divide the profits."

Tim whistled. "Huge profits on that place."

"Right. That's why I'm down here instead of in Boston. Meg, too."

"What does Jenny think of all this?"

Arden cocked her head. "You know, you seem just a tad obsessed with Jenny."

Tim averted his face, picking up a pebble and tossing it far out into the water. "Maybe. We're competitors."

"Surely there's room for more than one computer expert on the island."

"Oh, definitely. Plus, she's got a couple of contracts with New York–based firms. She set up a complicated site for about two hundred plastic surgeons and keeps that going, and does something for one of the big news blogs. So her major income doesn't even come from the island."

"You sure know a lot about her work."

Tim shrugged. "She knows a lot about mine."

"And . . . ," coaxed Arden.

Tim's expression grew stony. "She thinks she can just toy with guys. I don't trust her."

Arden waited for more, but Tim started gathering up the empty bottles and sandwich wrappers, stowing them in the cooler. He looked at the fat diving watch on his arm. "We should get back."

They sailed in silence, luxuriating in the day. It was nearly five when they secured the boat to the buoy, beckoned the launch, and were motored to the yacht club dock.

Arden thought perhaps Tim would invite her for dinner, or at least a drink, so she was surprised when Tim merely asked, "Would you like me to drive you home?"

Standing on the front porch of the club, Arden was a five-minute walk from the Lily Street house, and because of Nantucket's narrow one-way streets, a good ten-minute drive. Still, if Tim had spoken differently—if he'd said, "I'd like to drive you home"—she wouldn't have resisted.

"No, it's fine," Arden told him coolly. "I'll walk. It's

easier. Tim, thanks for the sail. I haven't been sailing in years, and this was a perfect day."

He smiled down at her. "I know. Perfect for me, too. I wish we could continue it, but I've got plans for tonight—not interesting plans, either, I'm sorry to say. I've got a customer arriving on the five o'clock ferry who's desperate for computer help. I've got to get home and shower and clean up so I can spend this fabulous evening with him."

Arden laughed. "Poor you." Her ego assuaged, she leaned up and kissed his cheek. "Another time, then."

"Arden."

She stopped.

Tim shifted from foot to foot. "Here's the deal. You're a total babe. I like hanging out with you. But these days I'm kind of off women. Romantically, I mean. I'd like to take you sailing again, but . . ." He grimaced, unable to find the words.

Arden took pity on him. "But no romance, right? Just friends?"

He nodded, visibly relieved.

"I'd enjoy a good male friend to sail with," Arden assured him. "No worries, okay?" With a little wave, she set off walking.

ELEVEN

"Are you busy, Liam?"

"Meg! I was hoping you'd call. How are you?"

Meg laughed deep in her throat. Only someone who'd seen her heaving her heavy book bags through the dirty winter slush of Sudbury College's campus could fully appreciate the stark contrast with her present surroundings.

"Well, Liam, I'm sitting on a bench at the top of Steps Beach, looking out over Nantucket Sound. A ferry is coming in, and I can count at least ten sailboats drifting out in the water. One has red sails."

"Okay, bye now," Liam joked.

"I'm surrounded by wild roses. The perfume is heavenly. I've got a great tan. I never tan, I usually burn, but I've gotten into a routine. I run on the beach in the morning and walk in the evening, when it's not so hot, when the sun's not so direct."

"Sounds perfect. Are you getting any work done?"

"Yes, O Voice of My Conscience! I work every morning after my run. In the afternoons, I work in the library on my laptop, just to get out of the house."

"How's it going with your sisters?"

"Not as bad as I'd feared," Meg told him. "We're all busy, and the house is so big that we don't get in each other's way. Plenty of bathwater and all that. We take turns cooking dinner for the three of us most nights, and yum, the seafood here is amazing. Fresh sea bass, or tuna, or bluefish—"

Liam groaned. "You're killing me."

"Oh, Liam." Meg pulled her legs up and wrapped her arms around them, cuddling the phone against her ear. "Tell me how you are. How are your summer school classes?"

"My fresh comp class is worse than usual. Our slacker student body becomes even more so in the summer. They miss half the classes and want me to give them A's anyway. But my lit class is good. Nice kids, lots of fun. Unfortunately, the air-conditioning in the building broke and you know our windows don't open. It's so hot and humid it's like teaching in a rain forest. Perfect for *Heart of Darkness*. I expect brightly colored macaws to fly out of the students' hair."

"I remember that heat," Meg said with real sympathy.

"I miss trapping you in your office, Meg." His voice was low, sweet, almost shy.

Something sexual, something spiritual, too, sped directly through Meg's body, catching her on a silken hook. For a moment she couldn't speak. She shifted on the bench. "Miss you, too," she answered brightly. "I'd better go. It's my night to fix dinner."

"Don't tell me what you're cooking," Liam begged. "Don't say a word."

"Spaghetti with red clam sauce," Meg told him, laughing. "What are you having?"

Liam whined with fake pathos, "Oh, I'm sure there are some leftovers in the back of the fridge."

"Mmm, probably a curled-up piece of old pizza," she teased. They said good-bye and clicked off. She felt oddly overheated in spite of the sea breeze.

Sitting at the kitchen table that evening with Arden and Jenny, Meg said, "I think we should throw a Fourth of July party."

"Here at my house?" Jenny asked, shocked.

"Yes, here at *our* house." Meg looked steadily across the table at Jenny. "When will we ever have the opportunity to have a Fourth of July party on Nantucket again?"

"But," Jenny objected, "you don't know anyone."

"Duh," Meg said. "We'd invite them down from Boston. I'm yearning for Liam to come down here. I miss him. He's my colleague at the college, my best friend, really. I don't think he's ever been to Nantucket."

Arden nodded. "Good idea, Meg. I could ask Serena; she's my best friend, a lawyer in Boston. Plus," she added, turning to Jenny, "I do know Palmer White and Tim Robinson."

Jenny chewed her lip. "Tim's not exactly my friend."

"Well, he's *my* friend," Arden cooed suggestively. She enjoyed teasing Jenny, the spoiled princess who had it all.

Jenny put her fork down on her plate very slowly. "Oh, really."

Arden smirked. "Yes. Really."

Jenny was clearly working to keep it together. "So you slept with him."

"I didn't say that," Arden replied silkily. "But we did go sailing and we're going to see each other again."

Jenny folded her hands in her lap and gave herself a moment. "Arden. I don't want to have Tim in m—*this* house. We're not friendly."

"Yeah, I know."

"You know?" Jenny lost all pretense of remaining poised. "Exactly what do you know?"

Arden relented. "Nothing, honestly." Holding up her hands, she admitted, "He just seems edgy about you. What's the problem?"

"I have no idea," Jenny said.

"You won't even know he's here," Arden argued. "We'll invite lots of people. We'll have some guests down from Boston—we can put a couple up in the front bedroom, and there's a pullout double bed in the den, and there's always the living room sofa. Plus, Jenny, you must have lots of friends on the island."

Jenny bugged out her eyes at them. "Of course I have friends."

"Fab!" Arden clapped her hands. "Then let's plan our party!"

"Darling," Nora said. "How's it going down there on the sunny isle of dreams?"

"Actually, Mom, it's good." Arden lay on her bed in the mermaid room, cell phone to her ear. "We're all getting along okay, and Jenny has taken me to parties where I've met some very interesting people."

"I knew you'd meet the right people there. Anyone special?"

"Well, there's a guy named Palmer White—"

"Palmer White!" Nora whooped. "Arden! Palmer White is *huge*. He owns everything! Tell me, tell me, tell me, tell me!"

"If you'd be quiet a moment, I will. And don't get so excited over him. Have you met the man? He's completely conceited."

"That's because he's brilliant."

"Mom, listen, I've met several other cool people, too. Like Genevieve Beaudreau—"

"Don't recognize the name."

"She's from Texas. I've had lunch with Bettina Winters, and I think she's going to let me use—"

"Bettina Winters? Is she married to Perry Winters?"

"If you keep interrupting me, I'll never finish," Arden snapped. Her mother huffed into the phone. "Yes. Yes, Bettina is married to Perry Winters, the drugstore mogul. They have a fabulous house down here, and about a thousand grandchildren, so she would *adore*, that's her word, to have me simplify her life."

"Darling, that's wonderful. I'm so proud of you."

"I'm excited by the idea, I have to admit. We're going to do a series about it, because they've decided to build a separate guesthouse on their property for some of the family. Also, they've been storing bikes, wheelbarrows, and so on in the same shed where they keep their kayaks and canoes, so it's a dream come true for before and after. I've got pages of notes."

Nora said, "I've got to come down sometime."

"Want to come for our Fourth of July party?"

"Sweet, I can't. I'm going to Tanglewood with friends. The *1812 Overture* and all those sexy cannon explosions."

Arden rolled her eyes. "Right. Another time, then."

"Hi, Mom."

"Meg! How are you?"

"Great. Loving it here. How are you? How are the boys?"

"I'm fine. The boys are backpacking through Europe, you know, and I haven't heard from them for three days."

"I'm sure they're okay, Mom. They're nineteen. They're big guys. They're in Norway now. That's a safe place, right?"

Cyndi said, "I suppose you're right."

"Listen, I'm calling to see if you, or you and Tom, would like to come down to spend the Fourth of July on Nantucket."

Cyndi was silent.

"In our house, of course. You'd have the master bedroom and bath all to yourselves."

Still silence.

"We've decided to throw a party. We're inviting

friends down, and I thought it would be fun for you and
Tom to come."

Finally Meg's mother spoke, squeaking up an octave
as she did when she was nervous. "The thing is, honey,
ever since the boys went off to college, your stepfather
and I have developed the most active social life. You
would be completely shocked. We belong to a bridge
club, and a book group, and a dinner club, where each
month someone hosts a dinner with a theme. Like Italian
food and wine, or sushi. I have to say the sushi didn't go
over very well."

Meg's shoulders slumped. She'd guessed what her
mother would say before she said it. Tom had never developed any kind of connection with Meg. Perhaps it
was her fault. By now it shouldn't matter. She was an
adult. She didn't need his affection. But she did want her
mother's attention and affection; she couldn't help it, it
was a deep, fierce craving. Perhaps that was why she favored *Little Women* so much, with the warmly maternal
Marmee, who worshipped her daughters, all four of
them; who spoke softly, gave moral instruction, was patient and even doting. Meg had actually wondered
whether she preferred the book because the father wasn't
there, just as her own father hadn't been there, just as, in
her deepest, most selfish heart, she wished Tom had
never been there to steal away her mother's heart, to give
her mother twin sons who took her devotion from Meg.

Cyndi said, "Meg, I'm so sorry, but we've got a party
already scheduled for the holiday. Tom will have to get
back to work the next day, anyway, so we really can't fit

even an overnight trip in right now. Perhaps later in the summer?"

"Okay, Mom. Just thought I'd check. I'll call you again to see when a good time would be for you both. Wouldn't you like a nice little free holiday on the island?"

Cyndi sighed. "The truth is—I might as well admit it—I don't think Tom would ever want to stay in Rory's house. That's just too—oh, I don't know—strange."

"But Dad *died*," Meg protested.

"Yes, but he slept in that house. Probably in the master bedroom you're offering us. I don't think Tom would ever want to sleep in Rory's bed."

"Okay, I get that. But there's a pullout sofa in the den," Meg persisted.

"Still, it was Rory's house. You need to be a little more sensitive, Meg, you really do."

Meg felt as if she'd been slapped. It took a moment for her to get her breath back. "All right, then," she said weakly.

"I'm sorry, Meg. It has nothing to do with you."

"Tom has nothing to do with me," Meg echoed.

"Don't put words in my mouth. Honestly, Meg, I think you're trying to pick a fight!"

Meg forced herself to back down. "I'm sorry, Mom. I don't mean to. I just wanted to ask you and Tom down for a visit. But I can understand why you might not want to come."

"Thank you for that, Meg. You know how I hate being caught between Tom and you. Listen, enjoy yourself. You've got the opportunity to spend the summer on the island. Then you'll be able to sell the house and have a good nest egg to buy your own house someday. The weeks will fly. We'll see you back in Boston in no time at all."

"Right. Well, okay, then, say hi to the boys when you talk to them. Say hi to Tom for me, okay?"

"Of course, Meg. Good-bye, sweetheart."

"Mom, how are you?"

"Jenny. Hi, sweetie. So good to hear your voice. The question is: How are *you*?"

"We're all getting along fine," Jenny assured her mother.

"I'm so glad. I really hope the three of you can bond, especially now that Rory's gone. You're all grown up, with your own lives. The past is behind us. It would be nice for you to have stepsisters you could share things with."

"It's a good thought, Mom. We'll see how it goes. Listen, the reason I'm calling is that we've decided to have a Fourth of July party. The three of us together. Sort of an all-day picnic and swimming at the beach, then a cookout at home and then the fireworks at Jetties Beach. Would you like to come down?"

"I'm delighted to hear you three are cooperating like this," Justine said. "That's wonderful. Let me think about it, will you? After all, Meg and Arden hold a serious grudge against me. I'm afraid I'd be the thirteenth fairy at the christening."

"That's silly, Mom."

"I don't think so. Are Cyndi and Nora coming?"

"No, I think they're busy."

"Mmm. Even more reason I shouldn't come. It will be all young people. You don't need a disconsolate old widow haunting the house."

"You're hardly—"

Justine broke in. "But I am, Jenny. I really am disconsolate. I miss Rory so much. I cry all the time. He was my soul mate. No, no, I can't do anything social for a while. You've got to give me time to grieve, honey. Okay?"

"Okay, Mom. I'm sorry you're so sad."

"I'll be fine. If you're happy, then I'm happy. I can't tell you how it cheers me that you and your stepsisters are getting along. I tell you what. I'll call Murray's Liquor and have them deliver a case each of red and white wine to your house for the party."

"Mom, that's not necessary."

"No, but I want to do it."

"But, Mom, most of the guys will want beer."

"All right, then, I'll have them deliver a case of beer, too."

"That's not what I meant—"

"I want to do it. For Meg and Arden as well as for you. If you can't drink all the wine on the Fourth, you can have it another time. Now I've got to go. I'm sorting through Rory's clothing; I want to give some to the thrift shop."

"That must be hard," Jenny sympathized.

"Not really. At least not so far. Your father had so many clothes, and he hadn't worn a lot of them for years.

Those are the ones I'm tossing. I do cry a lot, of course, but I cry a lot, anyway."

"Take care of yourself, Mom. Go out to dinner with your friends. See a movie."

"I will, Jenny. I do. You, too."

TWELVE

Monday night the three gathered around the kitchen table, which Meg had covered with a red-and-white-checked tablecloth. Meg served lasagna, green salad, and a buttery, garlicky bread. They drank an Italian Chianti with the meal.

"This is delicious," Arden said, licking her lips.

"Yummy," Jenny agreed. Leaning back in her chair, she asked, "How's your Alcott work going, Meg?"

"Okay." Meg put her elbow on the table and her chin in her hand, thinking. "Although I have to admit my research has got me in a slump about men."

"Why?" Jenny asked, tearing off a piece of garlic bread.

"Bronson Alcott allowed his oldest daughter to work herself sick to support him while he sat on his butt thinking great philosophical thoughts that no one cared about—"

"Meg." Arden leveled a look across the table. "That was a zillion years ago. Times have changed."

"But have men?" Meg countered.

Arden began to clear the table. Jenny stood up to help her. They worked together in silence, covering the left-over lasagna, stacking the dishwasher, wiping down the counter.

"Aren't men better fathers these days?" Arden clarified.

Meg gave herself a moment to consider. "I believe Tom is a good, faithful husband to my mother. He's a good father to his sons. He's reliable and trustworthy."

"How is he as a stepfather?" Arden asked. She turned from the sink, wiping her hands on a dish towel, watching Meg and realizing she'd never thought about Tom as Meg's stepfather before. Arden could scarcely remember the years before Gavin and Mike were born. When Arden's parents were first divorced, Cyndi used to babysit her while Arden's mother worked, but after the twins were born, Arden seldom was invited to Meg's house. "As I recall, Tom was kind of distant. Boring. I mean, he didn't ever pick me up or hug me. He didn't even really notice me."

Meg folded her arms across her chest. "Interesting to hear you say that. I don't think of Tom as my stepfather, actually. I called him that when I was in school, but I'm pretty sure he never felt any affection for me."

"I always thought you were treated like Cinderella in that household. After the babies were born."

Meg laughed. "You did? I guess you're right. But with sickly twins, Mom needed the help, and I was crazy about those little boys when they were babies. When they got older, not so much. They were all about each other, their own exclusive club. Then I got sent to boarding school, and at first I felt hurt by that, so shoved away. . . . That was a couple of years after The Exile." The lightness of laughter fell away from her face as her memories returned with their burden of sorrow. "I felt like I didn't belong anywhere. That no one wanted me." Tears filled her eyes. "Shit, I hate remembering those days."

"I'm sorry I brought it all up," Arden apologized.

"It's okay. Boarding school turned out to be good for me. I made some really close friends, and I learned I was hardly alone as a discard. At least half the kids I knew were from divorced homes. A lot of the kids whose parents were married didn't want them around, either. They were too busy traveling or working or something. I fit right in. I found my own little club." Meg's smile returned. "And I discovered I was smart. I hadn't known that before. I got a scholarship to Smith. That was just cool beyond measure; I can't begin to tell you what that did for me. For one thing, I didn't have to rely on Tom for a penny. Dad helped financially, of course. I worked waiting tables all summer, so I had enough money for clothes and stuff. I got a fellowship at Lesley University for my master's in English lit, and I started teaching at Sudbury College shortly after that. I've always been a hard worker. Independent."

"You should be proud," Arden told her.

"I wish . . . ," Meg began, then stopped and started over. "Mom and Tom and the boys came to my high school and college graduations. I think just that much was hard for them. The twins were a handful as children. Not bad boys, but active and mischievous." Meg smiled smugly. "They gave quiet old Tom a real workout. When they were in high school, they got into a lot of trouble—not serious stuff, but wrecking cars, skipping classes, that sort of thing. Now they're in college and doing well. They've settled down."

"Well, I'm glad for your mother's sake."

"I called Mom about our July Fourth party. She can't come. She and Tom have become social butterflies. With all the kids gone, they're partying with their own gang. She sounds happy and busy."

"So there you are," Arden said. "We know of one good man. He might not have been a good stepfather, but he wasn't abusive, and he's been good to his sons, and faithful to his wife."

Meg laughed scornfully. "That's a sad definition of a good man."

"Nobody gets everything," Arden pointed out. "Someone told me once to make a list of the ten things I want most in life. If I get the top three, I should shut up and be thrilled."

Jenny returned to the table. "Hmm. Interesting. What are your top three things? Husband, children, and what else?"

"Are you kidding? Husband and children?" Arden tossed the dish towel down and threw herself into a chair. "No children for me, thank you very much. I'm thirty-four. I decided a long time ago, when my father left me to marry Cyndi and be Meg's dad, that I'd never inflict the kind of pain on a child that I had dumped on me."

"It doesn't have to be that way," Meg said softly. She looked at Arden, whose perfect face was momentarily marred by bitter lines, and wanted to comfort her. "We had a lot of fun when we were little girls, remember? You were really nice to me when you came for weekends."

Arden looked surprised. "I was?"

"Don't you remember? You brought me so many baby dolls—"

"Yeah, but they were secondhand. Plus, I didn't like dolls—"

"That doesn't matter. You gave them to me. I was a little girl. It was a huge thing for me to get them! You brought me Barbie and Ken, and you gave me all the clothes you'd outgrown. Because you were three years older, I thought you were the coolest thing around. I'd wear your clothes even if they didn't fit. And you invented the best games. Remember our secret clubhouse behind the furnace in the basement?"

"I do." Arden burst into laughter. "Remember our babysitter, Patsy?"

"Oh, gosh, I'd forgotten about her. She was *awesome!*"

"Remember how when Mom and Dad went out to dinner or something, she'd dress us up in stuff she brought over and put on music and we'd do music videos? Remember when Patsy brought over all those bangles—"

"Walk like an Egyptian!" Meg warbled, undulating her arms.

"Everybody have fun tonight!" sang Arden. "We thought George Michael was so hot."

Meg cackled, "*You* wanted to marry him when you grew up."

"Okay, remember, I was, what, eight? Nine?"

"Bon Jovi," Meg crooned. "The band, the man, the hair!"

"I had a crush on Seal," Jenny confessed.

"Everyone had a crush on Seal," Meg said.

"Then suddenly it was all Alanis Morissette and people whining and complaining," Arden remembered. "What happened?"

"We grew up," Meg sighed. "What was that song she sang? 'You Oughta Know'?"

Arden snorted. "Well, now we know."

Not wanting to be left out, Jenny offered gently, "The three of us did have one nice summer together."

"We did?" Arden looked doubtful.

"Yeah," Meg agreed. "That first year we were here. Before the second bad year. We had fun."

"Wait, are we on the same planet?" Arden asked. "That first year, you and Jenny went into a teenybopper bonding thing and spent all your time painting your nails and sneaking into my room to try on *my* lip gloss. Then Justine would get mad at *me* for letting you wear it."

"I kind of remember that." Jenny planted her elbows on the table, resting her chin in her hands. "I know you had to babysit us a lot so Dad and Mom could go to parties and stuff. But that was always fun. We played statues in the backyard."

"Right!" Meg said. "Remember, Arden, you'd swing us around and we'd land in these ridiculous positions?"

"Some nights, especially if there was a storm, we'd play Spook. Meg and I would hide and you'd go through the house looking for us—"

"With special sound effects," Meg giggled. "You'd make creepy voices, Arden, and stomp hard like a monster coming up the stairs. I was really scared."

Arden grinned. "Yeah, I remember that. You two would scream like crazy when I found you."

"The show we did for Dad!" Jenny chirped. "Remember? We wore grass skirts and plastic leis over our bathing suits and did the hula to—gosh, what was that song?"

Meg shrieked with laughter. "'The Dock of the Bay'!"

"Oh man, I remember now," Arden said. "Michael Bolton! His hair was longer than yours, Meg."

"But the song is so good," Jenny said. "And our dance was *wicked cool.*"

Meg hummed a few notes of Otis Redding's quietly emotional song. Arden sang along, swaying in time, lifting her hands in a drifting motion.

Their voices faded. For a moment the kitchen was silently alive with memories.

"We told Dad we were island girls," Jenny said softly.

"Island girls." Meg nodded, a smile turning her face young. "Yeah. I remember."

"He loved our dance," Arden recalled. "He smiled so much, and when we told him we were island girls, he got all choked up."

"We made him happy then," Meg realized.

Again, they were all quiet, lost to memory.

Jenny spoke up. "You're right. We *were* all happy that summer. You know what else? The night of the meteors!"

"Oh yeah," Meg said. "That was, to use the word properly, *awesome.*"

Arden sat for a moment, searching her mind.

"How can you forget that?" Meg demanded of Arden. "You sneaked us out of the house! We went down to the beach and lay on the sand and watched all these meteors whizzing through the sky over our heads."

"It was like being in a spaceship," Jenny breathed. She closed her eyes and leaned back in her chair. "We have meteor showers every August, but that year it was sensational. I think I really began to believe in God that very moment."

"Yeah," Meg said, "because so clearly something else is out there, it was like messages written in star dust."

"And, Arden." Jenny opened her eyes and sat up. "We wouldn't have seen it without you. Remember? Mom said we couldn't stay up till midnight; that's when the showers began. So you stayed awake, and you tiptoed into my room and woke me."

"Me, too," Meg added.

"We didn't wear shoes. We stayed in our pajamas. We crept down the stairs—" Jenny shot a conspiratorial glance at Meg, and they both flushed with laughter at the memory of disobeying the strict Justine.

"We went out the back door. We didn't make a sound until we were a block away from the house." Meg put her hands to her mouth, caught in a warp of old gleeful guilt.

Jenny snorted. "Yes, and then we laughed so hard we almost peed our pants!"

"Let's go out for a walk now!" Meg suggested.

Arden rolled her eyes. "Duh. It's not August. No meteors."

"We don't have to have meteors. We can just look at

the lights of town and the lights on the boats in the harbor. Maybe have an ice cream cone."

"Good idea," Jenny said, standing up. "I'd love some ice cream."

Arden hesitated for one long second, then smiled. "Me, too."

THIRTEEN

Okay, she was an idiot, no doubt about it. Arden ripped open a new bag of Fritos with such fury the chips exploded all over the table.

Pride goeth before a fall, and her pride had sent her tumbling head over heels into disaster.

"Ernest," she'd invited, so sweetly, so sure of herself, "please come down to our Fourth of July party. I want you to meet some people. Some people with fab summer houses they want me to simplify on my show. You've got to meet them."

She'd wanted the Channel Six program director to see her in action, to *get it*, how good she was at convincing the hotshots and luminaries who summered on the island to allow her to redo a room in their house and let it be shown on *Simplify This*. She wanted Ernest to realize that no new kid on the block could hope to compare with her.

"I'm busy that weekend, Ard. You know how the wife

ties me up with social engagements. But tell you what, I'll send Zoey down. She can learn the ropes straight from the horse's mouth. Ha-ha, talk about a mixed metaphor."

"Oh." Arden thought fast. "We don't have any room for her to stay in the house, Ernest."

"That's okay. I'll have the station put her up at a hotel."

So there she was, the size-zero darling, flitting around the backyard, batting her long, dark lashes at all the men, pretending intense fascination at their conversation and allowing them to check out her perky cleavage.

"She's sweet," Meg had said earlier, when the Independence Day party started.

"You think everyone's sweet," Arden had muttered.

Meg blinked at Arden's harsh response. The three women had gotten along so well all day Sunday, getting ready for the party, making lists, double-checking supplies. They'd baked cheesecakes and topped them with strawberries, grapes, and blueberries in a red, white, and blue design. They'd gotten hysterical as they attached tiny lights to the hedges that walled in the backyard, only to discover they were miles away from any electric supply. Jenny had jumped in her Jeep and zipped off to buy heavy-duty extension cords. Then they'd had to put the tables over the cords so no one would trip on them, and that threw off their carefully devised layout. They'd worked like a team, excited and just a bit overwhelmed by all the people who'd accepted their casual telephone invitations.

Arden's best friend, Serena, came down for three days, sleeping on the living room sofa, keeping her clothes in

Arden's room. Meg's colleague Liam Larson—blond, handsome, and, Arden suspected, from a wealthy family— traveled to the island and happily used the sofa in the den because Jenny's friends, James and Manuel, were staying in the front bedroom, the master bedroom. The guests had been great, helping set up lawn chairs—and rushing off to buy more—covering the old picnic table and the card table with cloths, filling new garbage pails with ice, beer, wine, and soda. James and Manuel had made several bowls of sizzling salsa and a huge bowl of guacamole.

Jenny came in from the backyard, carrying an empty basket. "Oh, good, you've got more chips. We should just have had the Doritos truck back up to the yard and dump a load."

Arden laughed. "It's almost twilight. We'll start walking down to the Jetties for the fireworks anytime now."

They leaned over the sink, gazing out at the backyard.

"Good party, huh," Jenny said.

"It's a great party," said Arden. "Except . . . Oh God, there she goes, I knew she would—Zoey's sucking up to Palmer White."

Jenny watched for a moment. "She's not as cute as she thinks she is. Or as smart. Besides, Palmer White's got the serious hots for you."

"And that should thrill me, why?" Arden glanced sideways at Jenny. "What about you and Tim?"

"What about us?"

"Speaking of serious hots. I think he's really into you."

"Please. He hates me. I hate him. I'll tell you who I

think is interesting—that Liam Larson guy of Meg's. He's so handsome he almost looks gay."

"PC much?" Arden joked. "Forget him. He's all over Meg."

"Yes, but she doesn't seem to notice him."

"We need to talk to that girl." Arden wrenched herself away from the window and dumped another bag of chips into the basket. "Here. Let's take these out."

It was almost miraculous that this July Fourth was humid but not foggy. Almost all Independence Days over the past twenty years had been plagued by thick fog, postponing the fireworks for a night or two, but today was perfect.

As Arden set the chips on the food table, she felt a soft arm embrace her shoulders as a floral perfume swept around her.

"Oh, Arden, you are the best!" Zoey cooed. "I'm so grateful you invited me down to this party! I was just talking to Palmer White. *Palmer White!* He told me he introduced you to Ariadne Silverstone. *Ariadne Silverstone!* Oh, I would *die* to meet her."

"Well, we don't want that to happen, now do we?" Arden replied dryly, sliding away from Zoey's arm.

"What?"

"You said you'd die to meet her." Arden could see Zoey was still confused. "Oh, never mind. Listen, we're all going to walk down to the beach in a few minutes to see the fireworks. I'd suggest you use the john. It's not a long walk, but the streets will be congested with people so it takes forever to get there and back."

"Oh, you are so thoughtful!" Zoey trilled, and raced into the house.

"Dear God, am I really so old?" Arden spoke aloud, shaking her head.

"Not old," a man said. "Just experienced." Palmer wore preppy patchwork shorts and a red polo shirt. In the dimming light, his white teeth gleamed. "I suspect little Zoey's gotten a long way on her charm and pretend naïveté, and I'd bet money you employed those same tricks when you were her age."

"That's cynical," Arden said.

"Tell me you're not cynical, too," Palmer dared her.

Arden had to smile. "Okay. I *am* cynical. But in a good way." She considered this for a moment. "But I didn't use any tricks when I started out. First of all, to be honest, I never ever was as sweet and naïve as she seems to be. I was always ambitious."

"Zoey's ambitious, too. More ambitious than you are."

Arden stared at Palmer. "How do you know? What do you mean?"

"Think about it. You've got your Brad Pitt guy over there and your Ryan Gosling guy down at the end of the lawn. Not to mention quite a few other men and women. Who has naïve little Zoey spent the most time with today?"

"You?"

"Me. Once I told her I owned air space and stations, she was glued to my side."

Arden narrowed her eyes. "Come on, don't be so

jaded. Zoey's interested in the industry, and you know everything about television—"

"I'll make a bet with you. I'll bet that by the time the fireworks are over, Zoey will come back to my room with me."

Arden's eyes narrowed. "You're disgusting."

Palmer pretended innocent surprise. "Because I want to take a shapely young woman to bed?" Leaning close to Arden, he whispered, "How did *you* react when you met me? You're in the industry, too. Did you play up to me?" Before Arden could answer, Palmer continued, "*You* are the woman I'm interested in, and I've had to pursue you and bribe you with parties to get you to go anywhere with me."

"W-well," Arden stuttered, suddenly flushed with a peculiar, unexpected tingling at Palmer's words, "there you are. You had to bribe me with parties. So I'm just as ambitious as Zoey."

"Okay, I'll give you that. But you've got a softness to your ambition."

"I am not soft!" Arden told him.

He held up his hands to placate her. "Sorry, wrong word. How about kind?"

"I don't know what you're talking about." This man was getting under her skin.

"Let's take Ariadne Silverstone. I went through her house with you. I saw you in action. Which room in her house is the most cluttered and chaotic?"

"Her study."

"Right. Which room did you offer to help simplify?"

Arden had to smile. She knew where he was going, and she was surprised and pleased. "The kitchen."

"Why?" Palmer asked.

"Because her study is her safe place. It's her sanctuary. I could tell at once, and I didn't want to violate that. Besides, she knows what all those piles and scattered papers are; she could find anything she wanted in a moment. But she doesn't care about the kitchen. She really doesn't even care about the entire summer house. She's a lawyer. She cares about her work. The summer house is for entertaining guests, lobbying, having her children and grandchildren for a week or so. The kitchen is for staff. Ariadne doesn't even care what she eats. She lunches on saltines and V-8 juice and usually has dinner out with her husband or orders takeout. But she needs a decent coffeemaker that makes one cup at a time instead of the monster the staff uses for parties. The kitchen needs to be simplified so that much of the equipment can be stored when she's there alone with her husband."

Palmer was smiling at her with admiration in his warm dark eyes. "Exactly. You homed in on all sorts of deeply personal peculiarities of Ariadne's. You work with your heart, not just with your head. You know lots of viewers would drool to see her study, because it's so personal, and you steered away from that immediately, when Zoey would have pounced."

"That doesn't mean I'm *soft*," Arden protested. "I intend to go someplace in the television business. I am just as determined as Zoey—more determined, even."

"Are you?" Palmer's eyes met Arden's. All at once he wasn't smiling. He radiated power, intent, and an almost mesmerizing desire. "Then why don't you come home with me? Now."

Arden's entire body flushed with heat. She couldn't tell if it was anger or attraction. Talking to Palmer this way, with his piercing dark eyes fixed on her face and no hint of a smile on his lips, made her shiver. "The-the fireworks," Arden remembered.

"I'll give you fireworks."

She realized with a kind of thrill that this man could do exactly what he said. He was charismatic, and more than that, he was intelligent, shrewd, and discerning. He had a quality of concentration she'd found in few men. If he aimed that focus on her when they were alone together in bed . . .

"Hi, guys, I'm ready!" Zoey bounced up to them, all pert and bubbly.

At the top of the steps to the porch, Jenny clinked a fork against a glass. "Hey, everyone, it's time to go down to the beach for the fireworks. There's always a crowd, so we're bound to get separated. Find two or three people you want to be with and stick to them. If you don't want to sit in the sand, carry a lawn chair down, but please return it. And if you need to use the john, do it now."

"Oh, goody," Zoey trilled. "I don't need a chair, but you might, Arden."

"Right," Arden responded, deadpan. "For my old, aching bones."

"Arden." Tim Robinson appeared at her side, tall, wide-shouldered, muscular, and easy on the eyes. "I've got a blanket for us."

"Um, thanks." She tossed him a friendly smile.

Zoey ignored the hunky Tim. Linking her arm through Palmer's, she cooed, "You were telling me how you got into the television business. Did you study communications in college?" Silkily, she angled her body toward the gate, tugging Palmer along with her.

Palmer looked over his shoulder at Arden with a smirk. Arden shook her head at him, but smiled.

Meg and Liam were in the kitchen, covering any fresh veggies and salsa and stashing them in the fridge before going down to the beach. Meg glanced out the window and saw tall Tim Robinson standing next to Arden. At the far end of the yard, Jenny was laughing with her friends James and Manuel. Arden's friend Serena was carrying the last bowl of guacamole, and Zoey was flashing all she had at Palmer White.

"Liam." She clutched his arm. "Listen. Go out and talk to Jenny. Walk with her down to the beach, okay? Maybe even flirt with her?"

Liam pushed his glasses up his nose so he could get a clearer view of Meg. "What? Why?"

"Because she likes Tim Robinson and he's dating Arden. Jenny shouldn't be left with two gay guys even if they are her friends and cute."

"But I don't want to date Jenny," Liam protested.

"You don't have to *date* her," Meg said. "Just hang out with her."

"Then she'll think I want to date her."

"You're making this way more complicated than it is!" Meg complained.

Liam crossed his arms over his chest defiantly. "Is that why you invited me down here?"

"Of course not."

"Then why?"

Except for the glasses, Liam could have been carved from a medieval tombstone, with his long aristocratic nose and deep-set blue eyes. "You-you seem"—she struggled to find the right word—"*gallant*. Well, that's not why I asked you down here, but that's why I want you to help Jenny."

"First, tell me why you invited me down here."

"*Liam*," Meg began, helplessly.

Serena came into the kitchen and set the bowl on the counter. "Time to go." She was a brisk, no-nonsense real estate lawyer with short hair and long legs. Like Arden, she was obsessed 24/7 with her work; she'd already told Meg that she really didn't enjoy having fun.

Meg was grateful for the interruption. "You don't have to watch the fireworks."

"I came down for the damned fireworks, so let's go," Serena said, grinning at her own impatience. Her Julia Roberts grin changed her completely.

In a loose, informal group, the party strolled down to the beach. Police had blocked cars from the main roads leading to the Jetties, and crowds of people thronged eagerly toward the water. Kids in various yards they passed set off firecrackers; flags waved from poles and houses. In the harbor, boats motored close to shore for a better view of the spectacle.

As they left the pavement and began crunching over the low, sandy dunes, Liam reached out to take Meg's hand. She pulled her hand away. No, she argued in the silent turmoil of her mind, she was not going to have a fling with a colleague. She was not going to let this *child*, five years younger than she was and so spectacular he could get anything he wanted, think he could have her, too, just like that—like a toy or a car or a trip to Disneyland. He was brilliant, he was handsome, he was adorable, he should be with a fabulous woman, but she knew what she was, she knew what she looked like, and she knew anything she did with Liam Larson, PhD, would only end in complete and miserable disaster for her.

She stomped faster through the sand, calling out, "Serena, let me help you with the blanket."

Earlier that day, most of the party had gone swimming, but not Meg. She stayed home, cutting up strawberries, melons, and pineapple for a fruit salad, making a platter of tuna fish sandwiches for the group who returned home tanned and as starving as only a swim in the ocean could make you. Truth was, she didn't want Liam to see her in a bathing suit. Arden was as sleek as an otter, Jenny was curvaceous and slender, Serena was a stick— and Zoey, in her bikini, well, she was temptation personified. Meg could only imagine how she'd compare to those women in her black Speedo, her boobs bobbing along with each step. Uh-uh, no, never.

She believed someday she'd meet a good man, hopefully a professor, too, who would appreciate her charms, and who would be happy to wrap his arms around her and hold her close. She imagined he would be an older man. Perhaps he might even teach German, like the professor Jo March met and married in *Little Women*. Meg was not down on herself; she was realistic.

The fireworks began—stars, chrysanthemums, waterfalls, Catherine wheels, screamers—and the crowd yelled, applauded, and sighed at each one. The faces of those seated around Meg were lit by colored light, as if they were in a spacecraft flashing through the cosmos. The grand finale was an explosion of color and noise. The crowd cheered. Boats in the harbor sounded their horns.

Suddenly it was over. Everyone gathered up their chairs or blankets and made their way back through the sand toward their homes.

"I haven't seen fireworks in years," Serena said to Meg. "I'm always working on the Fourth of July. I'm always trying to catch up on something."

"I'm glad you could watch this," Meg told her.

"Me, too. It was sensational. And Arden knows so many fascinating people. You teach at Sudbury College, don't you?"

"Yes. It's a great place." Out of the corner of her eye, Meg saw, by the light of the streetlamp, Jenny walking close to Liam, gazing up at him with admiration, while Liam told her something Jenny evidently found fascinating.

So Liam had complied with Meg's odd request after all.

Although it seemed more like Jenny was attaching herself to Liam than the other way around. As Meg watched, Jenny tripped, grabbed Liam's arm to steady herself, and continued to hold on to him.

"—teach?" Serena was asking.

"Um, sorry, what?" Meg wrenched her attention back to the other woman.

"I was asking what you teach."

They were walking up a hill, and their party had fallen into pairs: Arden and Tim, Zoey and Palmer, James and Manuel, Jenny and Liam, Serena and Meg. As they passed other houses, music and the scent of barbequed food drifted out, and from an open window, a baby cried. The night was fully dark now. It was after ten.

"Mostly freshman composition," Meg answered. "I've had offers at universities, but I think community colleges are at the center of our country's future. The population is changing. Lots of our citizens are from other countries. They both need and are eager for adult education. Their dream is to create a new life for themselves here. Oftentimes, language is the foundation of their success." She caught herself. "Damn, way to sound pompous."

"Not at all," Serena said. "I'm impressed."

They arrived at the Randall house, all of them sitting on the porch steps or leaning against the railings to empty their shoes of sand.

"That was fabulous," James exclaimed. "Never saw better fireworks in my life."

"Oh, honey, now you tell me," Manuel joked.

Jenny announced, "I like to watch certain DVDs on certain holidays. I've got *Forrest Gump*, and *Armageddon*, and *Master and Commander*."

"*Master and Commander*?" Arden hooted. "Isn't that an English film?"

"Yeah, but believe me, Russell Crowe rocks that uniform," James said campily.

They all filed into the house, heading for the bathroom, the kitchen, the den. Meg stood at the kitchen counter, cutting slices of angel food cake and drizzling fruit and sugary fruit juice over it. Arden made a pot of decaf coffee.

Jenny had disappeared.

So had Liam.

As the rest gathered in the den with their desserts, Meg asked casually, "Where are Liam and Jenny?"

"They said they wanted to walk into town," Zoey told her, busy adjusting a pillow behind her back.

"Ooooh, *amor*," Manuel hooted.

"Okay," Arden asked. "Which DVD do we all want?"

Meg settled on the floor, leaning against the couch, an uncomfortable position, which suited her mood.

"Let me show you a special place," Jenny said as they left The Juice Bar with cups of ice cream.

"Is it far?"

"Just around the corner."

She led him toward the water, turned onto Easy Street, and walked to one of the three benches overlooking the small harbor enclosed by Steamboat Wharf and Old North Wharf.

The last big car ferry had arrived and unloaded. The steamboat lot was quiet for the night. In the cottages, lights glowed golden and music drifted from open windows.

Water lapped gently against the harbor wall.

"Nice," Liam said.

Jenny nodded, her mouth full of ice cream.

"Meg said she used to come here every summer as a young girl," Liam commented. "But when her parents got divorced, she couldn't come anymore."

Jenny sighed a deep, obvious sigh. "Tell me about you," she suggested. She angled her body toward him. "You're some kind of genius, right?"

Liam sniffed. "Hardly. Some kind of geek is more like it."

"Meg's in awe of you."

She heard him draw in a deep breath. "Well. Awe is not exactly what I'm going for."

Jenny smiled. "Okay." She ate some ice cream, thinking. "You're certainly handsome," Jenny said matter-of-factly. "And the two of you share the same interests. You're younger than she is, aren't you?"

"Yes, but so what? Lots of guys are younger than their girlfriends." With one deft move, he crushed his empty ice cream cup and tossed it into a trash barrel nearby. "If you only knew how tired I am of people judging me by my age. I never had any real friends in school because I was always younger than they were, plus they thought I was a freak."

"Are you? I don't mean a freak, but a genius?"

"I have a high IQ," Liam admitted. "I've got a good facility for transposition. But I'm actually just a normal guy."

"Who's had a book published and earned a PhD by twenty-six."

"I skipped a lot of grades in school."

Jenny sat silently, organizing her thoughts. "Don't you ever, because you're so smart, want to, oh, I don't know, change the world?"

"By which you mean go into science, cure cancer, or end world hunger?"

"Yeah, I suppose."

"Instead of teaching at a community college and writing books about poets." He looked at Jenny. "You're a computer geek, right?"

"I am. I totally get computers."

"Plan to save the world?"

"Gosh, no. But then I'm not a genius. No, I'm happy enough doing work that helps other people keep their own work going on." She grinned. "Plus, I like knowing secret codes and stuff that most people don't know."

Liam grinned back. "Yeah, I can see that would be fun. Kind of like I can read Greek."

"That's a profitable skill?"

"Not everything has to be measured by money." Liam stood up. "I believe that by teaching at a community college, I *am* saving the world." He stretched. "Now I'm sounding philosophical and boring. Let's go back to the house."

Jenny fell into step with him as they walked. "You and Meg . . . ," she began. "You're in the same field. Are you ever competitive?"

"Not really. Professors don't make much money. Since I have a PhD, I got shot to the top of the ladder. I'm a professor. A full professor, with tenure. I'll have a lot of input about the future of the department. Meg just has a master's, and she's ABD, all but dissertation, for her PhD. She's published essays, but no books. This book she's working on, though, just might make her name, might even make her some money. Certainly she could get some paid lecturing gigs out of it."

"You'd like it if her book got published?"

"You bet. First of all, it's a great thesis and subject. She's an assistant professor now; this might elevate her to full with tenure. More than that, it would make Meg happy, and more confident. Then she might actually stop being such an insecure little beetle, skittering away whenever I come near her."

Jenny let her head fall back as she laughed.

"Look." Liam stopped walking. "Talk to her for me, will you?"

Jenny raised an eyebrow. "You're kidding, right?"

"I don't understand."

"Meg's not going to listen to me."

"Yeah, she will. She feels closer to you and Arden than she does to her half brothers."

A handsome blonde woman in a stylish lime-green dress came from behind them, almost touching Jenny's arm as she passed on the sidewalk. "Excuse me," she murmured, her eyes lingering on Jenny.

Well, that was weird, Jenny thought.

Liam was still talking. "She's told me so, when we've talked on the phone over the past month." He started walking again.

Jenny skipped a step to catch up with him. She didn't want to let on how much his words delighted her. "Do you have brothers or sisters?"

"One of each." Liam laughed. "My brother's a marine, and you can imagine what he thinks of me, a literature professor. My sister's a doctor. If she wants to, she can curse so bad she breaks the china. She's married to a doctor. They have two daughters."

"You're the baby of the family?"

"Oh, please, don't use that word. I'm the youngest."

"I'm the youngest, too. Well, not really. I'm the same age as Meg."

They reached the house. As they went up the steps, their faces were illuminated by the porch light. "You know what?" Jenny asked. "I think you are amazingly handsome, and yet I don't feel the slightest sexual interest in you."

"Well, thanks for that. My self-worth continues to soar."

He leaned toward Jenny, and for a moment she thought he'd taken her words as a dare and was going to kiss her. Instead, he said, "You're not attracted to me because you're in love with Tim Robinson. Surely you know that."

Jenny bristled. "Oh, I am so *not!*"

Liam chuckled. "Sorry. It's okay, then, that he and Arden are, um, getting along so well?"

Jenny followed his gaze through the window into the den, where Arden and Tim sat on the sofa, side by side, with Tim's arm loosely draped over Arden's shoulders and her head pressed against his chest.

"I couldn't care less," she told Liam. Opening the door, she entered the house and strolled into the living room, trying to look smug and satisfied. "We went to The Juice Bar."

"Shhh," James hushed her. "Steve Buscemi's about to sit on the nuclear missile."

Tim didn't look at her. Meg, the third on the sofa, said, "Sit beside me, Jenny. I'll squash over next to Arden."

Liam settled on the floor, leaning against the side of a chair. Jenny wanted to say, casually, "No, thanks, I'm going to bed." But she liked the crazy movie, and she was not going to act as if she gave a fig that Arden was practically sitting on Tim's lap.

"Thanks, Meg." She squeezed in next to Meg and gave herself over to the movie magic. *Armageddon* it was.

The men went wild when the space tractor came over the hill, and everyone cheered when the crew made it back to earth. When Liv Tyler ran into Ben Affleck's arms, Jenny choked back sobs until she realized Meg, next to her, was weeping openly.

"It gets me every time," Meg confessed.

Jenny took her hand. "Me, too." They sobbed together.

The movie ended. The room was still.

"I am totally exhausted," James gushed. "Too many good-looking men in uniforms."

"I want a space uniform," Manuel pouted.

"I want to go to bed." Tim stood up, stretching. "What a day."

"It was fabulous," James agreed.

The group rose, yawning, searching out blankets, pillows, water glasses, and finally calling out good night.

FOURTEEN

She wasn't hungry. How could she be hungry after such a party? She shouldn't eat, anyway, she was already too fat.

But she was restless. She turned on the light on her bedside table and tried to read. Her mind wouldn't settle. The words flitted around, making no sense.

Liam and Jenny had been gone for over an hour, "getting an ice cream cone." Oh, sure.

Yet, she'd been the one to send Liam straight into Jenny's slender arms.

Okay. That was a good thing. That was the right thing to do.

Still, she was hungry. *Starving.* She didn't want anything sweet. Something substantial, salty. Maybe some of that potato salad.

It was one o'clock. She crept out of her bedroom. The master bedroom door was shut, with James and Manuel sleeping. Jenny's door was shut. Meg paused, holding her breath. No sounds coming from behind the door. So probably Liam wasn't in there with her. Not that Meg cared.

She stole down the stairs. The house was dark and quiet. She passed the living room and heard Arden's friend Serena sweetly snoring on the sofa.

In the kitchen, she took a moment to let her eyes grow accustomed to the dark. Opening the refrigerator, she scanned the contents; she squinted in the dim light. Plastic-covered containers were piled on one another. Beer and white wine lined the door. She shuddered. Maybe she wasn't hungry after all.

She shut the door, turned, and stifled a scream.

Liam stood in the kitchen doorway, wearing only his boxers.

He said, "Hey."

She said, "Hey."

"What are you doing up?" he asked in a low voice.

"Hungry," she whispered. "You?"

"Sunburn," he told her. "Thought I'd look for some lotion." He gestured toward the hall with his hand. "I looked in the bathroom down here. None there."

"Right." Meg couldn't help staring at the man. His lean, lanky form carried an elegance in its very stance. He looked like a nineteenth-century poet. George Gordon, Lord Byron, without the clubfoot. *Oh, just kill me now.* "I have some upstairs in my room," she said. "I'll get it."

"That's okay. I'll survive." He started to turn away.

"No, really. You're fluorescent." She smiled easily, moving toward him. "Come on up. I'll rub it on your back." She put her hand on his wrist, intending to tug him along, but her fingers ignited when they touched his skin, sending heat scorching through her like a wildfire. She jerked her hand away.

She was hideously conscious of him following her upstairs. She wore a discreet cotton nightie trimmed with lace on the bodice. It fell below her bum, but she wasn't sure it covered the tops of her thighs, especially from Liam's point of view behind her.

Quietly, they went down the hall and into her room. Her bedside lamp cast a soft glow over the small room and her bed, with the sheets tossed back.

Liam shut the door. "So we don't wake the others," he explained.

Meg's mouth was dry. "I'll get the lotion." She went to her dresser and searched among her makeup, jewelry, and creams.

Liam was bending over her desk. "What a great view."

"Sit down. I'll rub the cream in." *What am I doing!* she silently screamed at herself. If she touched the man, she'd be lost.

She touched him.

Liam sank into the small cane-seat chair, crossing his arms on her desk. Her laptop, a closed silver rectangle, lay surrounded by piles of books and papers. "You work here."

She dabbed lotion onto her fingertips, then gently swirled the lotion on his wide and rather bony shoulders. "I do," she agreed, although she could scarcely speak.

"Ah," Liam murmured. "That feels good."

She smoothed the lotion onto the base of his neck, where it got caught in the ends of his thick golden hair.

The knobs of his spine protruded against her hands as she spread the lotion down his back. His skin was hot to the touch. She knew from seeing him in his bathing suit earlier in the day that he had hair on his chest and belly but none on his back, but now she saw the lightest golden downy fluff where his boxers' elastic waist met his spine. He had a mole by his right shoulder blade.

Liam turned in the chair. He stood up. "You're not burned, and your skin is as pale as mine."

"I wear lots of sunblock," she told him. They had never stood so close together before. Her heart was trying to jump out of her chest and into his. She stood holding the lotion in both hands like an offering. "Want some on your nose?"

He shook his head. "No. This is what I want." He put his hands on each side of her face and steadied her as he brought his mouth to hers in a lingering kiss.

Her heart was leaping. She was trembling, and she had the most terrible fear that she was going to cry. She whispered, "Liam."

He took the bottle from her hand and set it on the desk. He put his hand on her wrist just as she had downstairs put hers on his, and led her to her bed. He sat down on her bed and pulled her to him, so that she stood there, caught between his long legs. He wrapped his arms around her waist and nuzzled his head into her midriff, her belly, her pelvis. It was the most tender nudging through the cotton, and she felt his need deep in her body.

She put her hands in his hair. Thick golden hair. She

leaned down to kiss the top of his head, and as she did, her breasts swung forward.

"My God, Meg." Liam put his mouth on her breasts, soaking the cotton and the lace, his lips and tongue skidding the wet lace against her nipples. He slid his hands up her legs, caught the waistband of her panties, and tugged down.

She stepped out of her panties. Liam stood up and pulled her nightie over her head. She stood naked before him. He dropped his boxers and he was naked with her. He put his hands on her shoulders and delicately drew her down onto her back on the bed, then knelt between her legs. She was trying as hard as she could to suck in her stomach, to make it look flat, which it never had been in her entire life, but when he eased himself down against her, she drew in a deep breath and forgot how she looked.

He didn't enter her immediately. He kissed her mouth again, and the sides of her face, and down her throat and across her collarbones, and the tips of her breasts, which made her moan and arch upward, and then he eased into her, slowly. He was longer and wider than she'd anticipated. She ached with pleasure. She couldn't touch his back or his shoulders—the sunburn—so she put her hands on his buttocks. Liam groaned helplessly and thrust forward fiercely, burrowing his head in the pillow next to her, turning his face so his breath was at her ear.

"Meg," he whispered. "Meg. Meg. Meg." She leaned her head back, throat exposed to the sky, and she was falling through space, clutching him to her, clutching this angel to her, and he lifted her to heaven as she fell.

She woke up at dawn's first silver light. She was curled around Liam, fastened to him, really, and drooling on his shoulder. Attractive.

Without moving, she surveyed their two bodies twined together. He looked like a *child*, so slim, clean, perfect, his skin tight to his bones. This lovely man was twenty-six! She was thirty-one. They weren't even in the same decade!

A shame with the same fiery intensity as fear raced through her. Last night she'd acted on impulse, and she acted on impulse again, sliding carefully backward from the bed, terrified that Liam's eyes would open and he would see her for what she really was in the morning light. The patchwork quilt had fallen to the floor. Picking it up, she wrapped it around her and scurried to the door, leaving the room, closing the door behind her so quietly it made only the smallest click.

She hurried down the stairs. Did she hear someone talking? Surely not; it wasn't even six o'clock. Frantically, she wondered where she could hide. Serena was in the living room. Liam's things were in the den. That would be the first place he would go when he woke. Everyone would go to the kitchen to make coffee.

Why was she so frightened? It wasn't logical, she knew that. But she needed a safe place to conceal herself, to give her heart a chance to steady, to let her thoughts lie down in peace. She went out the back door, and around the corner of the house to the driveway. She let out a low, near-hysterical laugh at how she must look, a tousle-headed woman wrapped in a quilt fleeing from a house like a heroine in a gothic romance. There, contemporary and immediate, was her car in the driveway, her old Volvo station wagon. She put her hand on the door, then stopped. Anyone coming out could see inside. In front of it was Jenny's Jeep, much higher than the Volvo.

Meg opened the passenger door of the Jeep and climbed into the backseat. She curled up on the seat, wrapping the quilt around her so that only her nose was uncovered. Now she was safe. No one would know she was here, unless Tim Robinson, so incredibly tall, happened to look in, and why would he?

Curled in a fetal position, protected by the sides of the Jeep, Meg felt safe. Her heart slowed, her breathing evened out, and she began to see the humor in her situation. Really, she was an idiot. Liam was a sweet man, and last night had been so unexpected, and she was so inexperienced, seldom having been with any man, that she mistook what most people would interpret as a casual hookup for something profound. She believed they were making love, but of course they were only having sex.

Yet, it had been wonderful.

She closed her eyes, remembering the sensations. Soon sleep possessed her.

"Where's Meg?" Liam asked.

The household was awake, gathered around the kitchen table drinking coffee and lazily eating Jenny's blueberry pancakes. Monday was an official holiday, but cool and foggy, with a dark sky threatening rain.

"Haven't seen her," Serena said. The others murmured agreement.

Arden cast a sideways glance at Jenny, standing at the stove in shorts and tee shirt. Arden had noticed how Jenny and Liam had gone off together the night before while everyone else watched *Armageddon*. Meg insisted she wasn't interested in Liam except as a friend, but as literary Meg would say, Arden thought the lady protested too much. It was obvious to Arden how Meg felt about her colleague; the desire in Meg's eyes gave her away. It would be cruel of Jenny to go after Liam, even if he was killer handsome and supersmart.

Arden wondered whether Liam had slept with Jenny last night. It wouldn't surprise her. Perhaps Meg had found out somehow, going to the bathroom or something, and, unable to face them this morning, had gone off to town for breakfast or down to the beach for a walk. Certainly Liam was twitchy this morning, jumping at the slightest sound, constantly turning to look at the door.

"*C'est dommage*," James cooed in French, pushing back from the table. "But I think Manuel and I must fly home. I've checked the forecast and we haven't a chance of getting more tan today."

"But, James," Jenny said, "I thought you wanted to check out the nude beach."

"I do, my sweet! But the temperature's fallen. No one's going to want to be nude today."

"I've got to get back, too," Serena added, stretching. She was still in her white terry cloth bathrobe.

"Oh, Serena," Arden protested. "Not yet."

"I've got piles of work to do. Since today's a holiday, I can go into the office and really dig in without anyone bothering me."

"You're a fine lot of friends," Arden snorted.

"Liam?" Jenny asked softly. "You're staying, aren't you?"

Arden's eyes flashed between Jenny and Liam like a searchlight.

Liam hadn't touched his pancakes. "I don't want to leave without saying good-bye to Meg."

Serena stood up. "Arden? Will you drive me to the airport?"

James waved his hand. "Arden, my sweet, drive me and Manuel, too, please?"

Arden hesitated. That would leave Jenny alone with Liam. But how could she refuse? "Of course," she said.

"I'll take a quick shower," Serena said.

"We'll pack," James said.

Manuel, who seldom spoke, smiled his sweet, glorious smile and followed James from the room.

Liam rose. "I guess I'll walk into town and buy some newspapers. Can I get anything for anyone?"

"Are you buying the *Times*?" Jenny asked.

"Yes. And the *Globe*." Liam was already dressed in khakis and a long-sleeved blue cotton button-down shirt. He went to the back door. "If Meg comes back, tell her I'd like to talk with her."

"Sure thing," Jenny said easily.

So maybe they hadn't slept together, Arden thought. Still, she hated that she had to drive people to the airport. She felt protective of Meg, although she wasn't sure why.

Carrying plates and utensils to the dishwasher, she realized she was probably focusing on Meg to keep from thinking about her own life.

But Jenny, scrubbing the huge frying pan at the sink, zeroed in on Arden's unspoken thoughts. "So have you heard from Zoey this morning? Or Palmer? Or Tim?"

"No." Arden dropped the knives and forks into the dishwasher rack with a clatter.

"Well, aren't you a little bluebird of joy this morning," Jenny said sarcastically.

Arden whipped around to glare at Jenny. "Did you sleep with Liam?"

"What? Shut up. You're nuts." Jenny glared at Arden.

"That doesn't answer my question," Arden pointed out.

"That question doesn't deserve a response," Jenny shot back.

Arden pounced. "Oh, so you did sleep with him!"

"What's wrong with you, Arden? *Of course* I didn't! As a matter of fact, during our walk last night, we talked about Meg. Liam's interested in her. He wants me to talk to her for him."

"About what?"

"Well, . . . he didn't actually say. He wants to date her, but she thinks he's too young for her."

Arden leaned against the counter, holding a dish towel in her hand. "Meg's scared."

"Can you blame her?" Jenny asked quietly.

"Ready to go!" Serena appeared, her short hair glossy

from the shower, dressed in black leggings and a black tunic, looking much more city than beach. Her laptop case hung from one shoulder, her briefcase from the other.

"I'll go up and sort the men out," Jenny said. "They're probably squabbling over how to fold their shirts." She left the room.

Serena dropped her cases on the table and crossed to the coffeepot. Pouring herself another cup, which she always drank black and strong, she said, "We haven't had a chance to really talk, Arden. In twenty words or less, how it's going for you this summer?"

Arden thought for a moment. "Well, you met Ariadne Silverstone. She's agreed to let me—"

"Oh, stop!" Serena interrupted. "I don't mean your show. I mean (a) your stepsisters or whatever they are and (b) your sex life." Before Arden could answer, she continued, "That Tim guy is sublime. I could crawl right up his long, tall body."

"Tim is a good-looking guy," Arden said. "Nice, too. We went sailing once. I don't know, Serena, the chemistry just isn't there. I don't know why."

"I know why," Serena stated in her bossy know-it-all way. "You three women are warped by your father. You don't trust men."

"What a news flash," Arden said. "I think I'd better sit down."

"Smart-ass," Serena said. "You don't have to marry the man. When's the last time you got laid?"

Arden ignored her. "As for Jenny and Meg, I think we're doing all right. We cooperated on this party; we get

through the days. Jenny's helped me make some contacts."

"Like Palmer White. If I were you, I wouldn't let that
Zoey snatch him up. He's a fascinating, powerful man."

"True," Arden agreed.

James appeared in the doorway. "We're ready."

Serena put her cup down. "My duffel's in the hall."

Jenny looked out the front door. "Meg's Volvo's behind my Jeep."

"Her keys are on the hook," Arden said, snatching
them up in her hand. "Okay, gang, let's load up the
train."

On impulse, Jenny announced, "I'll ride out with
you."

Arden drove through town and down Orange Street,
which became, after the rotary, a straight shot down Airport Road. James, a chef at a chic Boston restaurant, kept
up a camp account of his boss, the waiters, and the sous
chef until they arrived at the airport. They pulled luggage
from the hatchback, kissed, hugged, promised to meet
again soon, and then Arden and Jenny were left alone for
the drive back to the house.

"How did you meet James?" Arden asked as she pulled
away from the drop-off space.

"Here. In the summer. I was infatuated with him when
I was seventeen. He hadn't come out yet, and we had the
most romantic summer of my life. Lots of hand-holding
and sweet, gentle kisses. I thought he was such a gentleman, so considerate, not rushing me into having sex."
Jenny laughed at her memories. "I was so naïve."

"Actually, it sounds like an idyllic summer romance," Arden said.

"It was. I hadn't had sex yet, and I was terrified about it. James was the perfect boyfriend. When he came out in college, I was the first person he told. We've been close ever since."

"Do you like Manuel?"

Jenny shrugged. "Manuel doesn't say much. I think he might be a bit jealous because James and I are such buddies. But Manuel is faithful to James, and makes James happy, and that's what matters." She looked over at Arden. "How did you meet Serena?"

"At BU. She's smart as hell and aggressively ambitious. She was a scholarship kid from a poor family. She knew she wanted to be a lawyer and make a lot of money. She's got several siblings and no desire for kids of her own."

"Is she a lesbian?"

"No. She just doesn't want to get married and have children. I could understand that at the time, and I understand it now."

Jenny leaned her head back against the seat and sighed. "Not me. I want it all."

Meg came awake all at once, startled to find herself in the back of the Jeep. Her left leg was cramping, and she was simmering beneath the light cotton quilt. Blinking, she sat up. She had no idea what time it was because she wore no watch. She wore nothing, actually, except the quilt. Suddenly she remembered everything.

"Oh no," she moaned.

The day was overcast, the air thick with humidity. Perhaps everyone had gone into town for a big breakfast. Or, for all she knew, a big lunch. Whatever, and whoever was still in the house, she couldn't stay out here in the Jeep forever.

Tightening the quilt around her sarong-style, she slid out of the Jeep and padded barefoot around to the back porch and up the steps into the house.

No one was there. Then the front door slammed, and before she could do more than smell the enticing aroma of coffee, Liam walked into the room. He was carrying a stack of newspapers.

"Meg." He smiled when he saw her. "Where did you go?"

He was perfection itself. "Liam," she began.

Dropping the newspapers on the kitchen table, Liam came toward her and took her in his arms.

Meg shrank away, thinking of her morning breath, her frizzed-out uncombed hair, her foolish loss of control last night. Now that he had achieved his goal, he would perhaps believe he cared about her for a month, or maybe the summer, and then this fall, when the newly hired instructors arrived at the college, he'd meet someone his own age, or even younger, someone svelte and blossoming, and he'd drop Meg like the fat spinster she was.

"Meg?" He looked puzzled.

She had to be the mature one. She *was* the mature one. "Liam," she said coolly. "We need to talk."

"Meg, come on, talk?" Exasperated, he put his hands on his hips.

"Liam, last night was a mistake."

"You certainly didn't act as if it was."

"Liam, please." It was hard to be dignified wrapped in a patchwork quilt. "I want to be clear about this. It can't happen again. It won't happen again." She was verging on tears. She was trying not to tremble. But she knew the pain waiting for her somewhere in the future would devastate her past imagining. She could not let that happen. How could she do this? She had said before, when he'd asked her out, that she was too old for him, but he'd brushed that fact aside as if it were totally irrelevant. She had to do it differently this time. She had to be firm. It was very possible that she was in love with him, and that was like being hooked on drugs. It would only lead to disaster.

She *had* learned something in her life. "Liam," she said in a chilly voice, "last night was special, but the truth is, you're too young for me."

Liam flinched. She had hurt him. She had meant to.

"Meg," he pleaded. "Don't do this."

"Hi, guys!" Adorable pert little Zoey came in the back door, shimmering with youth and good cheer. Her white dress and heels set off the tan she'd acquired yesterday, and the day's humidity didn't lift one strand of her sleek dark hair out of place.

Meg managed to say, "Hi, Zoey."

Liam just stared. Well, any man would stare.

"Hi, Meg. Liam, I'm catching the fast ferry now. My car's in a lot in Hyannis. If you ride up with me, I can drop you in Sudbury on my way to Concord." When he didn't answer right away, Zoey cocked her comely head like a parrot. "We talked about this yesterday, remember? How it would save you from going through Boston?"

Liam nodded. "Right. Sure. I'll just get my luggage." He left the room.

Meg cleared her throat, but something still choked it as she asked, "Would you like me to drive you to the boat?"

"Oh, nonsense." Zoey flapped her hand. "We can walk."

Meg forced a smile. "In those high heels?"

Zoey seemed puzzled. "But I always wear heels. Well, of course except on the beach." She tossed her dark hair back. "Listen, where's Arden? I want to thank her for everything."

"I don't think anyone else is here just now," Meg said.

"Well, thank her for me, will you? Jenny, too? It's been just *super*." To Meg's surprise, Zoey zipped across the room and kissed her on her cheek. "I hope we meet again, Meg. Listen, when your book is published, we'll find a way to do a spot on you on our little television show."

So Arden's *Simplify This* had become "our little television show"? Meg felt dizzy.

Liam returned to the kitchen, wearing a backpack and carrying a small case. "I'm ready." His look at Meg was bland, a pretense of friendliness. "Meg, thanks for a great weekend."

"You're welcome." Meg could stab herself, she sounded so stilted.

"Bye!" Zoey twinkled her fingers at Meg and went out the door.

Liam followed.

"Have you ever stayed at the White Elephant?" Zoey asked Liam as they went down the porch steps. "It's totally cool, rather posh, and the breakfasts are incredible." Her voice trailed off as they went around the house toward the street.

Meg stood in the kitchen in the quilt, trying to breathe. In a moment, when she knew they were really gone, she'd allow the tears to come.

FIFTEEN

Arden and Jenny arrived back at the Lily Street house to find Meg sitting at the kitchen table, crying.

"Where have you been all morning?" Arden demanded.

"Why are you crying?" Jenny inquired in a gentler voice.

Meg sniffed. "I hate Zoey."

Arden nodded. "Join the club."

Jenny said, "Why are you wearing a quilt?"

Meg's shoulders shook as she sobbed. "I'm an idiot!"

"Have you had breakfast?" Jenny asked. She poured a cup of coffee, stirred in a lot of milk and sugar, and set it before Meg. "Drink."

"Thanks." Meg stifled her sobs, sat up straight, and took a sip. "This is delicious." She shot a suspicious glare Jenny's way. "Are you trying to make me even fatter?"

"Right," Jenny answered. "You found me out. I have a secret plan to make you big as a blimp." She stuck bread into the toaster and put butter and jam and a knife on the table.

"Meg, you're not fat." Arden poured herself a cup of coffee and sat down next to her. "I don't understand how an educated and beautiful woman like you could have such a poor body self-image. Haven't you seen the shows and read about women and body dysmorphia?"

Meg took another sip of coffee and regarded rail-thin Arden skeptically. The caffeine steadied her. She took a deep breath, then in the tones of a woman being led to the gallows, admitted, "I slept with Liam."

"Shut up!" Arden cried. "When? Where? How was it?"

Jenny said, "Wait. He went off with Zoey this morning."

Meg responded to Jenny first. "Yes, he just walked with Zoey to the boat. She's going to drive him back to Sudbury." She turned to Arden. "Last night. My room. Heaven, if you want the truth."

The toast popped. Jenny flipped it onto a plate and set it in front of Meg, then slid into a chair. "It was heaven?"

Arden echoed, "He went off with Zoey?"

Jenny said, "I have so been there." She cast a jaded look at Arden. To Meg, she said, "I think you need to settle down. This morning Liam was looking all over for you. Yesterday he asked me to talk with you about him. Clearly he cares for you, Meg. I think you're getting things all twisted around."

Arden added, "Plus, you said last night was heaven."

Meg sighed. "How many times can I say it? Liam is *twenty-six years old.* I'm thirty-one. He is not going to want to settle for an older, plumper female. It goes against a male's Darwinian nature. It's in their genes or their testosterone, whatever."

"I still think you should give him a chance," Jenny softly urged.

"Of course you would think that," Meg said quietly. "Your mother didn't go through what my mother went through when Dad left her."

Arden nodded. "Or mine. I can see Meg's point. Liam *is* young. *Twenty-six.* Better to end it now when it's relatively easy, when it won't hurt so much. At least she won't be publicly embarrassed. I mean, think about it, Jenny. What if Meg hooks up with Liam at the college, and then he dumps her for some grad student? Meg will still have to work *with him*, maybe even *for him*. He's got the PhD and the ambition. He could end up dean of her department. It could get messy and ugly for Meg."

"I disagree." Jenny folded her arms on the table and scrutinized Meg. "If Liam likes Meg the way she looks now, he'll never leave her."

Meg bridled. *"What?"*

Arden snickered. "I know what you mean, Jenny." She turned to Meg. "We're not talking about your weight. We're talking about that prim and proper Victorian virgin look you've acquired. Do you possess one shirt that doesn't button up to the top of your neck? And the slacks you wear, those baggy walk-in-the-woods khakis! Really, Meg, they're terrible."

"They're sensible," Meg shot back. "I can wear them with anything."

"Yeah, we've noticed," Jenny jested.

Meg drew herself up. "I teach at a college level. That

means I have to teach a lot of adults, some even older than I am. I need to look authoritative, like I know what I'm doing. I absolutely cannot look—" She paused, trying to clarify. "I can't look sexy, and I can't look as if I'm trying to look sexy."

Arden nodded, grinning. "Yes, I do see your problem. With a hot bod like yours, Meg, you must find it difficult not to look sexy."

"But that doesn't mean you have to look drab, Meg!" Jenny jumped up from the table and walked around Meg, eyeing her up and down.

Meg clutched the quilt more tightly around her.

"What do you usually wear to teach in?" Arden asked.

"I have a kind of uniform, really. So that I don't have to think about clothes and can concentrate on my work. I need the dean, among others, to understand that I'm a serious scholar and teacher—"

Impatiently, Arden interrupted. "Fine. We get that. So what's the uniform?"

"Either khaki trousers or skirt, a plaid shirt, and a corduroy jacket. Comfortable low-heeled shoes."

Arden and Jenny exchanged glances of horror.

Meg continued, "I have about ten shirts, and several jackets and slacks, so I can just snag what I'm going to wear each day and not worry too much about it."

Jenny touched Meg's glowing hair. "And what do you do with this?"

"I braid it and coil it at the back of my head."

"Very Louisa May Alcott," Arden said.

"Well, . . . yes," Meg agreed. "But I don't want it flying around while I'm teaching. It wouldn't be professional."

Arden stood up. "Meg, Jenny and I are going to do you over from head to toe."

"Brilliant!" Jenny cried. "Like *What Not to Wear*."

"What are you talking about?" Meg asked.

"Ever watch TV?" Arden asked.

"Not that much, actually. Maybe MSNBC or PBS . . . and I like *Simplify This*. That's the one show I watch regularly."

"You do?" Arden put her hands to her chest. "I didn't know that. Oh, Meg, that makes me so happy."

Jenny yanked at Meg's quilt. "Up. Dress. We're going shopping."

As the three women walked into town, Arden said, "See, Meg, this is just what I mean. Jenny and I are wearing sundresses. You might as well be wearing a short-sleeved paper bag."

Meg stopped dead on the sidewalk. After checking to see that no one was around, she told them in a loud whisper, "I have big boobs, all right? It would be inappropriate for me to make them a distraction when I'm teaching."

"But you're not teaching now," Jenny reminded her. "You're on an island. It's summer. And you have a waist as well as a bosom. Yet you wear shapeless tents that camouflage your figure."

"They camouflage my fat."

"Meg, didn't your mother ever show you how to dress?" Jenny asked sympathetically.

"She had two boys to raise, remember? She didn't have time to think about clothes, and neither did I."

"It's beginning to make sense," Arden said. "My mom has to look chic because she's a real estate agent who deals in high-end properties. So I learned a lot from just observing her. Jenny's mother, Justine, is drop-dead dazzling, and so is Jenny, so Jenny can wear her computer nerd gear with a pair of exotic earrings and look fabulous."

Meg cut in, "Don't forget, Jenny's slender."

"Don't forget," Jenny shot back, "you've got an hourglass figure that can make men blush."

Meg herself blushed at the compliment. "I never thought of it that way."

Jenny headed right to Zero Main, her favorite store. "When I have to go into New York for a business meeting, I come here and ask Noel to put me together."

When Meg saw Noel, she started to walk back out the door. "Jenny," she whispered, "that woman is tiny. She won't have anything here in my size."

"Give her a chance," Jenny said, locking on to Meg's arm.

While other saleswomen helped other customers, Noel joined the three sisters in a dressing room. Jenny explained the problem.

Noel quickly eyed Meg up and down. "You've got a movie-star figure."

Meg quipped, "Yeah, for 1930."

Noel said, "You have a tiny waist." She tapped her fingernail on her lip. "I'll be right back."

Jenny went out to help Noel carry the trial garments into the dressing room. Arden played handmaiden, zipping up dresses, returning them to hangers, handing Meg something new. Sleeveless Eileen Fishers worked the best, with short, bright jackets or shrugs and a scarf or costume jewelry around the neck. They pried Meg out of her Birkenstocks and into seductive sandals, some with actual heels.

"Bombshell," Arden announced.

"Try these embroidered tunics," Noel suggested. "They're all the rage. You've got great legs. Wear them with these pants."

Meg was breathless. She whispered to Arden, "This will cost so much money."

Arden said, "At the end of the summer, you're coming into a fat inheritance when we sell the house. Besides, you probably haven't bought any new clothes for a decade, right?"

Meg wanted to disagree but couldn't.

"Next," Jenny announced, "hair. Time for a cut and style."

"No!" Meg cried. "It's my one physical feature I'm proud of. It's such an unusual color."

"True, but when you braid and coil it behind your neck, you look like Heidi of the Alps. Come on."

"I'm hungry," Meg whimpered.

"Me, too," Arden confessed. "Let's get these bags home, grab a piece of fruit, and drive out to The Hair Concern."

"They won't have a free appointment," Meg said.

But they did. Tricia cut several inches of Meg's hair and showed her how to let it fall freely around her face. The change was alluring, even saucy, so she showed Meg how to roll it and tuck it to give it interest when she pulled it back with a refined clip at her neck.

By the end of the day, the women were exhausted and Meg was practically shell-shocked. They ordered a pizza and collapsed in front of a romantic comedy DVD.

Later, on their way to bed, Arden eyed Meg and said, "About your pajamas . . ."

Meg held up her hand. "No more. I need some time to adjust."

From behind Arden, Jenny joked, "Once Liam sees the new Meg, she won't have time to put on pajamas."

In order to prepare the arts coalition site, Tim and Jenny had to interview and photograph a number of visual and performing artists, as well as visit local art studios and galleries and meet the owners. The interviews they did on their own, dividing up the tasks, and they prepared a questionnaire for the artists and the gallery owners to fill out and submit. But they needed to see some of the work to get a sense of what the artists would prefer for their site, and they needed some brilliant photographs. Most of their professional collaboration thus far had been by e-mail or phone, but viewing and documenting local artists' work meant Jenny and Tim had to actually spend time together. They agreed to meet on Friday night, the night most art galleries had their openings.

At five o'clock, Jenny was paralyzed in front of the bathroom mirror as Arden swept in wearing a fabulous tight white cocktail dress.

"I'm off to the library gala with Palmer. What are you—what *are* you doing?"

"I look like a boy." Jenny stared at her image with huge frightened eyes. This was one of the rare times when she wished she knew something about her biological father. Had he been ugly or handsome?

"You could never look like a boy. You haven't worried about it before."

"I know. I don't know why I'm so anxious tonight. I guess because Meg is so stacked. Plus, I'm going to see all those artists."

Arden inspected Jenny's face. "What did you wear when you went out with Bjorn?"

"Bjorn liked everything natural. We usually were on a boat or swimming."

"Okay. Got it. Tonight, artists." Arden cocked her head. "Take off the black tee, put on your sequined tank top."

Jenny went into the bedroom, tossed off one shirt, pulled on the multicolored tank.

"Great. I've got just the earrings. Stay there." Arden went to her room, returning with long dangling gold earrings that hung almost to Jenny's shoulders. "Put these on. Now sit on the bed and hold still." Deftly, she brushed on eye shadow, bronzer, blush, and lip gloss. "Now look."

"Wow," Jenny breathed. "What a change. Thanks a lot. How did you do that?"

"Tomorrow. I've got to go. Have fun." Arden rushed out.

Jenny dropped her digital camera into a small clutch bag and headed out, walking into town to meet Tim at the East End art gallery. She didn't miss the admiring looks shot her way as she passed, and her spirits lifted. On Nantucket, the arts group was lively and sophisticated, internationally famous and edgy. The East End Gallery had once been a fisherman's shack. Tonight it would be crowded with millionaire art connoisseurs.

The gallery was already packed by the time Jenny arrived. Inside the shack, the artwork was displayed—tonight paintings by Gay Held and Michael J. Moore. Outside, tables were set up with a tuxedoed bartender pouring drinks and another laden with cleverly exotic finger foods.

"Well, hey." A stranger wearing bright yellow linen slacks and a patchwork blazer approached Jenny. "You look like you could use a drink."

The guy was good-looking enough and he knew it. Jenny quickly decided he was a creep. "Sorry, I'm busy." She stepped away.

Inside the gallery, she took time to study the paintings and took several shots of the crush of people grouped in front of the artwork.

"So you are working." Tim squeezed through the crowd to stand next to her.

"Of course," Jenny retorted, puzzled.

"Your friend in the fluorescent slacks didn't think so."

Jenny glared. "What's your problem?"

"Well, you don't look exactly professional," Tim said accusingly.

"Well, you do sound exactly like an asshole!" Jenny shot back, nearly shouting to be heard in the crowd. She

cold-shouldered him and pushed her way between par-
tiers to get out to the fresh air. For some reason, his
words had upset her. She thought she was going to cry.

She stood in line to get a glass of white wine. The evening was still hot, the sun only slightly lower on the horizon. The throng pushing in and out of the gallery made
her glad she'd worn the tank top.

Deciding to act professional even if she didn't look it,
she stepped back and began to snap photos.

Tim came up to her. He did look professional, in a
crisp white shirt and a navy blazer. "I'm sorry," he said.
When she didn't respond, he continued, "Really. I apologize. I don't even know why I said that."

"It's fine," Jenny told him coldly. "What do you think
of the show?"

"It's great. In fact, I saw a picture by Gay Held that
should be on the 'Paintings' link of the site."

"The one called *Monomoy*?" Jenny asked.

"Yeah, I think so. How did you know?"

"It's my favorite. Kind of hard-edged, not all dreamy."

Tim took her arm. "Come on. Let's be sure it's the
same one."

He led her into the gallery again. The crowd was thinning out so they were able to stand side by side, looking
at the painting.

"Yeah," Jenny said. "That's the one."

"I've already got a quote from Gay about her work."
Tim held up his pad. "Listen to this. 'The horizon line is
a consistent theme in my work. It represents a place of
rest and the notion of infinite beginning.'"

"'A place of rest and the notion of infinite beginning,'" Jenny repeated. "What a fabulous quote. That's what Nantucket is for people."

Tim smiled at her, and she smiled back. Collaborators. With an infinite beginning.

Arden had drawn up an Excel spreadsheet of island events, and all that July, she volunteered to help with fund-raisers—the Maria Mitchell Association Science Museum, the Nantucket Historical Association Whaling Museum, A Safe Place, the Atheneum, the Shipwreck and Lifesaving Museum. Willing to do any job, no matter how small or inelegant, she got to know all sorts of people, from the locals on the island to the wealthiest summer residents. She discovered she had a talent for simplifying events as well as houses.

"Don't set the bar up right here," she suggested sweetly to a trustee as she helped ready a party for The Homestead in the backyard of a brilliant gardener. "Put it over by the roses, so people aren't clogged in a bottle-neck just getting in. This way, too, they'll get to see more of this magnificent place and they'll be happier, more likely to donate."

"Don't spend your money on scotch and bourbon," she told a committeewoman planning a party for a private school fund-raiser. "Most of your guests are young parents. Only older people drink the hard stuff. The young marrieds want wine, maybe some Prosecco, even beer. They've been out on the water all day, they're stopping by here on their way to dinner, they have little kids who'll wake them at six tomorrow, they don't want to get bombed."

Because she was a minor celebrity herself, people listened and took her advice. She became sought after. By the end of July, her cell phone and e-mail were stuffed with messages.

She piled up guests for her show.

The Safe Place benefit was held at a benefactor's house on the cliff overlooking the gleaming sweep of the harbor. A large wooden deck with benches built into the railings extended into the green grassy lawn. Both deck and lawn were packed with women in silk, satin, and sparkling gems. Arden wore her fuchsia dress that night, the one with a short, flouncy skirt and a diamanté flower at the waist. Tight, brief, flashy, it was dynamite on her and she knew it.

Palmer had complimented her on it when he picked her up for the evening, but now as he approached her over the deck, his smile was amused.

"Arden," he said, "I'd like you to meet Winkie Linden."

Arden's breath caught in her throat. Winkie Linden was the widow of a former Massachusetts senator, dressed as always in her trademark black with a necklace of diamonds and pearls. Winkie herself was a jewel, a grande dame of eighty with pearly white skin, a nose like an eagle, and brilliant blue eyes. Briefly, she assessed Arden in her showy frock, and then, to Arden's relief, she held out her hand.

"I know about your show, Miss Randall. I've been meaning to contact you. I've got a rambling old summer house that's been in the Linden family for years. The Linden Society has taken all they consider relevant to their museum, but the house is still absolutely crammed with dusty old artifacts that don't leave room for anything new. I wonder, is this a project you could work with?"

Stunned, Arden replied, "I think so. Tell me more."

"Oh dear. Let's see. Old portraits of ancestors who were senators in Massachusetts in the 1800s. My grandmother's wedding gown. An early set of gardener's tools. Even"—Winkie smiled—"corsets and flapper dresses."

Arden nearly clapped her hands. "Oh, what fun. Yes, absolutely, we could do something on *Simplify This*. It sounds like we could do a miniseries and tie it in with our historical show, *Nest Eggs*."

"A miniseries?" Winkie's smile broadened. "What a pleasant idea."

"When could I come talk with you about it?" Arden asked. She took the widow's information just as another one of the late senator's admirers approached to introduce Mrs. Linden to his family.

"Well done," Palmer whispered to Arden as he strolled down to the lawn with her.

"You brought her to me," Arden told him. "Thank you for that."

"'You can lead a horse to water,' and so on," Palmer replied. "If she hadn't taken to you, she would have cut you dead. She's always been that way, makes snap decisions and acts on them. Obviously, she liked you."

"I'm surprised," Arden said. "This dress is rather flashy."

"You look very nice in that dress," Palmer told her.

"*Nice?*" Arden challenged.

"Would you like a stronger response?" Palmer challenged back.

An almost-famous singer, young and radiant, sidled up to Palmer. Placing a ring-studded hand on his arm, she said in a syrupy voice, "Thank you so much, Mr. White, for getting me that gig on Channel Six."

Arden arched a knowing eyebrow at Palmer and drifted away, leaving Palmer in the young woman's eager hands.

Arden didn't want to intrude on Zoey's territory, but could she help it if some younger people invited her to simplify their homes? When, at another benefit, Ludmila Soares, the fourth and most exotic wife of the owner of a major football team, confessed she was overwhelmed with organizing the summer home at the same time she took care of her two-year-old while she was five months pregnant, how could Arden not offer to help?

Ludmila, who had been a model, adored being on camera and was thrilled to show off her child and the seven-thousand-square-foot house she and her husband spent two weeks in every year. Another big catch for Arden.

To her delight, Arden was also making friends on the island with some of the clever businesswomen who ran the poshest shops in town. She didn't want to take the time to go to Boston to search for clothes to wear to the galas, parties, dances, and cocktail hours, so she stopped in at Zero Main to have Noel fix her up, and frequently drifted into Moon Shell Beach, where she got to know Lexi Laney, whose sensual silks and drifting shawls were not the sort of thing Arden could wear on television, but felt divine on hot summer nights. After observing the women who clustered in Lexi's store, Arden asked Lexi if she could take her out to dinner.

"Consider it business," Arden told Lexi, although she sensed a kindred spirit in the delightful workingwoman.

One late July evening, at a restaurant down by the harbor, Lexi and Arden settled by a window, ordered, then sat back to enjoy their vodka tonics.

"Business first," Arden said frankly. "I have a show in Boston—"

"Of course. *Simplify This.* I watch it all the time."

"I knew I liked you." Arden laughed. "I'm wondering if you have any suggestions for people with summer homes that might need an organizational touch."

Lexi sipped her drink. "Maybe. Let me think about it, okay? I have a question for you."

"Oh?"

"What's the deal with you and Tim Robinson?"

Arden let her gaze drift out over the boat basin, where yachts tied up to the docks bobbed in the calm water. "I go out sailing with him now and then. He's handsome, he's nice, he's smart—"

"But no chemistry, right?"

Arden checked Lexi's face. "Right. How do you know? Oh, are you interested in him?"

Lexi laughed. "Not at all." She held out her hand. "Haven't you noticed this?" She waggled a twinkling engagement ring. "I'm going to marry Tris Chandler. He runs a boatyard out in Madaket, and you've probably seen his teenage daughter, Jewel, in my shop. Anyway, yeah, I've seen you out with Tim on the water. That's why I asked."

"We're just friends," Arden said. "I've been too busy working to think of anything like romance."

"What about Palmer White?"

Shocked, Arden barked with laughter. "You do notice things, don't you?"

Lexi lifted an elegant winged eyebrow. "I've seen you at a lot of parties recently. Sometimes you're with Palmer. He's obviously hot for you."

"He's egotistical and insolent."

"Yeah, like Tommy Lee Jones with a tasty touch of George Clooney. He's a *man*, honey."

Arden sighed. "You're right. Palmer is an actual grown-up in a world of overgrown boys. He's powerful; he's used to getting his own way. I suppose he's sexy, too . . . but really, I don't want to get involved."

"Why not? How old are you?"

"I'm thirty-four. No, I haven't been married. No, I don't want children. I relish my career. The funny thing is," she added thoughtfully, "my two sisters are thirty-one and they haven't been married yet, either. Our father was Rory Randall—"

"I remember Rory. What a dreamboat. Handsome, and he could charm the birds off the trees."

"He could charm women into bed," Arden added cynically. "I suppose having him for a father made all three of us shy of trusting men."

"I understand." Lexi confessed, "I was married before. I was young, naïve, and reckless. It ended disastrously. I want to take my time with Tris before getting married again. He's divorced, too, so we're in no hurry."

"It sounds like right now you have it all," Arden said.

Lexi smiled. "You know, maybe I do."

SIXTEEN

For Meg, seeking refuge in books had started in boarding school, after she understood that not only had her father abandoned her for Justine and Jenny, but her mother had come to look at her with a kind of gentle regret, as if Meg were a tattoo she'd foolishly collected long ago.

Meg had found solace in the results of her intellect and hard work. She won praise from her teachers, and she became part of a gang of friends equally industrious and academic. Early on, she had decided that she wanted to be a teacher.

It was second nature for Meg to immerse herself in her work. Here on the island, she established a working routine and stuck to it, and gradually it encompassed her like a comfortable old quilt.

She rose every morning at six, crept out of the house in shorts and a tee shirt, and went for a half hour's run while the air was still sweet and cool. Back home, she prepared a cup of coffee, a piece of toast, and some fruit and took them up to her haven at the back of the house, where she opened her laptop, spread out her notes, and began to work.

The more she wrote, the more she became engrossed in her subject and even infatuated with it. May and Louisa May were sisters, talented, affectionate, competitive. The words flowed from her mind as she tapped away on her laptop, and real time ceased to exist as she lost herself in the past.

By three in the afternoon, she was flat with exhaustion. It was an effort to raise her body off her chair, to slip out of her shorts and tee, wet with perspiration from the heat and humidity of the little back room. She'd shower, put on one of her fabulous new sundresses, clip back her hair, and go out into the day, which filled her with a sense of sympathetic kinship, for much of Nantucket remained as it had in the nineteenth century when the Alcotts lived. Meg strolled the cobblestone streets and brick sidewalks, toured the historic houses, or sat in the library garden reading.

She couldn't resist being in touch with Liam. He had become so much a part of her life and her work. His voice brought her back to her real world, full of eager students, self-absorbed professors, worried administrators, and books—books online, on e-readers, on the shelves of libraries. But Meg made it clear when they talked that she couldn't deal with what had happened between them, that she didn't want to discuss anything as personal as a relationship, and he honored her request, as she'd known he would. So nearly every day she phoned Liam, or he phoned her. They e-mailed constantly, exchanging news about their work. Meg did not allow herself to think of him as anyone other than a colleague.

In the evenings, she, Arden, and Jenny took turns cooking dinner. Somehow this time of day had acquired a gentle feel of camaraderie. The sisters fell into the habit of enjoying a glass of wine out in the garden, or if the weather was rainy, in the living room, a more formal room than the den. They spoke about their work, but not in vague monosyllables. They each tried to explain to the others what it was they were doing, why they were excited about it, what the challenges were, what had been accomplished that day.

One stormy night, after a gloomy, chilly day, Jenny made a fire, Arden concocted hot chocolate from scratch, and they curled up in the living room to listen to Meg read the page she had written that day.

Meg read, "Love and work. For most of us, our lives are defined by love and work. It is a fortunate woman who loves her work and a blessed woman who does not find herself torn between them."

"Whoa!" Arden spoke first. "That's intense."

Jenny cocked her head. "Can you take some criticism? I think your writing sounds a bit old-fashioned, maybe stuffy. I wouldn't get through it."

Meg chewed the end of her pencil. "Yeah. I can see that. I guess I'm picking up the style of the times when Louisa May Alcott wrote."

"What you need is some newfangled media training. Or at least an attitude adjustment," Arden told her, shifting to straighten a pillow behind her back. "No one knows about May Alcott, but everyone's familiar with

Louisa May Alcott and will be fascinated to learn more about her. Also, you're delving into the topic of sisterhood, and God knows the world is full of sisters with complicated relationships."

"Arden's right," Jenny agreed. "Lighten it up a bit; make May's story more—what's the word?—*accessible* to the normal person." Seeing Meg's quiet retreat into reflection, she added, "I'm not trying to be harsh."

"I know," Meg said thoughtfully. "I'm thinking about what you've said."

These two women were paying the ultimate compliment: giving her their full attention, and their considered opinions. What she liked was sitting in this old house with the wind battering the windows, the rain slanting sideways at the walls, the fire flaring on the andirons, and the aroma of hot chocolate in the air; they might be the Brontë sisters.

For a moment, she felt at home.

At the end of July, Meg planned a picnic dinner for the three Lily Street women. When Arden and Jenny were ready in the sandals and swimsuits Meg had insisted they wear, she popped into the driver's seat of the Jeep and drove them all down to Jetties Beach.

It was six o'clock. The children had been taken home for baths and dinner and bed, leaving the long swath of golden beach relatively peaceful. The evening was still, with drowsy waves sliding against the shore and a few sailboats becalmed in the harbor.

Meg spread the blanket, planting the coolers on two

corners, and knelt to open one while she used the top of the other as a table. Shaking a thermos, she poured daiquiris into tall plastic cups and handed them around. She laid out a platter of finger foods—salty wrinkled olives, Brie on crackers, little tomatoes and carrots, marinated artichoke hearts, bluefish pâté.

"What's this all about?" Jenny asked, slightly suspicious.

"Nothing," Meg told her. "Everything." She gestured toward the ocean. "This."

A ferry was gliding toward the island, as stately as a grand white castle on the calm blue water. In the harbor, golden lights beamed from sailboats and laughter drifted toward the shore. High in the blue sky, a few puffs of cloud drowsed unmoving, as if they, too, were stilled by the heat. At the edge of the waves, a yellow bucket and a red shovel sat lonely and abandoned.

"Someone will come back for them tomorrow," Arden said, reading Meg's mind.

"We could use them. We could build a sand castle," Meg suggested. "A really enormous one, with lots of turrets and battlements and a moat."

"Then Arden could simplify it," Jenny joked.

Meg rose on her knees. "We should do it. Build a fantastic castle for kids to discover when they arrive tomorrow morning."

Arden snorted. "Please, don't make me move. This is too blissful."

Meg sank back down. "You're right."

"And you're high," Arden told Meg.

"Kind of," Meg agreed. "My work has been going so

well. I've gotten a lot done. This place is great for working. I'm cut off from so many distractions."

"It's turning out to be helpful to my work, too,"
Arden said after taking another sip of her daiquiri. "My
contact list is crammed with new names. I've got my camera crew coming down in August to do a few shoots. Except for Ariadne Silverstone, the homeowners are young.
So take that, Zero Zoey."

Meg clapped her hands like a girl. "Arden, I just remembered! Your career in journalism started here on
this island."

Arden lifted an inquisitive eyebrow. "Oh yeah?"

"Arden. Remember when you were ten? You wrote the
Lily Street News."

Arden chuckled. "I'd forgotten all about that."

"What was the *Lily Street News*?" Jenny asked.

"A newspaper Arden wrote on Dad's computer," Meg
said. "Arden went up and down the street, interviewing
people, asking them if they were summer residents,
where they were from, if they had kids or dogs or cats,
and what new things they were doing to their houses or
yards."

"Then I'd print off copies and take them around to the
houses. Put them in the mail slot or boxes. It was actually
rather professional. I put in the names and times of the
new movies and events at the library," Arden said.

Meg said, "Back then, I thought it was brilliant. Now
I think it is adorable. Mr. and Mrs. Edward Jones of
Houston, Texas, have a new member of their family with
them this year: Poppy, a Jack Russell terrier puppy."

"But I made a typo and printed 'Poopy'!" Arden

whooped. "I had to print a special edition with the correction."

"And you made *me* deliver that edition to the Joneses' house in case they were angry," Meg added.

"I knew they wouldn't take it out on a sweet little seven-year-old." Arden sighed, lost in memories. "I only did it for about a month. Someone in the neighborhood thought it was *inappropriate* for the daughter of a real estate agent to be cruising the area asking questions about houses."

"You've got to admit, they had a point," Meg said.

"Some people were cool with it," Arden reminisced. "They invited me into their homes, showed me around. Especially the Wiltons. They were so proud of all the historical stuff that I could scarcely understand back then."

"They were nice, the Wiltons," Meg agreed. "They'd invite us into their house on a rainy day and serve us tea and cookies, in real china cups and saucers, remember?"

"Oh, and remember their grandson? What was his name?"

Meg snapped her fingers. "Josiah. You and I thought it was the most hysterical name, although he told everyone his name was Joe—"

"But his grandparents insisted on calling him the whole horrible thing. Josiah." Arden bit into an olive and chewed thoughtfully. "He was really cute, wasn't he?"

Meg nodded. "I wonder whatever happened to him."

"I don't know," Arden said. "We lost touch with him after we were exiled from the house."

Jenny shifted uncomfortably on the blanket. After a

moment, she said, "The old Wiltons died when I was about fifteen. Whoever inherited the house sold it. No Wiltons live on Lily Street."

"'The unplumbed, salt, estranging sea,'" Meg murmured. Seeing the glances of the others, she gave the quote's attribution: "Matthew Arnold. Staring out at the water while remembering people who've been separated from us made me think of that line."

"It wasn't the sea that estranged us from this island," Arden pointed out, her voice flat, empty of anger. She didn't need to say that it had been Jenny's mother.

Jenny pretended to ignore Arden's remark. "Actually," she said, "the sea is becoming less and less unplumbed. James Cameron's already explored the deepest part of the Mariana Trench in a private submarine."

"I heard about that," Arden said. "I'd like to do that myself. Think of all the creatures you could see that have never been seen by humans before. Maybe down there, they'll find intelligent life on this planet," she joked.

"I'd settle for spotting a whale in the waters around the island," Meg said.

"We should go on a whale watch sometime," Jenny said. "They have them all summer."

"Good idea," Meg said.

"Whales." Arden didn't sound enthusiastic. "I guess I'm not much of a nature fan as you two. Even this"— she spread her arms out, indicating the entire beach and sound—"is not really my scene. Those whale watches are expensive. I prefer my fish on a plate, with an endive salad on the side."

Jenny grinned. "You'd prefer to get laid."

Meg held up her thermos. "More daiquiris, anyone?"

Arden extended her glass.

"Palmer's interested in you," Jenny said. "I've seen the way he looks at you."

"That would be complicated." Arden shied away from discussing her ambivalence about that particular man. "He's in the business. I don't want to reach the top by lying on my back."

Jenny snickered and looked to Meg. "Isn't that a mixed metaphor?"

Meg and Arden smiled. They settled in to eat seriously, sharing the various sandwiches Meg had made: cheese, avocado, and chutney; crab salad; BLTs. The blue sky deepened to an indigo hue and a breeze rose, lifting the edges of the blanket and ruffling their hair.

"I got some more movies from the library today," Meg told them. "Three or four brand-new chick flicks."

"Just what I'm in the mood for," Jenny said.

Arden finished her sandwich and dusted crumbs off her hands. "I'm in the mood for a mystery."

"I've got a few of those, too," Meg told her smugly. "Plus strawberry cheesecake."

After a while, they gathered up their things and slowly stepped over the sand to the parking lot, where they stopped to put on their sandals. A blonde woman in her late forties walked up behind them, a towel tossed over her shoulder.

"Hello, girls," she said in a sultry voice as she forked right to her own car.

Politely, they murmured greetings.

In the car on the way home, Arden asked Jenny, "Do you know that woman?"

"No," Jenny said, "but I think I've seen her before, on our street. Maybe she lives on Lily."

"She only said *hello*," Meg snorted. "We're on the island. People are friendly."

"Something seemed strange about her," Arden said. "I'm paranoid, right?"

"Only someone paranoid would think that," Meg teased.

The three of them laughed, easily, together.

SEVENTEEN

Jenny and Tim were sitting in Genevieve's home office, holding their breath while the three of them studied her computer screen.

"Hmm, yeah, I think this is a bull's-eye, exactly what I was hoping for," Genevieve decided. Before they could relax, she added, "Now, what if some of the artists want to add something on the site's blog?"

"We're e-mailing them all with instructions," Jenny replied.

"Will they be able to call you if they need help?" Genevieve asked.

"They'll be able to e-mail us," Tim said.

"Yes, darlin', but some of them like to be able to actually hear a friendly, helpful voice on the phone."

"In some cases," Jenny offered pleasantly, "it takes a long time to help someone—"

Genevieve didn't hesitate. "Keep track of the time you spend on the phone calls and I'll pay you a consulting fee,

extra to the basic commission." Before Jenny could speak
again, she added, "If you have to drive to their homes, of
course I'll pay your driving time and gas. Okay?"

"Sounds good," Tim answered.

The words were hardly out of his mouth before Genevieve rose. "Fine, then. I've got to dash. Keep in touch.
See yourselves out, darlins." With a swish of her silk
dress, Genevieve made her exit.

Jenny flashed a wry smile at Tim. "For a big woman,
she moves fast."

They closed their laptops and stood up.

"So we're good?" Tim asked Jenny.

"Seems like it." She slipped the laptop carrier strap
over her shoulder.

They went out into the hall, where the maid waited to
open the front door for them.

"Thanks," Tim said, and they went down the steps
into the bright summer day. After the air-conditioned
house, for a moment the humid July heat stunned them.
They stood on the brick sidewalk, gathering their thoughts.

Jenny was aware of Tim next to her, so tall, smelling
of a citrus aftershave, something he seldom wore; she bet
he'd put it on for the appointment with Genevieve. He
wore a button-down shirt in a dreamy blue that matched
his eyes, a red tie, and khakis. He looked so damnably
masculine, adult, and handsome Jenny's knees went
weak. A wave of sensual pleasure passed through her as
one of those unexpected moments of good health and a
fine sunny day stilled her normal need to rush. She let
her head fall back, closed her eyes, and gave a silent
thank-you to the universe.

"You look like you're ready to be kissed," Tim remarked.

Her head snapped back up so fast she almost cracked her vertebrae. "What?" She hoped he didn't think she'd been coming on to him.

"Nothing," he muttered, backing away. "Just—good, it's good that Genevieve's happy with the site, right? See you."

Puzzled as much by her emotions as by Tim's words, Jenny watched him walk away.

It was her night to prepare dinner. To forget her problems, Jenny chose a complicated recipe for paella with lots of different seafood. She tossed in extra spices because she was in that kind of mood.

The evening was hot and humid. The women loaded up their plates, filled their glasses with wine, and carried everything out to the patio to eat. At first, they hardly spoke, absorbed with the delicious meal, but after a while they sat back in their chairs, content and sated.

"I could get used to this," Arden mused. "Cooking only every third night. Eating homemade gourmet meals instead of what I usually eat—takeout, or a bag of popcorn and a pear."

"I enjoy cooking," Jenny admitted. "It takes my mind off other things."

"Like what?" Arden asked.

Jenny gave herself a moment to think while slowly sipping her wine. "Well, . . . it's complicated."

Arden chuckled. "Who is he?"

Jenny nodded. "You're right, it's a man, but not how you think."

Meg looked concerned. "Are you okay? Are you sick?"

"No. What I'm talking about is something you two, with all the things you have to crab about, will never need to consider." Jenny fiddled with her napkin for a moment, then lifted her chin and blurted, "I don't know who my father is."

Arden snapped, "Dear God, you're always making it clear that Dad is *your*—"

"My birth father." Jenny put it right out there in the evening air.

"Your biological father," Meg clarified.

"Right. The guy who knocked up my mother."

"For heaven's sake, haven't you asked Justine?" Arden demanded.

Jenny toyed with the last forkful of rice. "She refuses to talk about it."

"That's ridiculous," Arden said.

"She says I have a father. Rory is my father, and I don't need another."

Arden plonked her elbows on the table. "Jenny. Reality call. Ever heard of biology? Genes? What in the *hell* is Justine thinking?"

Jenny's mouth tightened. "I know you hate my mother, but—"

Meg interrupted. "Jenny, what Arden means is that you need to find out who your biological father is for medical reasons. What if he has some kind of genetic disease?"

"Disease?" Jenny shrieked. "Why would he have a disease?"

"I don't mean disease, necessarily. I mean, you need to know what traits he passed on to you genetically. Because you could be passing them on to your children."

"This is the most depressing conversation I've ever had," Jenny moaned.

"Look, don't head right for the fatal stuff," Arden suggested, keeping her voice mellow. "I'm thinking of normal issues like high blood pressure. Late-onset diabetes. Thyroid problems. Even things like dyslexia or bipolar disorder."

"We all have something," Meg added sympathetically. "That's just part of being human."

"Plus," Arden insisted, "I think it would do you good to meet your biological father. Just to set eyes on him." After a moment, she challenged, "Don't tell me you're not curious."

"I *am* curious," Jenny admitted quietly. "I mean, that's why I brought it up."

"Then do something," Arden urged. "Find him."

"I know. I *know*." Jenny made a face. "But I don't know how to go about it."

Meg patted Jenny's hand. "You have to convince your mother to tell you who he is."

"What if she continues to stonewall me?"

Arden grinned wickedly. "Scare her. We'll look up some diseases and find some creepy symptoms. Tell her you've been shaking or twitching or whatever—"

Jenny glared at Arden. "There is something so very wrong with you!"

Arden laughed.

Meg persisted in her gentle voice: "Jenny, I don't think you should put it off. Why not get serious with Justine? You have a right to know."

Jenny picked up her wineglass, but it was empty. She set it back down on the table. "I can't just call her up and demand that she tell me."

"I agree," Arden said calmly. "Something like this should be done face-to-face."

A rush of relief swept through Jenny. "Right. And Mom's in Boston and I'm down here, so I'll have to wait until the fall. I don't even know why I brought it up."

"Jenny, you could go to Boston tomorrow," Meg pointed out.

Jenny shook her head violently. "No, because we have to live here together for three months or the house won't be ours."

"Please." Arden rolled her eyes. "Dad didn't stipulate that we could never leave the island for three months. Just that we live here, and we're doing that."

Jenny chewed her lips.

Meg said, "Jenny. You really should go talk to your mother. Now's the time."

Jenny shoved back her chair and paced around the table, thinking. When she sat back down, she said with a touch of triumph in her voice, "Fine. And you should tell Liam you're in love with him."

Meg tossed her fiery hair away from her shoulders. "Jenny. We've been through this."

Slyly, Jenny said, "You know, I looked at your notes."

"What?"

"You left them on the dining room table the other day. The outline."

Meg put her hand to her forehead. She knew what was coming.

"What are you talking about?" Arden asked.

"I read your outline. You tell us everything about your precious May Alcott, but did you tell *us* about who she married?"

"No. Why should I?" Meg demanded defensively. "The subject has never come up."

"Please," said Jenny.

"*What* are you talking about?" Arden asked again.

Jenny faced Arden with a victorious grin. "Meg's revered May Alcott married a man fourteen years younger than she was!"

"Aha." Arden sent a piercing glare Meg's way. "And you're worried about loving a man a mere five years younger?"

"It's more complicated." Meg wriggled.

"How?"

"Ernest Nieriker was not May Alcott's colleague, almost boss. Besides, May died in childbirth about a year into their marriage, so Ernest didn't ever get the chance to leave her for a younger, slimmer woman."

Arden slapped her hand to her forehead. "You are one twisted sister!"

"Don't be so freaking superstitious!" Jenny scolded. "Whatever happened to May Alcott is not going to happen to you just because you're writing a book about her."

Meg nodded unhappily. "I know."

Jenny said, "I'll tell you what. I'll face off with my

mother. I'll make her tell me about my birth father. But only if you go up and talk with Liam about your feelings and your fears."

"Those two things aren't comparable at all!" Meg objected.

"Well, we both don't want to do them," Jenny told her.

"Then what does *Arden* have to do?" Meg asked.

Arden snorted. "Why should I have to do anything?"

"Because *we* do." Meg crossed her arms over her chest.

"What do you want me to do?" Arden asked.

Meg thought. "Ask Palmer White to dinner."

"Please, no."

"Why not?" Jenny asked.

"He's not my type," Arden finished, squirming uncomfortably in her chair.

"Why not?" Meg asked. "You've certainly spent a lot of time with him this summer."

"He's arrogant, opinionated, bossy, and a workaholic," Arden said.

Jenny cleared her throat loudly.

"Okay, I am, too," Arden agreed. "But Palmer's high-powered. Type A. He's at the top of the ladder. I'm still working my way up and I want to deserve any advancement I get." She turned the conversation back to Meg. "Well? Are you going to talk to Liam?"

Meg equivocated. "He's up there, I'm down here."

"So invite him down here," Jenny told her. "If you need an extra bed, there's the front bedroom, empty and waiting. If you really need an extra bed."

"Or go up there," Arden suggested. "I'll hold the fort down here."

"I know!" Meg clicked her fingers. "Jenny and I will go to Boston if you invite Palmer here for an intimate little dinner while we're gone."

"That is so lame," Arden sighed.

"I don't think so." Jenny was grinning now. "It makes lots of sense to me. If Meg and I have to do something difficult, so do you." She leaned toward Arden, getting right in her face. "Or are you scared of him?"

Arden rolled her eyes. "Fine. I'll do it."

EIGHTEEN

The car ferry was booked, so Jenny and Meg agreed to pool their money to rent a car when they got to Hyannis. The plan was for Jenny to drop Meg at her apartment in Sudbury and pick her up in three days, keeping in contact by cell phone.

Zipping north on 495 in the cherry-red Toyota, they chose a rock station featuring Coldplay, Arcade Fire, and Foo Fighters, tacitly allowing the music to prevent any kind of serious conversation, which in both cases would probably have been a long, repetitive shriek of: *What am I doing? Should I go back? Is this the right thing to do?*

Jenny left Meg at a white gingerbread Victorian where Meg rented an apartment two blocks from the campus. Meg insisted she'd be fine without a car; she could walk to a small health food store for what she needed, and if she called Liam—*when* she called Liam—he could drive her anywhere she had to go. Or just come to her apartment, as planned.

Justine still lived in the French provincial mansion she'd shared with Rory in the posh Boston suburb of Belmont. Its grounds were stunning, with lots of topiaries, a "water feature," and even a few statues. As a real estate agent, Rory insisted he needed to live in a house that would inspire respect. Jenny had a room of her own for her occasional visits from the island.

Parking on the familiar circle drive, she pulled out her overnight bag and walked around to the back of the house. Here, glass doors opened into the fragrant, lush conservatory, which led to the Mexican-tiled steam, sauna, and shower room Justine relaxed in after exercising in her private gym.

Justine wasn't there. It was just around one, so perhaps her mother was in the kitchen fixing herself lunch. Jenny headed that way.

Canned laughter led her toward the small private den—as opposed to the larger, slightly overwhelming media room, with its movie theater seating and enormous screen.

Justine was curled up on the sofa in a winter robe, eating Smartfood popcorn from the bag and staring listlessly at a talk show.

"Mom."

Justine jumped so fast half the popcorn flew from the bag. "Jenny! You startled me!"

"Oh, Mom, you look terrible." Jenny entered the room with a sinking heart.

Justine's hand went to her unwashed hair. "I haven't organized myself for the day."

Observing other bags of junk food, empty cans of

diet soda, and slithered stacks of tabloid magazines that occupied all the other surfaces in the den, and smelling the unmistakable odor of an unclean woman's body, Jenny understood that Justine hadn't organized herself for many days.

"Where's Estrella?"

"I told her to take a month off with pay so she could go back to the Dominican Republic and visit her family. I don't want anyone around. Right now I don't need a housekeeper." Justine set the popcorn bag on the coffee table. The bag slowly slid off onto the floor. "Jenny, what are you doing here? Why didn't you phone?"

"It was very spur-of-the-moment," Jenny said. Sitting on the sofa, she reached out to take her mother's hand. "Mommy. Look at you."

Tears welled up in Justine's eyes. "I miss Rory. Why should I bother about anything when Rory's gone? Who cares what I look like, what anything looks like, without Rory?"

Jenny started to argue, but changed her mind. "Let's get you showered and dressed, okay?"

With almost childlike willingness, Justine allowed Jenny to lead her by the hand through the echoing chambers of the mansion and up the stairs to Justine's suite. Jenny pulled her mother's slightly disgusting sticky robe off and tossed it into the laundry hamper. She guided Justine toward the shower and turned on the water. Slid the door shut and waited. After a moment, she heard a sigh ease from her mother as the hot water washed over her, providing its generous, natural relief.

While Justine showered, Jenny went into the bedroom

and changed Justine's stale and wrinkled sheets. She gathered up miscellaneous items of clothing for the laundry hamper and stuffed even more bags and boxes of junk food into wastebaskets. The surfaces of the end tables, dressers, desk, and bookcase were thick with dust.

"Miss Havisham, I presume," Jenny muttered.

Justine had a closet full of silk robes and kimonos to swish around in back in the days when she watched Rory eat breakfast as she drank her juice and green tea. Jenny chose a kimono in what she knew was her mother's favorite shade of lavender. She wanted Justine to feel well groomed and serene. She handed the kimono into the now-steamy bathroom, waited a few moments, entered the bathroom, and found Justine combing out her long, dark hair.

It shocked her that so many gray roots showed on her mother's head. Jenny hadn't realized her mother colored her hair. Hadn't realized her mother was getting older.

She dropped a pair of feathered mules by her mother's feet.

"Let's go downstairs for some coffee," Jenny suggested.

For an hour, Jenny treated her mother with the attention and kindness due a grieving widow. She made a pile of cheesy scrambled eggs and toast and set the plate in front of her mother. She phoned the agency and asked that a substitute housekeeper be sent over. She arranged for a hair appointment, facial, massage, manicure, and pedicure for Justine. She punched in the numbers of several of Justine's good friends and set up lunch dates. She watched color appear in her mother's cheeks and the glaze disappear from her eyes.

When she'd done what she thought she could for Justine and sensed her mother had achieved some kind of self-control, Jenny said, in a smooth, sweet tone, "Mom, I need to tell you why I'm here."

Justine smiled. "Oh, Jennykins, you know you're always welcome."

"I know, and I'm glad. But I have a specific reason for coming here today." Her pulse throbbed uncomfortably in her throat. This was harder than she'd expected. "Mom, I want you to tell me who my biological father is."

"That doesn't matter—" Justine began, moving her hand as if brushing away a fly.

"But, you see, it does matter. Rory will always be the man who cared for me and raised me, but another man's genes are in my body, and I need to know who he was." When Justine's lips shut tight, Jenny's temper flared. "Were you promiscuous? Were you sleeping with so many men you can't narrow it down, or you didn't know their names?"

Justine's eyes blazed. "Jenny, what is wrong with you? How can you be asking me these hideously insulting questions!"

"I'm asking you because when I was a little girl, you told me you didn't know where my father was, and I had to be satisfied with that. But I'm older now, Mom."

Justine shifted on her chair, folding and refolding the fabric of her kimono about her. "Of course I knew your father's name."

"Tell me."

"Why?"

"Because I need to know his health record. Does he have a family history of diabetes, cancer, mental illness . . . ?"

With a start, Justine's face changed. She went white. "Jenny. Are you ill?"

"I'm fine, Mom. Not ill. Perfectly healthy. But I've been talking with Meg and Arden, and they encouraged me to find out who my biological father is."

With a sniff, Justine flipped the brilliant silk sails of her kimono over her legs. "Those girls always make trouble."

"Please. Don't start. Don't try to sidetrack me. I don't want a grand sentimental reunion with my birth father. It's a reasonable request. I need to know about his medical history." She crossed her fingers behind her back. There was so much more she hoped to learn. Merely to see his face would be a dream come true.

"He's perfectly healthy."

"He is? How do you know?"

"Well, I don't know *now*. But he was, back when you were . . . conceived."

"Mommy, I'm not trying to embarrass you or make you sad. I just want you to tell me his name, and anything else you remember about him. I'll search for him. I'll do the investigation. It might be that I can do this all online. I won't even have to meet the man. But I can e-mail him about his family medical stuff. Don't you see?" When her mother didn't answer, she played her ace. "I mean, what about when I have children? Some traits skip a generation."

Justine's head whipped up. "Are you pregnant?"

"Are you kidding? I haven't had sex in months."

With a momentary flash of her normal charm, Justine said, "A simple yes or no would have sufficed."

Jenny exhaled a sigh of relief and leaned back in her chair. She sipped her coffee and waited.

With a decisive little shake of her head, Justine faced Jenny straight on. "All right." Her face softened, and a gentleness brightened her features as she allowed herself to remember. "I was in love with him, Jenny. I want you to know that."

Jenny only nodded, not wanting to stop her mother's words.

"He was in med school. I was just nineteen. I was in college at Tufts. I was a virgin. Saving myself." Tears sparkled in her eyes, but now she was smiling at the same time, and she let her head fall back in a kind of luxurious swoon as she surrendered to her memories. "William Chivers. Willy. We met in a coffee shop in Harvard Square. He was my first real sweetheart, and I was his. Oh, I'm sure I was not his first sexual encounter, but I was his first real love. He was tall, dark, and handsome, all of that. Only"—she laughed, and her long hair swung from side to side—"he always smelled like antiseptic. Well, med school, you know."

Jenny was breathless at this image of her father, her real father, a medical student named Willy. Gooseflesh broke out all up and down her arms and legs. She could almost *see* him.

"He was enchanted by the technology of medicine," Justine continued. "I'm sure that's where you got your affinity for computers. He wasn't brilliant, though; I mean he had to work hard to keep up with his studies. We both knew that when he became a resident, the work would be relentless and we wouldn't see each other as much." She hugged herself, and now the words flowed as she gave herself over to memory. "Six months. We were together six months. Jenny, we loved each other so much. We were so romantic with each other. We said such exaggerated things, like 'Our passion will last till the end of time,' you know the sort of things young lovers say, but I meant it and I know he did, too." A shadow crossed over Justine's face. Her eyes closed. She murmured. "I was fortunate in my first and last beloveds."

Jenny waited. She had his name. She could start there. She wanted to hear more, though.

At last, with a little shiver, Justine said, "Well, I got pregnant. I was on the Pill. I don't know how it happened. He was interning at Mass General. His supervising doctor was ruthless, a perfectionist, a bully and a tyrant. Will and I saw each other less and less. He was so stressed-out. He was always *exhausted*. But Will had such enormous ambition. He wanted to become a transplant surgeon; his grandfather had died of liver disease."

Jenny's hand flew to her mouth. Justine was so caught up in her thoughts, she didn't realize what importance her words might have for Jenny.

"I was nineteen, Jenny, remember that. *Nineteen*." She nodded, and now the tears that came were tears of sorrow. "For three months I hardly saw him. When I did see him, he was nauseated with fatigue, which was kind of funny because I was nauseated for a completely different reason, although he didn't know it. He could hardly see straight. We didn't fight, but we . . . drifted apart. I broke off with him. I left school and went to live with my grandmother in western Massachusetts. I suppose he could have found me if he'd tried, but he would have had to make an effort to do it. In my heart I wanted him to try to find me."

Jenny reached over to touch her mother's hand. "You must have been terrified."

Justine nodded. "My grandmother helped. She absolutely thought you hung the moon. The early years were sweet, really. But when Gran died, I had to find a way to make a living. You were old enough to go to school. I returned to Boston to work. I did try to find out where Will was—and I finally located him. By then, he had married someone else." She pressed her hand over her eyes. "I'm sorry you didn't have a father when you were a little girl."

Aiming for lightness, Jenny said, "Oh, I think I turned out all right."

Gratefully, Justine smiled. "And Rory was a wonderful father to you."

"Yes. Yes, he was." Jenny waited a few seconds. "Do you know where Will Chivers is now?"

Justine averted her face. "Google," she mumbled.

Jenny laughed. "I know. It's irresistible. I've looked up all my old boyfriends." Quickly she added, jokingly, "Not that I *ever* slept with any of them!"

Justine was still in her own world. "Will's in Boston. He's at Mass General. He's married, he has two children. He lives in Back Bay. I've walked past his place, a row house on Beacon Hill. Very posh."

"You've never seen him again in all these years?"

Justine shook her head. "No. Kind of odd, really. Boston isn't such a big place. But I'm glad I've never run into him. I went on with my life. I had you. And I wouldn't have missed being with Rory for anything in the world."

"Mom, I'm going to go see him."

Justine had stopped weeping, but she looked very tired. "I suppose I can understand that. Fine. Someday. Perhaps in the fall, when—"

"No. I mean I'm going to go see him today."

Shocked, Justine choked out a harsh laugh. "Goodness. Couldn't you write him a letter first?"

"I have to get back to the island. I have work to do. Plus, the whole legal matter of staying on the island for the summer."

Justine drew her fingers over her forehead. "Jenny, this is a lot to throw at me, especially right now."

"I know, Mom. But you're okay, really, aren't you? I mean, you're grieving, but you're okay?"

Justine's face reflected her struggle to be honest. "I feel better with clean hair and some real food. I don't want you to worry about me or think I've gone off the deep end. I'm just sad."

"I'm sad, too, Mom. I miss Dad every day. But I'm going to try to see Will Chivers."

Emotions flickered over Justine's face. "When are you going back to the island?"

"I'll stay here tonight. We could go out to dinner. Maybe even a movie. There's a new comedy with Steve Carell. You like him, don't you? Wouldn't that be fun?"

"I guess." Justine sagged in her chair. "God. Will Chivers." She closed her eyes. "I think I'd like to take a nap now."

"I'm going to try to see Will Chivers," Jenny repeated.

Rising from the table, Justine waved a listless hand. "Fine. You can tell me about it later. I don't think I can take anything more just now." She left the room.

Jenny took her time cleaning the kitchen. She washed the skillet and dishes by hand, letting her thoughts settle. Then she sat down at her mother's computer on the small kitchen desk and searched for liver transplant physicians in Boston.

And there he was.

William Chivers, MD, Massachusetts General Hospital, chief of transplantation.

He was thirty minutes away.

Her biological father.

A small photo on the hospital website showed a slender balding man with glasses and a kind face.

There was a phone number, but she didn't want to phone him. That didn't seem right. Nor did e-mail. She didn't want to wait, either. Now that she'd come so close, she didn't want to wait another second. She looked at her watch. It was a little after two o'clock.

She hurried out to her rented car and drove.

Again, she played music to cover the panicky absence of thoughts, or perhaps it was a collision of thoughts, like white being all colors. Urgency pressed on her skin, pinched her lungs, abraded her lips against each other as she drove along the crowded roads, carefully not speeding, but still deftly steering around slow-moving vehicles, sputtering trucks, and old people clutching the steering wheel with both hands.

The Longwood Medical Area along Brookline Avenue was a complicated stretch of brick buildings, parking garages, fast-food restaurants, medical supply stores, pharmacies, and doctors' offices. She parked on the fourth floor of an echoing garage, took an elevator to the street, and crossed over to the entrance to the hospital.

Inside, at the information desk, they told her the location of Dr. Chivers's office: wing L, second floor.

Jenny marched through the long corridor, head high, aiming for a resolute and slightly officious walk, as if she were supposed to be here. No one stopped her. No one even looked her way. Probably he wouldn't even be in his office, she thought. It was summer, after all. Probably he wouldn't be back from vacation for weeks. Maybe months.

Still, her heart tripped and fluttered. Her breathing went wonky, uneven. She could feel her toes, fingertips, and lips going numb. Well, if she had a heart attack, at least she was in a hospital! A nervous giggle rose in her throat.

There was the door. Transplantation Offices.

She ran her fingers through her hair. What was she wearing? God, how did she look? *All right, all right, calm down,* she told herself. She was wearing a simple blue linen dress, no jewelry, and sandals with a low heel. She looked *fine.*

He wouldn't be there anyway.

She opened the door.

She stepped inside a room filled with chairs and coffee tables littered with magazines. Almost every chair was occupied. Her heart sank. Of course patients were waiting to see him. Well, she'd waited thirty-one years. She could wait a few more hours.

The reception counter was in the middle of the room. It was high and forbidding. Behind it, several women tapped on computers and barked the names of medications at each other.

"May I help you?" one of the women said.

Jenny was trembling. "I'm here to see Dr. Chivers."

"What time is your appointment?"

"I don't have an appointment. This is personal. I'm a relative." She waited to be stonewalled, refused as a fraud.

"Down the hall, turn left, past the water fountain." The woman went back to her computer.

Jenny went back to the hall, turned left, and walked. So he wasn't on vacation. So he was here. Her mother had been right. She should go home, slow down, write Dr. William Chivers a letter, and do this thing with some kind of ceremony and dignity instead of flapping in like a startled chicken lost in a maze.

William Chivers, MD.

His name was on the door.

She pushed the door open.

This room was small and quiet. Behind a desk a secretary sat wearing headphones, tapping at a computer. She was an older woman wearing a pink flowered dress and a pink cashmere cardigan. She looked up at Jenny and smiled with lips painted the perfectly matching shade of pink.

"Hello. May I help you?"

"Hello. I'm wondering . . . I'd like to see Dr. Chivers." Jenny wound her fingers together tightly. She cleared her throat. "It's personal." Quickly she added, "It's not about a medical thing."

The woman in pink tilted her head sideways, blinked, then picked up the phone. "Dr. Chivers? A young lady is here to see you. It's a personal matter." After a moment, she said, "Thank you, Doctor." To Jenny, she said, "Please take a seat. He'll be available in a moment."

Jenny's legs were stiff as she made her way to a chair, and her body folded like a series of snapping sticks. She had barely sat down when the woman in pink said, "You may go in now."

Jenny couldn't breathe. She was trembling. Fear rushed through her. What if he denied being her father? What if he said he didn't even know her mother? What if he was enraged and ordered her out of his office? Dr. William Chivers had no reason to want to know her. Why should he, after all these years, be presented with someone who could only be a problem to him? What if he thought she were coming after him for money? What if—

She walked to the door. It was pulled open from the inside, and a man stood in the doorway, looking tired, kind, and curious. His white hair formed a circle around the exposed pink top of his scalp. His forehead was scored with lines of wrinkles. His eyes were brown, he was tall, he was slender, his Adam's apple protruded sharply. He wore a tan summer suit, a white shirt, a blue tie.

Jenny's lungs were frozen. Her vocal cords were paralyzed. She opened her mouth to speak, but she was terrified that she was going to cry, or fall apart in hysterical laughter. She forced a smile as she looked up at the man.

Dr. William Chivers's eyes widened as he looked at Jenny. His mouth dropped in surprise. He looked stunned.

He said, "*Justine.*"

NINETEEN

Steam practically boiled out of Meg's apartment on the third floor of the graceful old Victorian when she pulled open the door. Hurriedly, she flicked on the dials of the two small air-conditioning units that made it bearable in the small space, but the old machines were clunky and inefficient. It would be at least an hour before the place was tolerable. She'd forgotten what it felt like here in the summer, inland Massachusetts, far away from sea breezes.

She tossed her bag on her bed, kicked off her sandals, and faced herself in the mirror. Was she going to do it?

When she called Liam last night, she told him she was driving up to Sudbury. That she wanted to see him. He said he'd pick her up at six and take her out to dinner.

She wasn't sure she could wait.

She wasn't sure she could keep herself from running away.

To cool herself off, she took a long shower and shampooed her hair. She put on a Coldplay CD to listen to while she slathered on moisturizing lotion. Wearing only her undies, she slowly unpacked, finally lifting out her secret purchase, a white sundress dotted with strawberries. On the hanger, it appeared all innocence. On her body, it was dynamite.

When she tried it on in Vis-A-Vis, the saleswoman kept asking, "Are you okay? Can I bring you something else?" Meg had been mesmerized by her reflection in the mirror. The dress curved in and out, accentuating her waist. It dipped low in front, exposing more of her breasts than she'd ever dared—but then, she'd never dared. How grateful she was to her sisters, both of them so stylish and of the moment. Spending this summer around them taught her that she was stuck in the past, so entrenched in the 1800s she hadn't even noticed herself ripe and ready in the present.

"I'll take it," she'd told the saleswoman. "And perhaps a little shrug?"

The saleswoman brought her a white shrug. "What about adding this?" she suggested. Stepping behind Meg, she'd clipped on a gold chain with dangling multicolored stones.

Meg had laughed out loud. "Or we could just draw an arrow to my breasts," she said.

"Believe me," the saleswoman had said, "in that dress you don't need an arrow."

Meg clasped on the necklace now. She stepped into her high-heeled sandals.

She smirked at herself in the mirror. She could do this.

But when Liam knocked at six o'clock precisely, Meg's limbs went into lockdown. She could scarcely make it to the door.

She opened it. Liam wore cream flannels, a yellow linen long-sleeved shirt, and a blue tie. He looked so classy—suddenly, with her loose hair and low-cut dress, she felt like a tart.

Liam gawked. "Good Lord."

"Would you like to come in?" Meg asked invitingly. "I've got some cold Prosecco. We could have a drink before we go out."

Liam stepped inside and shut the door behind him, but didn't sit down. "I don't understand, Meg."

"Excuse me?"

"I think you need to clarify your intent."

Meg's heart drummed triple-time as she felt his intense scrutiny. Oh, he was so handsome, so unreasonably handsome. His thick blond hair, his aristocratic profile, and the way he carried himself—he was like a prince. Or a king. King Arthur.

No, she thought, not King Arthur, because Guinevere betrayed him for Lancelot, and Meg would never betray Liam.

"Liam—" Meg reached out to touch his arm, but he stepped back.

"Meg, the last time we were together, we made love, and I thought we were—" He went still, blushing deeply. "I thought it meant something. Then you told me that it was a mistake, that I'm too young for you. Now you show up looking like *this*?"

Meg flinched. "I was wrong, Liam. I mean, I was telling the truth, but I was acting out of fear. Please, sit down. Can we talk about it?"

Liam sat at the end of the sofa. Meg poured the wine into chilled glasses and handed one to him. Liam watched her, waiting in silence.

"Arden and Jenny made me do this," Meg began. With an awkward laugh, she added, "All this, the new clothes and hairstyle, and calling you." She peered at him from under her lashes. "Do I look okay?"

"I don't care what you wear," Liam said brusquely. "You're a knockout no matter what."

"Oh." His words gave her the courage to go on. "But, Liam, it's true, you *are* younger than I am, and that frightens me."

He nodded. "I can understand that. I suppose the most difficult thing about being precocious—because I have to admit, I was precocious intellectually—is that people assume I'm emotionally challenged. Still, I don't think our dean would have given me tenure if she thought I wasn't capable of handling any job she threw my way."

"True," Meg agreed.

"Eleanor's a shrewd judge of character, don't you think?"

"She is."

"When she hired me, she definitely reckoned I'm trustworthy."

Meg understood what he was tacitly telling her, that

he was a man who could be faithful. "I know what you mean, Liam. Still . . ." She faltered in the face of his steady, patient presence.

"I suppose the only thing that would allow me to prove my adulthood even more definitively would be to get married and have a family."

Meg stopped breathing.

"My parents got married when they were twenty-four," Liam continued in his mellow, quiet way. "They've been married for twenty-seven years. I came along when they were only twenty-five, and my sister a year later. Somehow they muddled through."

"Yes, but they were wealthy," Meg reminded him.

"I've got some assets of my own," Liam confided. "It's because my grandparents left me some money that I can act on my ideals."

"You should go into politics."

"Don't make fun of me, Meg."

"I wasn't," she protested.

His voice was low and solemn, his expression resolute. "I'm not a child. I'm not a playboy. I'm not a pretty boy who wants his face on TV. I don't want to sleep around. Believe me, I've slept around. I started early and accepted every opportunity, and there were plenty."

Meg's face went hot. She looked away, stunned by the fierce volcano of jealousy erupting inside her. No denying it: She was in love with this damn man.

"I can't change the way I look or the way my brain works. But I can use them. I can use them for what *I* want. You know what I want. You know what I want for work, and you know what I want for my life."

Meg nodded. "I know you care about teaching. About community colleges . . ."

"Right. You and I are philosophically attuned on this matter. I like challenges. I like diversity. I like mixing it up. I like teaching classes at night and on weekends, when people who work can attend. I like writing poetry and reading about nineteenth-century poets, and using the Internet to teach basic language skills."

"Renaissance man," Meg teased.

He didn't return her smile. "I certainly hope so." He was serious suddenly, as intent on her face as if studying his own future in a crystal ball. "I hope I can do great work and at the same time share a great passion." He hesitated, then added, "And if that sounds sappy, I don't care."

"Not sappy," Meg said, almost whispering.

"So can we agree that I'm not emotionally young?"

Meg nodded.

"Does that mean you're willing to take a chance on me? A serious chance?"

She looked into his eyes. The intensity between them was like the pull of music. "Yes," she said.

He smiled. "Of course you realize I'm taking a chance on *you*," he continued, relaxing back against the sofa, aware that he had her now. "Some people would tell me I shouldn't be with a woman so terribly old, and especially one so, um, what's the word I'm looking for?"

Meg waited for him to say *fat*.

"*Ravishing*," Liam finished. "That's it. People might say I can't trust a woman who looks like you to be faithful to me. You'll be going to academic conferences where all sorts of intellectually dashing men will hit on you. Especially if you go around looking like that."

Meg couldn't resist preening just slightly. "So you like the dress."

Liam stood up. "I'd better take you out to dinner before I show you exactly how much I like that dress."

TWENTY

Arden waved good-bye to Meg and Jenny, watched them walk off toward the ferry with their backpacks and duffel bags, then shut the door. She had a lunch date with a summer resident, a prospect for her show, so she dressed carefully and prepared her proposal, then walked down to town for the meeting.

It was after three when she returned to the house. When she opened the door and stepped inside, the house was sleeping, silent as a cat in the afternoon sun.

They were gone.

She didn't remember ever having been alone in this house before. She threw herself onto the living room sofa, kicked off her sandals, rested her feet on a pillow, and scanned her memories. She'd been in the house long ago with Meg and Jenny, babysitting them when her father and Justine went out. Perhaps when Meg and Jenny went off to town to buy magazines or ice cream, she'd been alone in her room, but Justine had always been there.

It was so quiet. The windows were open, but the wind was flat today, useless for sailing, not even enough to cause the curtains to flutter. The heat drugged the birds into silence. Her eyes closed.

She woke around four, with sweat pooled between her breasts. The front of the house got the afternoon sun, and the room was stifling. Yawning, she padded barefoot down the hall to the kitchen. As she ran herself a nice, cool drink of water, she stared at the backyard, shadowed by the surrounding trees. She looked at her watch: 4:05. She didn't have to cook dinner for the three of them tonight, and no one would be cooking for her. She wouldn't be watching a DVD with them or yakking or playing poker like they did when it rained. She could eat a pint of ice cream in her underwear if she wanted.

An irresistible urge surfaced right beneath her heart, the sort of inquisitive temptation that drove her professional curiosity to check out other people's houses.

She could look into their rooms.

First, she called Meg on her cell phone.

"Hi, Arden," Meg answered. "Is everything okay?"

"Of course. Just wanted to be sure you got there all right."

"That's sweet. Yes, we're here, and I'm kind of busy now. Can I call you back?"

"No, don't bother. I'll see you tomorrow."

Arden clicked off her phone and climbed to the second floor.

It was hotter here. Arden paused, deciding which

room she wanted to enter first. She knew much more about Meg, and besides, she thought Meg was just less interesting, really, with all her old-fashioned bookish stuff.

Jenny had left her door open. Arden paused in the doorway. It would be just like complicated, technological Jenny to create some kind of invisible trap that would provide evidence that Arden had entered her room while she was gone, then she could have proof that Arden was, if not a thief, at least a snoop, and Justine's accusation would be justified.

But Arden couldn't resist. She squinted, checking for a thread, a hair, strung across the doorway. She'd seen that on TV. Nothing.

She stepped inside. No sirens went off, no flashing alarm. Jenny was such an odd duck. She'd had this entire house to herself for years, but she kept her workstation with all the computers, printers, scanners, whatever, on one side of the bedroom, leaving little space for the antique spool bed and dresser.

The bed was neatly made with a light quilt pulled taut. A clock and a book called *Chaos* by James Gleick were on the night table.

Arden turned to the end of the room occupied by desks, tables, computers, and other electronic devices. Jenny had tied a color-coded plastic tab around each cord corresponding to the color-coded list of machines they connected. Of course she had.

Arden sat in Jenny's chair. She considered turning on the computer and trying to access Jenny's e-mail. No, Arden couldn't risk leaving any electronic fingerprints.

Her eyes scoured the room.

She went to the one dresser, an old walnut Empire thing Arden remembered from her childhood. She pulled open the drawers. Extreme neatness.

First drawer: socks. Winter socks on one side, little white sneaker socks on the other.

Next: underwear arrayed as if in a magazine ad, bras lying cupped together in shades mostly of black, white, and beige. Camisoles.

Next: tee shirts, pressed, folded, and layered in wrinkle-free hues of black, white, gray, brown, and blue.

Finally: sweaters. One thick Irish cream cardigan. A couple of cashmere pullovers. A couple of cotton cardigans and a few crewnecks.

Wow. Here was a woman with a rich sensual life.

Finally, the closet.

Jenny's pants were clipped to pants hangers, her shirts hung next to them, dresses farther down the closet rack. On the floor, her shoes stood side by side in neat rows. At the back of the closet, a box. Arden squatted, reached in, removed the lid. Love letters hidden inside? No—old headbands, barrettes, and other hair accessories from the days Jenny wore her hair long.

Irrationally miffed, Arden dragged the desk chair over to stand on while she checked out the shelf at the top of the closet. Purses, evening bags, neatly folded pashmina shawls—well, at last, thank heavens, a sign of some bit of luxury!—a couple of saucy hats, flannel pajamas.

What a disappointment. Jenny was a beauty. She had to keep some sentimental old notes and photos of former boyfriends somewhere. Perhaps she had a trunk in the attic.

With a sigh, Arden left Jenny's room and headed to the back of the house to the small room she'd once used, the room Meg had now. Her excitement had dissipated. The long summer evening spread before her in all its steamy languor. And here she was, alone.

Listlessly, she pawed through Meg's dresser, finding nothing unusual. Meg's new sundresses hung from the rack in a rainbow of fabric. She smiled, happy to think of Meg appearing before Liam in her new guise.

Still bored, Arden went back down the hall, wondering what to do now. At the top of the stairs, she stopped.

The door to the master bedroom was shut, just as if someone were in there. It was a little bit creepy, really. On impulse, Arden opened the door.

She stepped inside. She'd seldom been in this room. Her father didn't own the house when he was married to her mother, Nora, his first wife. It was only three years later, when he'd left Nora to marry Cyndi, that his real estate business soared and he was able to afford the Nantucket house. Arden hadn't come in this room during the summers she visited her father, Cyndi, and Meg. She'd been a child, and the room was off-limits.

Only one summer had she been in the room, when her father was married to Justine. She'd peeked inside, of course. It had been fragrant with Justine's perfume, the armchairs draped with her discarded lingerie, all lacy and, to an adolescent's impressionable mind, tantalizingly sexy. Mysteries shimmered in the air, and the enchantments of the woman who had stolen her father's loyalty.

Arden walked around the room now, touching the posters of the canopy bed, the back of the armchair, the bureau. It all still gleamed with secrets, sensuality, choices made long ago and forgotten.

Justine's red velvet jewelry box stood on the dressing table. Arden slid onto the bench and lifted the lid. Inside—nothing. Of course not. Justine must have taken all her jewelry with her to her Boston home after Rory's death.

Because it wasn't Justine's house any longer. It belonged to Arden, Meg, and Jenny.

Arden rose and slid open the doors of the closet. Extending deep into the walls, it was crammed with clothing: Justine's colorful summer wardrobe and Rory's equally vibrant attire. At one end of the closet, a shoe organizer held sparkling sandals and well-worn deck shoes along with knee-high rubber waders.

At the other end of the closet was a row of shelves where Justine kept extra sheets, towels, and blankets. Arden ran her hand over the linens, feeling only the smooth softness, enjoying a sense of illicit possession, wondering who would keep these sheets if Justine didn't take them. Certainly Arden and Meg wouldn't want the sheets their father had slept on with Justine.

Turning, Arden caught her heel on something. She clutched at the inner wall to keep herself from falling.

Looking down, she saw she'd nearly tripped on a loose board. Squatting, she started to wedge the board back into place.

Then she stopped.

She lifted the board. Beneath the closet floor lay a black velvet jewelry pouch.

Arden's heart thudded so fast and hard she thought she might faint.

She lifted out the pouch and dumped the contents into her hand. Even in the darkness she could spot the glimmer and gleam of real gold and a large diamond-circled emerald.

Justine's necklace. Oh. My. God.

She left the closet, sat on the bed, and inspected it in the light. Yes, this was it, the necklace, the necklace Justine had accused Arden and Meg of stealing, the reason she'd exiled them from the house and island.

Jaw clenched, Arden returned the jewelry to the pouch and stomped down to her own room and her cell phone.

Jenny couldn't take her eyes off Dr. William Chivers. He appeared to be as stunned as she was. People had told her she looked like her mother, but never before with such immediacy.

She forced her numb lips to move. "I'm Jenny. Justine's daughter."

A flush of warmth moved over the physician's face, and a smile broke out like the sun from behind clouds. "Of course you are. Please come in." He shut the door behind her, gestured her to a sofa in a small consultation area, and punched the phone on his desk.

"Barbara. No calls."

He seated himself in an armchair across from Jenny,

taking care to pinch the crease of his trousers as he sat. He waited, an amiable expression on his face.

Jenny's mouth was so dry she couldn't speak. She was trembling.

Williams Chivers noticed. Patiently, as if she were someone from another country, he said, "My goodness. You look just like her. How is she?"

"She's fine. Well, not so great just now. Her husband died." Jenny's words were slow to arrive and felt shapeless in her mouth.

"I'm sorry to hear that." His eyes were gentle, his face full of compassion.

"You're my father," Jenny blurted. Now the words rushed out. "This is weird, I know, and I apologize, but I'm thirty-one now, and my—friends—have convinced me I need to know about my biological father because so many characteristics are passed along through the genes. Mother—Justine—never told me until today who my biological father was. For years she was married to a wonderful man, Rory Randall; he adopted me, he was my real father, I thought of him as my real father, but of course, I don't have his genes. I don't mean to upset you or embarrass you or cause you any problems at all, and I won't tell your wife or kids or anyone, but I really think I need to have some idea of your medical history."

She sat back in her chair, exhausted.

His hands had been clasped together, but now he put one hand over his heart, as if to still it. He seemed to sink into a private reverie. "Give me a moment."

Jenny waited.

Dr. Chivers spoke slowly, remembering. "The last

time I saw her, we fought. I don't recall the reason. Something inconsequential. We fought, we parted in anger. I was busy, I didn't phone her for a few days. . . . When I did call, she wasn't there. She'd just vanished, without a word. I tried to find out where she'd gone. I didn't have much free time, I was at Mass General then, but I did everything I could and came up with nothing. I thought . . . I thought she'd stopped loving me." Suddenly he bent forward, resting his elbows on his knees, burying his face in his hands.

Jenny sat silently, respecting his mood.

After a moment, he lifted his head. "Could you tell me your birth date?"

"March 18, 1982."

He nodded. His eyes searched her face. "It's as if she cloned you. I don't see much of me in your features at all, which is lucky for you."

She smiled and lifted her dark hair off her ears. "What about these?"

The tops of her ears were slightly tipped, peaked like an elf's. Like William Chivers's. Justine's were perfectly rounded.

"Oh dear." He chuckled. "Poor you."

"You're being so kind."

"My dear child," William Chivers said, "why wouldn't I be kind?"

At his words, emotions unclenched in Jenny's heart like a flower opening to the sun, unfurling petals she'd never even known existed, delicate silken shades of hope, regret, and a profound, stirring, powerful need.

This man was her father.

This man was her father, and he accepted her.

"I'm sorry," she whispered, for tears were streaming down her face and her shoulders were shaking. "I didn't know—I wasn't sure whether you'd be glad to see me or if you'd turn me away or tell me I was wrong—"

William Chivers rose and crossed his office to a table with a pitcher of water and glasses on a tray. He poured the water and brought it to Jenny.

"Take your time," he advised her. "No hurry. Of course you are upset." He sat back down in his chair and waited, hands folded in his lap.

A box of tissues sat on the coffee table between them. He held them out to her. Jenny took a few, blew her nose, wiped her cheeks. She took a sip of water and made an effort to still her shaky breathing.

Lifting her eyes, she studied his face. She saw her own emotions reflected in his eyes and in the sudden blotchy patches on his skin.

"Are you married?" she asked.

"I was. My wife died two years ago."

"I'm sorry."

"Thank you. We have two children. My son, Roger, is in medical school at Harvard. My daughter, Penny, is studying to be a veterinarian."

Her arms broke out in goose bumps. She had a brother and a sister! A half brother and sister, but still!

"Do you have siblings?" he asked.

She paused, then said softly, "Two sisters."

"I'm so glad. I wouldn't want you to be an only child. I was an only child, and it's lonely."

She wanted to tell him everything. She wanted him to

know that she *had* been lonely, for ten years, until Rory brought Meg and Arden into her life, and then she'd only really had them for two years, until Justine sent them away.

He was speaking now. "Where do you live?"

"On Nantucket. I'm here visiting my mother. She lives in Belmont. She's widowed, too."

William Chivers took a deep breath. "I didn't realize she lived in the Boston area." He studied the floor for a moment, seemingly fascinated by the pattern in the carpet. "I have some phone calls to make, and paperwork to finish," he told her. "But I wonder, do you think you could have dinner with me tonight?"

Her throat was choked with tears. She could only nod.

TWENTY-ONE

When the doorbell rang, Arden swore under her breath. She'd been pacing the house, cell phone in one hand, jewelry pouch in the other, and completely forgotten that she'd invited Palmer White to dinner.

She stuck the pouch in the drawer of the hall table, smoothed her hair, and opened the door.

Palmer stood there with a bottle of wine in his hands. He was casually but expensively dressed in chinos and a red rugby shirt that gave a glow to his cheeks and made his dark eyes glitter.

Seeing her face, Palmer said, "You forgot?"

Arden shook her head. "Of course not. Come in. Sorry, I'm kind of rattled. I—it's complicated—never mind."

"Want help hiding the body?"

"No, no." She smiled. "But I'm afraid I didn't manage to get dinner started yet. It's been that kind of day."

Palmer held up the bottle of wine. "We could start with this while we recon a new plan."

"Brilliant idea." She led Palmer to the kitchen, found glasses, handed him the corkscrew. "Do you like Szechuan? We could order some in."

"Doubt it. I don't think there's a Szechuan place on the island."

"Well, we are not having pizza." Arden opened the refrigerator and peered in at the steaks she'd planned to marinate and grill. "I can cook," she said over her shoulder. "Well enough, anyway."

"I'm sure you can," Palmer said. Gently he pulled her away from the refrigerator, shut the door with one hand, and wrapped her against him with the other.

She felt his heart beating steadily against her, and his breath was warm on her face. With a sigh, she laid her head on his shoulder and sagged into his supporting arms. To her surprise and relief, she realized she was crying, not in great agonizing sobs, but in silent acceptance. Crying on Palmer White's shoulder seemed like receiving an unexpected mercy.

"Sorry," she apologized after a while. She walked over to take a tissue and blew her nose. "How do you like our dinner so far?"

"Best I've ever had." Palmer's voice was low and kind.

They sat inside, on the sofa, because it felt so good to kick off her sandals and curl up on the welcoming cushions. What could she tell him? she wondered. That she'd discovered the pouch of jewelry Justine had accused her of stealing?

That she'd found proof that Justine had purposely lied in order to exile her and Meg from the island? That it was an unbelievable relief it hadn't been Jenny who had taken the necklace to make her mother get rid of them? That as much as she had adored her charming father, she wished he were alive for just one minute—no, make that five—so she could shout at him, rail at him, tell him how much misery he'd caused in his lifetime, how much chaos!

Simplify this.

All of this was private knowledge that should be shared only with Meg and Jenny. Arden didn't know Palmer well enough. She didn't know if she could trust him not to spill out the Randall family gossip after too many glasses of wine beneath a hot summer sun to twenty or forty of his best friends.

"I played tennis today," Palmer told her.

She gawked at him as if he'd said he'd visited the moon. She was so absorbed in her own melodrama she'd forgotten other people had lives.

She focused on Palmer. "How'd you do?"

"I won. I usually do. I'm fast, and I'm powerful." He waggled his eyebrows. "Wanna feel my biceps?"

Arden glanced at his tanned muscular arm pushing up the fabric of his cotton sleeve. He did look strong. He did look healthy. He did look—uh-oh—attractive.

"Tell me about your family," she invited.

"My family?"

"Yes. Because my family is so bizarre. It would be nice to hear about someone whose life isn't wacko."

"You think my family's not wacko?" Palmer grinned. "I think that may be the nicest thing you've ever said to me."

Arden dropped her head in her hand. "Oh, damn, I have been slightly snotty, haven't I?"

"Not snotty. Let's say cautious."

"Women in our family tend not to trust men," she told him. Waving her hand, she pressed, "But I need a break from my family for a while. Tell me about yours."

Palmer leaned his head back, as if searching for the information on the ceiling.

"My father's a hedge fund manager. My mother's a social worker. I'm a media space manager. My sister Hadley's a nurse working in Africa." After a moment, he added, "My father is six feet tall. My mother is five feet six. I'm six feet tall. Hadley, who is two years younger, is six feet three."

"How was it for her, growing up?" Arden asked.

Palmer shook his head. "Not easy. She got her height early, and her boobs, too. She always knew she'd be tall. She was tall in kindergarten. With our mother recounting seriously upsetting scenes from her day at the dinner table—and I realize she was a little off base to do so, but maybe this will assure you that all families are wacko—Hadley started volunteering as a Big Sister early on, and at youth shelters and safe places. Right after school, she'd bike off, or later, when Dad gave her a beat-up old sedan, which was exactly what she wanted, she'd drive that.

After high school, she went to nursing school, and then she signed on with a volunteer relief agency."

"She sounds admirable."

"She is admirable, but she's no saint, and she's not boring, and she attracts her share of men. She's actually quite a bombshell now that she's an adult. She's engaged to a doctor, and in a couple of years they're going to settle down in Boston and start a family."

"Nice." Arden reached forward to pour herself more wine.

"Feel better now?" Palmer asked.

"I do. Thanks. Sometimes my family life overwhelms me."

"I've got a proposition for you that would take you far away from all that." Palmer's eyes were sparkling.

Arden leveled a skeptical look at him.

Palmer laughed. "Well, of course, I'm always up for that, you might say. But no, this is a business proposition."

"Oh yeah?" Now she was interested.

"I recently bought a TV station in Houston. I need someone to jazz it up. I need a morning show most of all, something to appeal to women."

"And you thought of me?" Arden was stunned.

"You're a smart woman. You can learn fast. Plus, you've got a real presence, you think on your feet, you've got sex appeal, you've got a great laugh. I want you on my team." He paused, then added slyly, "And I guarantee the pay is good."

Arden stared into space, her mind buzzing. *Houston*. One thing she knew from reading *W* and *Vogue* was that the parties were stupendous, the clothes and houses out of this world. They knew how to live in Houston; they weren't paralyzed by ancient Yankee rules of make it last/ wear it out. The women's jewelry was more than one set of grandmother's pearls; the men's wardrobe consisted of more than one old blue blazer. Lots of money in Houston . . .

"I have a contract with Channel Six."

"Since I own it, I'm sure we can work that out." Palmer stood up and held out his hand. "Let's go out to dinner. Someplace really posh so you can contemplate my suggestion in seductive luxury."

Arden hesitated. "Well . . ."

"Don't worry," Palmer said with a quirky smile. "You can pay."

She took his hand, knowing at that moment she was just perhaps maybe falling a little bit in love with him.

Weirdness, she was utterly weird, but she didn't want to drive the thirty minutes back to her mother's home in Belmont to change clothes. For one thing, it was close to rush hour and the traffic would be horrific, but more than that, Jenny did not want to share one fraction of this event with anyone, not even her mother—*especially* not her mother—not yet.

William Chivers was Jenny's father, her biological father, and he wanted to take her out to dinner, to get to know her, and she wanted to get to know him.

She wanted him all to herself. She wanted him to *look*

at her, his daughter. She wanted to hear everything about him, to see if he held his fork the way she held hers.

But they were meeting at the Harvard Club for dinner, and she felt wrinkled in her blue linen dress. She hurried over to Newbury Street, slipped into the first boutique she came to, and quickly found a svelte sleeveless black dress. She bought heels to wear with it, even though she had a pair of black shoes almost like them back on the island.

She passed the time until dinner walking around the public gardens, pretending to enjoy the flowers, the children playing games, the man throwing a Frisbee for his dog. But all she could think of was William Chivers.

They were seated at a table near the window, with a respectable amount of space between their table and others. Light music played, something classical. William Chivers wore the same tan suit, white shirt, blue tie. The maître d' knew him, as did the waiter. He requested his favorite white wine and made small talk while they checked out the menus and ordered their meals. Then they sat back in their chairs and studied each other.

"Please," Chivers said. "Tell me about yourself."

Shyly at first, Jenny spoke about the easy things: her work, her schooling, her life in the Nantucket house. She was hesitant to say her mother's name, or Rory's, as if that would break the frail cobweb bond between herself and this new real father.

"And men?" Chivers asked. "Or women?"

"I broke up with a man a few months ago. He was a

really nice guy, but perhaps a bit too beefcake." She blushed, remembering sex.

"Tell me about your sisters."

The waiter set their entrées in front of them, giving Jenny a moment to gather herself.

Delicately, she requested, "First, could I hear something about *your* life?"

"All right." He sipped some wine. "I'm old enough now to reflect on my past. So I can say with some pride that I've had a rewarding career as a transplant surgeon. I have saved lives. I've been less of a success as a father." His eyes were sad. "My relationship with my children was never close. Entirely, I'll be the first to admit it, my fault. It has improved since their mother died. By the way, before I forget . . ."

Putting down his fork, he reached into his breast pocket, took out an envelope, and handed it to Jenny.

She accepted it, confused and slightly alarmed.

"It's a sort of medical history of my side of the family," Chivers explained. "I made a copy for you to keep. You can study it at your leisure, but I can assure you there are no hideous genetic diseases in our family. Although"—he hesitated—"there might be a history of OCD. Obsessive-compulsive disorder." With a twitch of his shoulders, he added, "Also a bit of anxiety." His eyes twinkled. "I have often heard it reported that I prefer people under anesthesia."

Jenny chuckled. "You've always lived in the Boston area?"

"Yes. Back Bay. I can walk to Mass General." Sighing, he continued, "Peggy, my wife, had hoped that would mean I'd be able to spend more time at home, but it didn't work out that way. I found family life rather stressful, I'm afraid. Two children—well, with children, very little is under complete control."

Jenny had to duck her head so he would not see that this made her guiltily happy, that he hadn't been such a perfect father.

"I provided financially, and of course I attended school events and graduations. I took everyone on vacation for two weeks to Cancún or Hawaii. Unfortunately, I remained in the hotel room reading medical journals. In my field, there is never enough time to keep up with new techniques, new advances." He cut a piece of haddock and chewed it thoughtfully. "I sound as if I'm stating my claim to the entrance through the Pearly Gates before Saint Peter. Not, my dear, that you resemble Saint Peter in the slightest."

"Good to know," Jenny said.

"Let's get back to you. I'd like to hear about your childhood."

He wanted to know about Justine, Jenny understood, and now she was ready. "Mother got married when I was five, but I don't remember much about her first husband except that Peter didn't especially care for me. They got divorced after about a year, and I was glad. Mother got married again, when I was ten, to Rory Randall. He adopted me, so I took his last name. Jenny Randall." She savored the words. "He died this spring."

"You loved him," Chivers said.

"Very much." How to describe Rory, his energy, his magic? "He was a real estate broker, here in Boston, very successful, and he appreciated people, which must have been one of the reasons for his success. He possessed a singular, remarkable *charm*—it was such fun to be with him. He had terrific ideas, enjoyed playing games—life was a game for him in a way. He was handsome. All my girlfriends at school had the silliest crushes on him. He'd take us all out for ice cream in his convertible with the top down and would let a lot of us smash in together, not caring whether we wore seat belts, so even when we were twelve, we felt kind of like we were living dangerously."

"You were," Chivers said dryly, and Jenny caught the flash of disciplinarian in his expression.

"He didn't do that often," Jenny hurried to add. "He wasn't a careless man." She paused, wondering if her words were true. "Although . . . well, my mother was his third wife."

"So he was careless with women?"

"With his wives, yes. He was a bit of a . . . *philanderer* is perhaps too strong a word. But he left his three daughters the Nantucket house. If we three manage to live in it together for three months this summer, we can sell it and split the proceeds. It's generous of him. He was always financially generous."

"Tell me about your stepsisters."

Jenny took a big sip, almost a gulp, of wine. "Actually, they're okay."

"You seem to imply there's some discord among you."

Jenny paused thoughtfully at his formal words. "*Discord*. Well, at first there wasn't, then there was, and now we're working it out, or I hope we are. We've drifted apart since we were young. The reason is complicated, but I'm sad about it. I hated being an only child growing up, and this summer, getting to know Meg and Arden again, it's been a dream come true being around them. My *sisters*."

Chivers raised his eyebrows questioningly. "Do you want to stay living on Nantucket?"

"Absolutely. The island is my home. I've lived there for years now. My friends are there, my work."

"And the house? Will it be hard for you to leave it?"

"Gosh, yes." Jenny put her fork down and gave herself a small, comforting hug at the thought. "It is the most *wonderful* house." After a moment and a reassuring sip of wine, she continued, "But it's far too big for one person. And realistically, Arden and Meg should have their third of the proceeds from the sale. It's only fair."

"It's what your father did stipulate in his will, correct?"

Jenny leaned forward. "Could I tell you a secret I haven't told anyone else?" she whispered.

"Yes. I'm good at keeping secrets."

Jenny scanned the room, as if expecting Meg and Arden to pop up at another table. "When my father was dying, in the hospital, I got to spend some time with him, which I'm so grateful for. Anyway, I asked him to add that stipulation to his will. Actually, I typed the letter on my laptop and printed it off, and he signed it and discussed it with his lawyer."

"Really. How curious."

It felt so good to let the secret out. The words spilled from her like a waterfall; she felt light-headed and breathless. "I've always wanted to be closer with Meg and Arden. My mother didn't want me to have anything to do with them. I'm an adult now; I'm making my own money and doing just fine. I don't need money. I want my sisters. I thought this would be a brilliant way to force them to spend time with me—a sustained, concentrated time when we could get to know one another. And it's working really well. I don't mean we're all jolly friends forevermore, but we're muddling along. We *are* definitely getting to know one another. We're laughing, and talking about stuff, and I know after this summer we'll keep in touch, see each other, e-mail—be a *family*—and that means more to me than any money in the world."

Chivers shook his head in amazement. "What an unusual person you are."

"Meg and Arden can't know this. They'd get upset, tell me it's just another way I've manipulated matters to my own ends, even if it means this way they'll get one-third of the sale of the house."

"So no one else knows?"

"No one." Jenny smiled. "Perhaps when we're all old, sitting in our rocking chairs on some porch somewhere, I'll tell them. Then they'll peck away at me like a pair of old hens, but by then it will be too late."

"I doubt that either one of them will make much of a fuss about receiving so much money."

"Oh, they'll say Dad would have left them a third of the house anyway, and perhaps they'd be right. He didn't even have a will until he had the heart attack. He had his lawyer come in and draw one up while he was in the hospital bed. I don't know how he would have disposed of the house, but I don't think he would have stipulated that the three of us live there together for the summer." Remembering, Jenny's eyes filled. "He liked my idea. He saw immediately how perfect it was."

Chivers laid his knife and fork in exact parallels across his empty plate. "I wonder if my own son and daughter are capable of such generosity. Or such cleverness."

"I wish I could meet them," Jenny admitted hesitantly.

"You do? Yes, of course you do, it's a natural instinct. All right, then, you shall. We'll arrange it. Not until after August, I think. You've got enough drama going on for the summer, and I have some plans myself. Vacation, I mean, nothing as exciting as what you're up to. But I need time to contemplate all I've come to learn today."

Jenny froze. Perhaps he thought she was unstable, impulsive, even a bit daft, showing up as she had at his office, clear out of the blue without so much as an introductory phone call or note, and now knowing the crazy thing she'd done with the house. Perhaps he wouldn't want to be associated with her.

As if reading her thoughts, Chivers reached over and patted her hand. "Jenny, I am so glad you found me. I hope we will stay in touch for the rest of our lives. I believe I'm a more deliberate man than your stepfather, but I am a resolute man. You can trust me. Now that we are in each other's lives, we will remain that way."

She would not make any kind of a scene in this elegant restaurant, with her distinguished father sitting across from her, but she could not hold back the tears. She carefully removed her hand from the table so she could open her purse, find a tissue, and wipe her eyes.

"Thank you," she told him quietly. "I would like that more than I can say."

Meg awoke in a strange bed. It took her a moment to realize she was at Liam's. She'd been in his apartment before, but never in his bedroom. She closed her eyes again, allowing herself to savor the moment. The aroma of warm male next to her, and the sound of his breath. The appearance of his room, all navy blue and antique wood, elegant, as he was.

The memory of their night in bed together. The words they had murmured to each other. Words of love.

Liam shifted next to her in the bed. "Good morning." He bent to kiss her.

"Morning breath," she warned.

"Me, too," he told her, and then they didn't talk again for a long time.

She showered and dressed while he prepared a light breakfast of coffee, bagels, and cream cheese.

"I have to go back to Nantucket today," she told him.

"You're sure?"

"Because of our father's silly inheritance clause. It's not for much longer. Just till the end of August. Will you come down and visit me?"

"How many times can I come?" he asked. When she blushed at his double entendre, he said, "Would you like me to drive you back to your apartment?"

"That would be good. I have to pick up a few discs and folders I need for my book."

"How are you getting back to the island?"

"Jenny's going to pick me up around ten thirty, so we can make the one o'clock fast ferry."

"Okay, then, I guess I'd better let you go."

"No," Meg said. "Don't let me go." She blushed again. She wasn't used to flirting with him in this delicate, amorous way. She certainly wasn't used to sitting across the table from him in a low-cut sundress.

He drove her to the Victorian house and stopped in front. "Shall I see you in?"

"Thank you, no." It seemed they couldn't stop gazing at each other, smiling at each other. "I think I can find my way from here."

She put her hand on the car door.

"Meg." Reaching out, he took her arm and turned her toward him. "This isn't a frivolous thing we've got here, you know."

She nodded, close to tears.

"It's as serious as it gets," he continued. "At least it is for me."

"And for me."

Leaning forward, he kissed her. "I'll see you soon. And please, buy more of those dresses."

She laughed and nearly skipped from the car, up the walk, and into the house. Had she ever been this happy? She didn't think so. She fairly flew up the stairs to her room at the top, unlocked it, and went in. She needed to find—oh, where had she left that one folder on the Paris art exhibition? As she rummaged through the piles of paper on the ornate antique table she'd bought for a desk, she remembered she'd left the folder at the college.

Slinging her bag over her shoulder, she set off for the

college, only a few blocks away, where even her small cell of an office was centrally air-conditioned. She could check any snail mail that had piled up in her absence, find the folders, and be back home in time for Jenny to pick her up.

The main building housing the college's administrative offices was a dignified edifice of brick and stone built in the early nineteen hundreds by a flourishing national men's club that by 1970 no longer had any local members. The state bought it and refurbished it, constructing less attractive cement block wings for classrooms and instructors' offices. Later on, plantings had been added to soften the harshness of the annexes, and now in summer, trees and bushes cast a lush green shadow over the sidewalk as Meg took a shortcut to the door to the liberal arts section.

She had just stepped inside, onto the hideous gray-green linoleum, which must have been bought at discount, when she heard her name called.

"Meg! Just the person I want to see!"

Meg froze in place. It was Eleanor Littleton, PhD, head of the liberal arts department. A brilliant woman with a quick wit and a depth of knowledge, she had not been equally blessed with beauty. But she had great charm and genuine respect for the college and its students.

Meg turned. "Eleanor. Hello."

Eleanor came down the hall toward Meg, carrying, as usual, a stack of folders up against her bosom. She wore a plain tan sleeveless dress and sensible heels.

"I thought you were gone for the summer," Eleanor said. "And don't you look pretty."

"Thanks. I *was* gone. Well, I am. I just returned for a day or so."

"I'm glad. I want to talk with you about something. Come with me."

They strolled side by side down the long, empty hallway, chatting about easy topics—the weather, the Red Sox, new books—until they entered Eleanor's large and precisely organized office.

"Sit down, dear." Eleanor gestured toward a chair as she took her own behind her desk.

Dear, Meg thought. That was a good sign.

Stacks of folders, papers, and envelopes covered Eleanor's desk, but they were neatly arranged, edges tidily aligned, topped with colorful paperweights. Eleanor crossed her arms on her desk and said, "I'll get right to the point. Your freshman writing students perform better on national exams than the students from any other class in this college."

"Oh!" Meg smiled, pleased.

"I've been looking at the syllabus, reading assignments, and worksheets you've compiled for your students. I'm impressed."

"Thank y—"

Eleanor held up her hand. "Wait. I've talked this over with the dean of liberal arts, and we've come up with a plan. Writing is not the favorite subject of many of our students, but it is the most necessary. Many of our students are ESL, or come from high schools with abominably low standards, or have been out of school for a long time. But you know all that."

Meg nodded.

"Frank and I want you to turn your class material into a bound document that we can distribute to all our freshman writing instructors."

Meg's jaw dropped.

"We understand this will take some work on your part. We're prepared to compensate you in two ways. First, we're offering you tenure as a full professor. Second, we'll increase your salary."

Meg was speechless.

"We wouldn't expect you to have it completed until the beginning of the spring semester in February. We would expect you to continue to carry your teaching load as well as put the text together. You'll have the rest of the summer, and the month of January during midwinter break. Do you think you can do it?"

Meg bit her lower lip, thinking of her cherished May Alcott project. She was so far along; she couldn't abandon it now. But it was a stunning compliment to her that both Frank Ruffalo and Eleanor Littleton found her freshman writing preparations so good they wanted to turn them into a textbook used by the entire freshman writing faculty. And tenure? And a raise? Why was she even hesitating? She would find a way to do it all. The fall semester would have plenty of weekends and evenings when she could work.

"Eleanor, I'm so pleased." As the realization of it all set in—tenure!—she wanted to jump from her chair and perform a victory dance, but attempted to retain her dignity. "It's wonderful to know my students have done so well, comparatively. You know I'm committed to this college and to working with these students. I'd be so glad to have tenure, and of course to have a raise."

Eleanor clapped her hands on the desktop. "Well, great. Just what I was hoping you'd say. Now, what I propose is that you work on this directly through me. Some of our other instructors are going to feel slighted by this, or at least propose suggestions, additions, alterations. You could be overwhelmed with politics, egos, suck-ups, and so on. Don't deal with any of them. Tell everyone to come straight to me."

Meg's eyes went wide. "Oh. I hadn't even thought. . . . But do you want to deal with all that?"

Eleanor smiled her endearing crooked grin. "Absolutely. You're good at teaching, I'm good at administrating. Frank and I are thinking that once the handbook's completed, you might teach a couple of seminars to our instructors before each term begins. So we don't want them to hate you. It's fine if they hate me."

"Eleanor, you're amazing."

"Hah. Thanks. I'm experienced, that's what I am. I've been doing this a long time. Also, I go to conferences where we discuss research on negotiation and strategy. Most of all, I've learned not to take campus politics personally. If I want to get things done, I've got to be prepared to take the flack. For our less fortunate students, education can be an economic challenge, but it's nevertheless an absolute necessity. We need to make adult education as appealing as possible, which you do in your classes."

Eleanor stood up and extended a hand across the desk. "You realize the tenure bit has to be passed by a committee, *blah blah blah*, but consider it done. I'll start e-mailing you about the composition syllabus soon."

Meg shook her hand. By the time she'd turned to leave the office, Eleanor was tapping numbers into her phone.

Back at her own office, Meg just sat for a few minutes, giving herself time to absorb it all. Tenure. A raise. A book! She was a good teacher. She was a *really* good teacher!

She wanted to celebrate.

And she wanted to celebrate with Liam, who would know exactly how fabulous this all was.

TWENTY-TWO

Jenny and Meg agreed to remain on the mainland for one more day, and Meg told Jenny she'd make her own way to the island by bus and boat or plane. They arrived home to find that Arden had prepared a picnic dinner for the three of them. Once Jenny and Meg had unpacked and caught up with their e-mail, they slipped into shorts and tank tops, piled the Jeep with coolers, blankets, and baskets of food, and drove the long six miles to Madaket. This area of the island was the least known, because on Nantucket, six miles was considered far away, especially when you could bike or walk from town to several other beaches.

They got up to a speedy forty-five miles an hour on the straight part of the road, but closer to the western tip of the island, the road curved, and after they passed the creek leading to Long Pond, where several boys were crabbing, they slowed to maneuver the curves. Handsome shingled houses lined the two-lane road, creating a small village with even narrower roads leading off to Madaket Marine and the harbor on the calm, less surfy Nantucket Sound side. They parked near a tremendous sand dune that rose up like a shifting wall between the paved road and the long stretch of white-gold beach on the west side of the spit of land.

Lugging the coolers and beach blankets and baskets, they went barefoot up the dune and down, and along the sweeping western finger of the island. Their feet sank into the warm sand. In the distance, a group of people were gathered for their own picnic, but since few families with children ever came here, where the surf was rough and treacherous, much of the beach was empty and quiet.

They set up camp, helping one another flap out the big blanket, holding down each corner with a cooler or basket, and finally, flopping down onto the blanket to ponder the blue Atlantic. It was calm today, as if stunned by the summer heat, and the surf rolled in lazily, making gentle shushing sounds.

Meg got to her knees, opened her beach bag, and brought out a bottle of champagne. "Now," she began.

"What?" Jenny asked. "Champagne? Wait! I brought champagne, too." She opened her cooler and took out a bottle.

Arden laughed. "So did I. Plus," she added smugly, "*I* brought glasses."

"Did anyone bring any food?" Jenny asked.

"Of course." Meg opened her basket to display a platter of cheese, crackers, and fruits. "I've got sandwiches, too."

"But *champagne*," Arden said. "We each brought champagne? What's going on?"

Meg puffed out her chest. "Meet the new *tenured* head of freshman English at Sudbury College."

"Congratulations!" Jenny said.

"That's wonderful," Arden agreed. "I'm not sure how you went to see Liam and ended up with tenure, though."

"I saw Liam, too." Meg smirked. "How can I put this . . . ? My new style was a great success." Suddenly her cheeks were red. "I spent both nights with him. We talked so much about so many serious things. I think— I believe he loves me. I know I love him. And I don't think I'd have had the courage to take this risk and trust if you two hadn't helped me believe in myself. If you hadn't helped me sort of reinvent myself. So thank you." Fearing she'd sounded sappy, she hurriedly asked, "Arden, why have you brought champagne?"

Arden said, "First, a toast to you, Meg." She poured the bubbly.

The sisters toasted and sipped, toasted and sipped again. They sat back, Indian-style, legs crossed in front of them, like Girl Scouts by a campfire as they talked. Arden explained about Palmer's offer of a job in Houston.

"But Arden," Meg said with a pout. "Houston's so far away!"

"Airplanes," Arden reminded her. "Plus, I doubt I'll stay there forever. It might be a stepping-stone to someplace else."

"Moving all over the place?" Meg shook her head. "I couldn't live that way."

"Fortunately, I can," Arden countered. She turned to Jenny. "Now, you."

Jenny cleared her throat. Very seriously, she said, "I met my biological father." She waited a few beats, letting the suspense build. "William Chivers. Transplant surgeon. In Boston."

"Shut up!" Arden cried. "How lucky are you? He could have been some alcoholic old taxi driver who'd been hot when he was young but fell so far off the wagon he turned into a reprobate."

"I know." Jenny was smug. "It's almost miraculous, isn't it?"

"How did you find him?" Meg asked.

"I talked to my mother. I convinced her to tell me what she knew, and as it turns out, she knew a lot." Jenny spilled out the story, which now seemed sugared with romance, of her mother's love for a dedicated medical student, her accidental pregnancy, and her decision to disappear.

They poured more champagne, clicked glasses again, and set the food out on the blanket. They talked about freshman English, Houston, and William Chivers. They talked about marriage, careers, and future families—the one Meg wanted with Liam, the half brother and sister Jenny was going to meet. The sun, slowly rolling lower in the sky, gilded their limbs and haloed their faces.

When they opened the second bottle of champagne, Arden pulled a bottle of sparkling water from her bag. "I'm going to be the designated driver," she told the others. "I get dehydrated quickly, so it's water for me from now on."

"Good," Jenny said. "More champagne for us."

"Also," Arden said, "not to rain on this glorious parade of events, but I've got one more bit of news."

Jenny leaned back on her arms, letting her head fall so that her throat was exposed to the setting sun and her black hair swayed against her neck. "Can't imagine what it could be. Can't imagine I'd even care right now."

Meg was curious. "What's the news?"

"I found the necklace."

Jenny snapped upright. "Where?"

Meg gasped. "Justine's necklace?"

Arden sat very straight, legs crossed in front of her, hands on her knees, her face somber. She looked like a chief, or a ruler, or a judge.

Jenny squinted suspiciously. "I don't believe you."

"Believe me," Arden said.

"Where was it?" Meg asked.

Arden put her hands to her heart in a token of apology. "Jenny, I'm sorry, but I found the necklace beneath a loose board in Justine's closet."

"What were you doing in her closet?" Jenny demanded.

"Searching. While you two were gone, I searched your rooms."

"Why, you little sneak!" Jenny cried.

"Call me whatever you want, but I did find the necklace."

The sun was sinking lower now, and the ocean, gilded by its light, faded to dull gray.

"Where is it now?" Meg asked.

"In a safe-deposit box in the bank."

Jenny sighed. "We have to tell my mother."

Softly, Arden said, "Jenny, I'm sure your mother already knows where the necklace was."

Jenny flinched as if hit. "What are you implying?"

"I'm not *implying*, Jenny, I'm saying it straight-out. It's the only logical explanation. You've got to see that."

Jenny's lip quivered. "You're accusing my mother of *pretending* it was stolen? Why would she do that? She prized that necklace."

"I think she hated me and Meg more," Arden said quietly.

"That's not true," Jenny protested.

Meg joined in. "Jenny. It makes sense. She accused Arden and me of taking it so that she could get rid of us, and she did get rid of us."

Jenny was trembling now, her eyes tearing up. "I can't believe it."

"It's not as if your mother hasn't lied before," Arden pointed out. "She lied to you when she told you she didn't know who your biological father is. She lies about big things, Jenny, significant things; she's willing to fabricate whatever she needs in order to get her own way."

Trapped, Jenny said in a low, choked voice, "I hate you, Arden."

"Hey," Meg pleaded. "That's not fair."

Calmly, Arden accused Jenny: "Come on. You know in your heart this is true."

"No," Jenny disagreed. "I don't believe it."

"Then let's get your mother down here and ask her, point-blank."

Jenny lurched backward. "Are you kidding? She's just

lost her husband. If you could see how she is now, she's bereft, she's lost weight, she's *grieving*."

Gently, Meg reminded her, "We are, too. Rory was her husband, but he was our father."

Jenny shook her head fiercely. "No. I won't subject her to an inquisition." Standing up, she said, "I want to go home. Now. I don't want to be here anymore."

"Running away from the truth, Jenny?" Arden's voice was not unkind.

"Stop it, Arden. Give me time to think. This is all too complicated. You've ruined the evening. You've ruined *everything*."

Arden shrugged. "This isn't the first time I've been accused of that by a female in your family."

Jenny bit back a response and began piling food, glasses, bottles, corks, into the nearest basket. Meg and Arden did the same. They trudged back through the sand and up and down the high dune to the Jeep. A breeze brushed their skin as the sun sank below the horizon.

Frustrated, alienated, troubled by their own thoughts, they didn't speak on the ride home. Without a word, they carried the baskets, blanket, and empty bottles into the house and disposed of them in the appropriate places.

Jenny shook out the beach blanket and hung it over the railing of the back porch. Arden rinsed out the champagne bottles and put them in the glass-recycling bag. Meg put away the uneaten food and shook the baskets out over the sink.

Then there they were, in the kitchen, together.

Arden leaned against the counter, arms crossed over her chest. "I've decided that I want my mother and Meg's mother to be here, too, to hear what Justine has to say when she comes down. Justine owes us all an apology."

"I told you. I won't do it." Jenny's voice was shaking but strong.

Meg said, and her voice was trembling, too, "Jenny. I totally agree with Arden. Furthermore—"

"*Furthermore?*" Jenny interrupted. "Oh, please, could you be more academic?"

"Furthermore," Meg continued, unfazed, "if you don't do what Arden suggests, I'm going to pack and leave this house tomorrow. You won't get any of the money from the sale of the house."

Stunned, Jenny went silent. Then she laughed. "Yeah, well, that means *you* won't get any of it, either."

"Which should show you how important this is to me," Meg said.

Jenny stared. She opened her mouth to snap out a snotty retort. She paused. She wanted to tell these two bossy, opinionated smart-asses that *she* was the one who had convinced her father, their father, on his deathbed, to write the letter that stipulated they would each inherit a third of the house as long as they all stayed together one summer. She had wanted a relationship with these women so much, she had been willing to give up whatever chance she had of inheriting the entire thing.

In the far reaches of her confused thoughts, a golden banner of truth flew past as if pulled by an airplane. The banner read: *Your mother did lie to you about your birth father. All these years, she knew who he was, and she told you she didn't.*

Justine *could* have hidden the jewelry to get her own way. It was possible.

Jenny took a deep breath. "All three mothers down here in this house at the same time? It will be a screaming match."

Arden said, "So we'll scream."

Jenny slowly passed her eyes over Meg and Arden. Their faces were tight, their expressions argumentative, their postures tense. Anger radiated from them like a kind of force field.

So we'll scream.

She had had so little of this, Jenny thought, this fierce thrust and yank of family altercation, the daily squabbling, making up, hugging, laughing, bickering, fussing, stomping, snorting, and simple collapsing side by side on the sofa. She'd seen it happen in her friends' families. It had frightened her. But now she saw how it made people whole, how life was made of dark and light, yin and yang, quarrels and peace. This was how a person learned to forgive. It was how a person learned to care so deeply their heart was laid open as if with a knife. She'd been protected all her life by her mother. It was time she came out from under her mother's wing and became herself.

Jenny said—and now her voice was calm, not meek, but full of courage—"All right. I'll call my mother."

TWENTY-THREE

"Arden, darling."

"Yes, Mom, it's me, with the call you've been waiting for."

Nora chuckled wickedly. "Oh, you mean you're marrying Donald Trump?"

"Gross! Blech! No, Mom, I'm not marrying anyone. I'm calling to invite you down to the island, to the house."

"Do I hear a drum roll in my future?"

"Maybe. Jenny and Meg have agreed to give you the listing."

"Fantastic!"

"We're having Cyndi and Justine down then, too."

"Cyndi and Justine? Please tell me we're not going to sit around a campfire beating drums and singing about Rory."

"You're a cynic, you know that?"

Nora sighed. "Honestly, honey, the idea of being around Cyndi isn't so terrible. I've always gotten on with her, you know that. She babysat you for a while when you were a little girl, before she got overwhelmed with her own babies. But Justine. The last time I saw her—well, except for Rory's funeral and the reading of the will, when we only nodded—was when she sent you packing from the island. I didn't like her then and she didn't like me, and nothing's changed."

"Actually, something has changed, Mom. You'll be pleasantly surprised."

"By what?"

"If I told you, it wouldn't be a surprise."

"I hate surprises."

"Fine. We'll give the listing to an island realtor."

"Oh, you're good."

"Learned from the best."

"All right, darling. I'll come. Whenever you say."

"I've got some other exciting news of my own, too. It will knock your socks off, and I'm not telling you until you come down here."

"Does it concern Palmer White?"

"It does. But we're not getting married if that's what you're thinking."

"A mother can hope."

"Yes, marriage worked out so well for you."

Nora's voice softened. "Hey, sweetie, I did get *you* out of the deal." She continued, "Just tell me when you want me."

"August fourteenth. That's a Tuesday."

"What an odd day to choose."

"It has to be the middle of the week because Cyndi goes away on the weekends, little family trips."

"Oh, whatever works," Nora agreed.

Arden hung up the phone with a smile.

"Hi, Mom. How are you?"

"Oh, Meg, it's you. I'm fine, honey, just so busy. You know how summers are."

Meg took a deep breath. "I'm about to complicate your life even more."

"Oh?"

Meg could hear her mother rustling around. It sounded as if she was unpacking groceries. She could see her in her mind's eye, the cell phone held to her ear with one hand while with the other she lifted juice, bread, eggs out of the bag and put them away.

"I want you to come to the island. I want you to stay here with me. Just one day and one night. August fourteenth."

Cyndi laughed. "Yes, well, I want a fifty-carat diamond, but I'm not getting that, either."

"Some really wonderful things have happened to me, Mom. I want to tell you about them."

"I'm sure they can wait until you're back up in Boston."

"That's not the point. Mom, listen to me. Seriously. You *have* to come down." Meg had hoped she wouldn't have to play this card, or play it so soon in their conversation. She'd even been foolish enough to hope that her mother might pause and admit that it would be nice to spend just a little time with her daughter, to get away from all those men. But, of course, that had been wishful thinking. "Mom, if you don't come down, I won't get my share of the money from the house."

"That's ridiculous." Cyndi was indignant, and she dropped something—it sounded like a bag of chips.

Meg could sense her mother bending over to pick up whatever she'd dropped from the floor. "It may be ridiculous, but it's true. We're only asking for that one day and night."

"Why?"

"Why that day and night?"

"No, why do I have to come down?"

"First of all, Mom, I'm not inviting you to *hell*." Why couldn't her mother ever choose *her*? Meg wondered. Why was it always her husband and her sons?

Cyndi sighed audibly. "Meg. I don't have time for this conversation."

"Justine and Nora will be here."

"So what? I don't care if I ever see them again in my life."

"The point is, we're having an important conversation. Lots of things have happened. We need a kind of council of war, or brainstorming session. Look, you can fly over, spend the evening and the night, and fly back the next morning."

Cyndi slammed a cupboard door shut. "All right, I'll come. But you've got to know it's going to create havoc with my schedule. I'm sure Tom will be upset."

"Oh, Mom, thank you! I'm so excited that you're coming down. We'll treat you like a queen. You'll have fabulous food and we'll have such a good time."

"I've put it on my calendar, Meg. Okay? I have to go now."

Meg hung up the phone. She felt as she always did after a conversation with her mother, both happy and sad.

"Hello, Jennykins. What's up?"

Jenny was sprawled on her bed with the bedroom door shut. "Lots of things, Mom, but to find out, you're going to have to come to the island."

"Oh, sweetie, you know I'm not ready to do that yet. All I can think about is Rory, and if I see the house, our room . . ."

"You can have my room, Mom. Listen, I wouldn't ask you, but it's important. It's *crucial*."

"Jenny. Are you ill?"

"No, no, it's nothing like that. It's—" *It's that I'm betraying you and inviting you into the lion's den*, Jenny thought. But what was her option? "Meg, Arden, and I are inviting all our mothers down here for one last big family night before we sell the house."

"Family night?"

"Well, we are all kind of related." Jenny had an inspiration. "For one thing, we want to let everyone choose something from the house to keep before it all goes to an auctioneer."

"Why should anyone else have anything from that house!" Justine demanded indignantly.

"Meg's mother, Cyndi, was married to Dad when he bought the house," Jenny reminded her mother. "She chose some of the paintings, and I think she actually made some of the curtains that are still hanging."

"God, they'll be a thousand years old and faded. She's welcome to them." But Justine was mollified. "Still, I don't understand why Nora should get anything. She never was in the house."

"No, but she was Rory's first wife. She might like a memento."

"I've never heard of a first wife wanting a memento of her ex-husband."

"Plus," Jenny continued, "we've all got a lot of things to talk about."

Justine went quiet. Then, warily, she asked, "What things?"

"Who gets to handle the sale of the house, for example. Nora wants to do it, of course. She's the logical choice since she's a real estate agent. Actually, you and Cyndi don't really have a vote in this—it's up to me, Meg, and Arden—but it's just one of the things we'd like your input on."

"Why can't I just agree over the phone? I don't care who handles the sale of the house. I'm so sad we have to sell it; I'll never be in it again, and I don't want to be, not without Rory."

"But *I'll* be here, Mom." Jenny paused. "Please. Just one night." After a moment, she coaxed, "It might be helpful for you to be back on the island. The sea air, the memories, even things in the house you've forgotten."

Justine sighed. "All right, Jenny. For you, I'll come."

———

Nora, not unexpectedly, was the first mother to arrive. She wore an ecru DKNY suit with a short skirt and no shirt so that her stunning cleavage, while not quite exposed, was definitely alluded to. Her hair was shorn crisply short and colored in a variety of shades of blonde that went well with her gold and diamond jewelry. No dummy, she chose high heels with wedge cork soles, which wouldn't get stuck in the brick sidewalks but still gave her slender figure more height.

Arden was at the small airport to meet Nora's plane, and she watched admiringly as Nora sauntered toward the terminal. She saw others, of all ages, watching Nora admiringly, too.

"Mom." Arden hugged her mother and leaned in to kiss her cheek.

Nora tilted her head away so Arden wouldn't ruin her perfect makeup. "Darling." She pointed to the window where the luggage was being unloaded. "That's my case. The pink leather."

Arden hefted the case from the carousel and rolled it along as she ushered her mother out to the waiting car.

"Could you turn up the air-conditioning?" Nora asked the moment she sat in the passenger seat.

"It's not that hot here, compared to Boston," Arden pointed out as she flicked the blower on.

"I don't like heat," Nora reminded her daughter. "I'm not crazy about beaches, either. Just lying there, getting skin cancer and sand in every crack? No thank you."

"I can see why you've never sold a house on Nantucket before," Arden said wryly.

"I've been here, of course, for parties, and weddings,

and I've done some shopping. Good little boutiques, I've got to say. I've found some nice things." Nora scanned the scenery as Arden drove. "More houses since I was here last. Some good professional landscaping, too. The town must be spending some money."

"You're the first mother to arrive," Arden told Nora. "So you get to choose the bedroom you want. Meg, Jenny, and I are going to take the den and the living room sofas, and I assume Justine will want to sleep in the bedroom where she slept with Rory, so you can have my room or Jenny's."

"I saw there's a house on the market on Polpis Harbor going for fifty-six million dollars," Nora remarked. "That should help the sale of the Lily Street house. Do you have the town tax assessment?"

"I don't, but maybe Justine does."

"I've got a couple of buyers interested," Nora said. "Both have families and like the idea of being in town. I hear the Dreamland Theater is completed. That will be a big draw to families, having a decent movie theater that can show first-run summer films. Oh, wait, I've got an important text." Nora fastened her attention on her iPhone.

Arden pulled into the driveway of the Lily Street house, behind Jenny's Jeep.

Nora had been here before—back when she and Justine got into a shouting match—but now, as she slid out of the Volvo, Nora took her time scrutinizing the house.

"Trim's in good repair," she said. "The shrubbery needs a decent smartening up. Let's see, nothing expensive, you can just plant a few fall flowers, but *not* mums."

"Let's go in the house and get you settled, Mom," Arden suggested. "You'll want to choose your room."

Not surprisingly, Nora chose Jenny's room, because it was the biggest room at the front of the house. Justine would sleep in her own bed in the master bedroom. When Cyndi came, she could take Meg's room and Meg could have the den.

"Jenny and Meg are out in the backyard," Arden told her mother. "Come out and sit with us."

"In the heat?"

"It's four o'clock. The house is shaded by the trees. It's pleasant. I'll make you a drink."

"When do the others get here?"

"Any minute."

"I think I'd rather give myself a good look through the house while I can," Nora decided. She took out her iPhone and snapped a picture of the windows in Jenny's bedroom. "Jenny will have to get rid of all this ugly computer furniture before we show the house."

"You can make a list for us," Arden began.

Nora crossed the hall and clicked pictures of Justine's room. "Oh dear, Justine's a bit chintzy, isn't she? This is like a little girl's room."

"Not everyone prefers chrome and leather," Arden informed her mother. "I think it's a delightful room."

"You can change the bedspread." Nora made a note in her iPhone. "Something not floral, and a dark color. Maybe navy blue."

Nora stalked down the hall to the mermaid bedroom. "Now, this is charming. This is a selling point."

"Before the others get here, Mom," Arden interjected, "I thought I'd tell you my news."

"Oh, right." Nora slid past Arden and went down the hall to check out the large bathroom. "Hmm. Old-fashioned, but the tiles are ceramic, so it seems historic. That will work."

"Palmer White has offered me a job in Houston."

Nora snapped to attention. "*Houston?*"

"He's bought a new TV station. He wants me to do a morning show."

"Oh my goodness!" Nora hugged Arden tightly. "Darling, I'm so proud of you! This is fabulous! Houston is a dynamite city. The oil money, the banking money, the whole livestock thing. You'll have so much fun!"

"I'm kind of nervous about it," Arden confessed. "It's so far away."

"*Nothing* is far away these days," Nora told her. "Get on a plane, do some work or read a book, and suddenly you're somewhere else." She turned her back on Arden. "God, I wish *I* lived in Houston. The real estate is killer. Wait till you see the houses. They know how to do it stately and sumptuous in Texas." She opened a door at the end of the hall. "Oh. This little cell must be Meg's room. Maybe we can bill it as a walk-in closet."

Jenny met her mother at the Hy-Line fast ferry. Justine had made this trip many times before and still had several trips left in her ticket book. Justine wore white capris, white sandals with glittering stones, and a magenta halter top that showed off her sleek figure. Her long black hair was pulled up into a cooling high ponytail. She looked more like Jenny's sister than her mother.

Jenny and her mother embraced, and Justine gave her daughter an extra hug, because it was an emotional moment for her, being on the island without Rory.

"Are you okay, Mom?" Jenny asked.

"I'll be fine."

"How was the crossing?" Jenny asked as they strolled over to the luggage rack.

"Smooth as silk. They serve a decent white wine on the boat, surprisingly. Your father used to like it, too, although he usually had a beer."

"Here, Mom. I'll pull it." Jenny reached over for the handle of Justine's rolling suitcase and they walked together down the parking lot, took the shortcut near The Tavern, bumped over the Belgian blocks, and came out on Easy Street.

"Has anyone else arrived yet?" Justine asked.

"Nora has. Arden drove out to pick her up about thirty minutes ago. I'm sure Nora's looking the house over so she can take the listing."

"Nora." Justine's mouth tightened. "It breaks my heart that we have to let it go," Justine said. "So many wonderful memories. I had dreamed of being a grandmother here, taking your toddlers down to the beach to play in the sand." They turned up Broad Street, strolling past the Brotherhood, Bookworks, and the Jared Coffin House. "And yet," Justine continued, "it might be better to sell it, since Rory's gone."

"I don't have a choice," Jenny reminded her mother. "It was what Dad wanted."

Rounding the corner onto Centre Street, they headed toward the Congregational Church, with its famous high pointed steeple.

"Do you have any idea where you'll live after the house is sold?" Justine asked.

"I'm keeping my eye out for a little house I might be able to afford."

"Really? On Nantucket? Everything is so overpriced. Are you sure you want to stay here?"

"To be honest, no, I'm not sure. I think I want to stay, but now that I've met . . . William Chivers—"

Justine stopped dead on the sidewalk. She put her hand to her chest. "Did you like him?"

"I liked him a lot. I want to meet his other children. His wife died two years ago." Jenny watched her mother more closely when she spoke.

"I'm sorry for that. I wouldn't want him to be lonely."

The two women, mother and daughter, stood in front of the long walk of steps leading up the hill to the high white church. The street was dappled with shade and fragrant with honeysuckle and roses. Jenny suddenly realized that she was taller than her mother, perhaps only an inch, but it surprised her.

"You look good, Mom," Jenny said. "Much better than when I saw you in Belmont."

"I looked like hell warmed over then," Justine said. "Felt like it, too." Reaching out, she stroked her daughter's cheek. "You're such a splendid young woman."

Jenny smiled. "Thanks, Mom." A knife of knowledge stabbed her heart: She was delivering her mother to the jury, judge, and executioner.

Although the hard truth might well be that her mother had betrayed her, and Meg and Arden, first.

Pulling the suitcase, Jenny walked on toward Lily Street.

By five o'clock, Nora had left the house to saunter up and down the street, checking out the neighborhood, making notes of what was new and what was worth mentioning. Justine had the door to her room shut and was resting on her bed.

The three girls—for today they thought of themselves that way—were gathered in the kitchen, preparing platters of finger food. They'd agreed the six of them might never get past drinks and munchies and to an actual dinner table.

Meg was making deviled eggs from her mother's recipe. Arden unwrapped expensive cheeses and fanned wheat crackers around them, with a small pot of pickles and one of olives on the board. Jenny sliced the crusts off bread and put together cucumber sandwiches, chutney and cheese sandwiches, and salmon sandwiches. They filled the ice bucket and carried it to the living room. They set out a variety of wines and liquors and the appropriate glasses. They splayed napkins out on the coffee table. They had discussed having drinks outside in the cool of the backyard but decided the conversation might not be anything they'd want the neighbors to overhear.

"So we're just waiting on Cyndi?" Arden asked, although she knew the answer. She was talking for the sake of talking, to fill the room with a sound other than their rather nervous breath.

"She'll be here any moment," Meg said defensively. Her mother hadn't been able to state exactly when her plane would arrive and had insisted she'd take a taxi. Meg was just a little afraid that Cyndi would be a no-show.

But as they carried the platters into the living room, someone knocked on the door.

Meg ran to answer it. "Mom!" she cried. "You're here! Come in."

"The three of them are here now," Arden whispered. "I need a drink."

"I need one more," Jenny murmured.

Meg ushered her mother into the living room. Cyndi collapsed wearily on the first chair she saw. She wore the air of an exhausted martyr, someone who'd just finished scrubbing the convent floors instead of a happy woman who'd just arrived at a resort island.

"Hi, Cyndi." Arden shyly approached her stepmother and kissed her forehead.

"Hello, Arden."

"Hello, Cyndi," Jenny said.

"Hello." A bitter note rimmed Cyndi's voice as she replied to Jenny.

Of all three mothers, Cyndi was the one who had aged the most. She'd gained weight, and appeared to have chosen an inexpensive dress to emphasize the point. Her sandals were cheap and worn. She'd allowed the yellowish gray to stain her once auburn hair, and she wore no makeup. Looking at her, it was impossible to believe that

Rory Randall had left Nora for this woman or that Meg, with her glorious mane of strawberry-blonde hair and voluptuous beauty, had sprung from this woman's DNA.

"How was your trip?" Meg asked.

"Exhausting. The plane bounced all over. I nearly threw up."

"But, Mom, today is so calm. Even the sound is like a mirror."

Cyndi shrugged. "I was in the sky, and I can assure you it wasn't calm up there."

"Can I get you a drink?" Arden asked. "Or perhaps you'd like to go to your room to freshen up?"

"My room." For a moment, Cyndi lurched out of her apathy and moved her eyes over the living room furniture, taking in the crisp blue-and-white décor Justine had so carefully chosen. Her thoughts flittered clearly across her face: Once she had owned this house; once she had lived in it during the summer with her husband, Rory, and their daughter, Meg.

Before that marriage-wrecker Justine ruined everything.

"Where is *my* room?" Cyndi inquired.

Meg hurried to tell her mother, "Let me take you up. It's the sweetest room, at the back of the house, near the biggest bathroom. You can wash up, rest from your trip, and unpack."

"I brought only a nightgown. I'm leaving tomorrow morning."

"Oh, okay. Well, anyway, let me show you where you'll stay. I'm giving you my room upstairs—" Meg turned to leave.

"It's not worth it, making you leave your room for the night," Cyndi protested. "I'll just sleep on one of the sofas in here."

Meg froze. Why was her mother acting like such a martyr? Certainly Cyndi wouldn't want to sleep on a living room sofa tonight, not after the discussion with all the mothers that was planned.

"Mom, I've already put clean sheets on the bed."

"All right, then, if you insist." Cyndi rose and followed Meg as if being led to the guillotine.

"Well, she's turned into a cranky old shrew," Arden whispered to Jenny when Meg and Cyndi were out of hearing.

"She'll cheer up tonight," Jenny replied with quiet dread. "When we gang up on my mother."

TWENTY-FOUR

It hadn't been so long ago that the six women had been in the same room together, but the circumstances had been quite different. Last May, they'd met at the lawyer's office to discuss the memorial service and hear the reading of the will.

They had all known Rory had already had a heart attack, but none of them had imagined that his great heart could actually give out so soon. Stunned by his death, the group of women had been formal, respectful, and grieving. Justine had hidden her swollen eyes behind sunglasses and had barely been able to walk. The three daughters were also stricken with sorrow, snatched unaware from the routines of their daily lives by the death of their father. Nora and Cyndi, while not inconsolable, had been considerate, even reverential, in the face of death. They had come separately with their daughters to the reading of the will. They had left separately, without speaking to Justine or Jenny. They had not kissed or touched or hugged.

A memorial service was planned for Rory in October, when the frenzy of the summer was over and the people who lived on the island would have the time and the psychic space to attend to the loss of this beloved man. Tonight, once other matters were dispensed with, the daughters were hoping they might also be able to discuss this.

But now it was time to take care of the other matters.

Arden, Meg, and Jenny had strategized the meeting with the care of an international summit conference. They'd moved the furniture into arrangements that would prevent the mothers from having to sit next to or too close to one another. They'd put end tables beside each chair with napkins waiting, and also, discreetly next to the low bowl of flowers in the middle of the coffee table, a dainty box of tissues, in case anyone was to burst into tears. Surely someone would. Their platters of finger food covered the rest of the coffee table, and a table behind one of the sofas held the ice bucket, glasses, and drink mixers.

They'd also worked out a plan of action.

At six o'clock, they carried everything into the living room. Shortly after that, they heard steps on the stairs, and Justine appeared.

"Oh, thank God. Drinks." Justine walked to the table and prepared herself a vodka tonic with the authority of the woman who had been the owner of this house for years. She still wore her white capris, her magenta halter top, and her jeweled sandals, but she'd redone her makeup and brushed her long black hair out of its ponytail. She was magnificent.

Jenny dithered around, making drinks for herself, Meg, and Arden, wondering aloud if she should have prepared some sangria, asking Meg if they'd remembered to refill the ice trays.

"I'm sure I did," Meg told her. "I'm going up to get Mom."

A few minutes later, Meg and Cyndi entered the room. Cyndi had combed her gray hair, smoothed her wrinkled skirt, and applied lipstick, which only made the rest of her face look paler. She stopped when she saw Justine, her chin jerking up defensively, as if blocking a blow.

"Hello, Cyndi," Justine said smoothly, carrying her drink to a chair.

"Hello, Justine." Cyndi looked everywhere but at Justine, seeming confused about what to do next.

"Sit here, Mom." Meg settled Cyndi on the end of the sofa farthest from Justine.

"What can I fix you to drink?" Jenny asked Cyndi. "We've got everything."

"Oh, water will be fine," Cyndi said.

"Come on, Mom, have some wine. We've got Prosecco, which is sparkling, and cool and light on the alcohol."

Cyndi allowed herself to be convinced. "Fine."

Jenny was handing the flute to Cyndi when Nora stalked down the stairs and into the room. She'd changed into a turquoise tunic thick with embroidery and matching turquoise sandals. Even her earrings were turquoise, dangling and bright.

"Hello, everyone," Nora cooed. "Oh good, drinkies." As silkily as a lioness, she lounged down onto the end of the other sofa, stretching out her long, sleek legs. "Fix me a g and t, will you, Arden?" No sooner was the ice clattering into the glass than Nora was beaming her easy smile around the room. "Good grief, check us out! What a bunch of luscious babes. One thing we've got to admit, Rory Randall had great taste in women."

Justine's mouth quirked up nervously.

"Although you, Cyndi," Nora continued brashly, "could use a serious makeover."

Cyndi bristled. "I have sons. I'm busy all the time, doing laundry, attending soccer games. It's not like I have time to sit around filing my nails."

"Obviously," Nora stated flatly. Flashing her attention on her own daughter, she demanded, "Okay, so when do the fireworks begin?"

Arden sat down next to her mother. Meg poured herself a glass of wine and sat on the sofa near Cyndi. Jenny took her own wine to a chair near Justine. And there they were, the six of them together.

"I'll go first," Meg announced. "I have just been offered tenure at Sudbury College. I'm getting a raise. Plus, my freshman English syllabus will be the standard, and I've been put in charge of the freshman English program."

Cyndi smiled. "That's wonderful, Meg. I'm sure that will help you get a position in a real college."

Meg's pale cheeks blushed crimson. "Sudbury *Com-*

munity College *is* a real college, Mother. To my way of
thinking, it's more important to our country's future
than many of the four-year colleges. Our students learn
the skills that will help them get jobs and be valuable
members of our society."

Cyndi's smile soured. "You sound like a pamphlet."

Arden's head jerked up. "Hey. Give Meg a break.
More than that, give her a damn compliment, Cyndi.
She's just had an enormous responsibility placed on her
shoulders and a huge tribute paid to her skill as a teacher."

"And there you are," Justine said smugly. "The real
Arden Randall. Ready for a fight."

"What?" Arden stared, mouth open.

"Justine," Meg began, "Arden wasn't trying to start a
fight. She was championing me, something I wish you—"

"This is perfect." Jenny stood up suddenly, startling
everyone. "I was going to wait to get into this, but it seems
we're all in the mood for confrontation, so I'm going
to dive right in. Mom"—she faced Justine, her hands
clenched at her sides—"we've found the necklace."

Justine went white. "You did?"

"*I* did," Arden said.

"You would," Justine muttered darkly.

"What are you accusing my daughter of now?" Nora
demanded.

Jenny didn't allow herself to be sidetracked. "You hid
it yourself, Mom, in the back of your own closet. It's
time you admitted it and apologized to us all."

"I don't know what you're talking about," Justine
sniffed. "Of course I didn't hide my own necklace. Why
would I do that?"

"So you could get rid of us," Arden said. "Me and Meg."

"Mom." Jenny knelt before her mother and took her hand. "Please. *Please* just admit it, won't you? We want to get past this."

Justine averted her eyes. The other mothers sat frozen, as if afraid to break a spell.

Everyone waited. One beat. Two.

"Fine," Justine said. "I hid it. I was sick and tired of dealing with Arden, and you all have to agree that that year she was a miserable, nasty, disobedient little hellion."

"I can attest to that," Nora said dryly. "Still, manipulating events to oust her from the house seems a pretty severe reaction."

"Making us all believe Arden was a thief was a pretty severe reaction," Cyndi cut in. "I was afraid to let Arden come to our house to hang out with Meg because of what she did. I was afraid she'd steal something of mine."

"But why did you make me leave, too?" Meg asked Justine. "*I* didn't do anything."

Justine lifted her eyes and scanned the room. What she saw in the faces of the other women was not anger so much as curiosity. After all, it had been so long ago. These girls, these daughters, were close to the age Justine was when she'd had to deal with Arden and Meg. These girls were now women.

Justine sagged just a bit. She ran her fingers over her forehead, and then she tried to explain. "Listen. I was Rory's *third* wife. Both you girls were his real, biological daughters. Jenny needed a father. I wanted Rory to think of her as his daughter, his *real* daughter. You both were, well, *in the way.* I was insecure, I was jealous, I was young."

"You were a grown woman," Nora reminded her, but her voice held no malice.

"Oh, when is *anyone* grown-up?" Justine asked. "I thought I was an adult when I gave birth to Jenny. Legally, I was an adult when I turned twenty-one. But I had a brief marriage in my twenties to a guy who hardly noticed my sweet little girl, and we divorced after a year. That destroyed my self-confidence. Perhaps it made me feel not so grown-up. Certainly not so smart. You were always so capable, Nora, swanning around like you owned the world, and you, Cyndi, why, you had Tom and your two sons. Neither one of you needed Rory the way *I* needed him, the way Jenny needed him for a father."

"Self-preservation," Nora said, nodding her head. "I can see that."

"No," Meg objected. "*Selfishness.* You wanted Rory all for yourself and Jenny. You took him, and this house, and our Nantucket summers away from Arden and me. Maybe Arden deserved it for being a pill that year, but *I* never deserved it. Do you think *Tom* was a father to me? Hardly."

"He was your stepfather," Justine reminded her. "He was *there.*"

"Not for me, he wasn't," Meg shot back.

Cyndi hung her head and pleated her skirt with her fingers, shrinking into herself.

Justine glared at Jenny, who had returned to her seat on the sofa. "So this is why you wanted us all down

here?" she asked her daughter. "To humiliate me in front
of everyone? To hurt me, when I've just lost the love of
my life."

"He was the love of our lives, too," Arden pointed
out quietly.

"He was your father!" Justine tossed her black mane
of hair, and her dark eyes blazed. "He was only your *father*, not the angel of your heart. It's not my fault if Rory
preferred Jenny to the two of you. Jenny was lucky she
had his affection at all. Our passion was all consuming. *I*
was Rory's one real, true soul mate."

In the midst of the tense silence, a loud knock sounded
on the front door.

"Now what?" Nora demanded. "What other delights
have you girls arranged?"

Arden snapped, "I have no idea who it is."

"I'll see." Jenny rose, went into the front hall.

They heard a female voice.

When Jenny returned to the living room, her face was
white. "She says her name is Marcia Kirkpatrick."

Justine frowned. "Marcia—? Oh, you mean his office
manager here on the island."

A woman appeared behind Jenny. She was perhaps
forty-five or fifty, slender, with tumbling blonde hair.
Without invitation, she stepped around Jenny and right
into the room.

"You're the blonde!" Arden said in surprise.

Meg nodded. "Right. We've seen you everywhere."

With a toss of her head, Marcia announced, "Yes, I
am the blonde. And I was more than Rory's office manager."

Justine drew back. "What do you mean?"

"For heaven's sake, what do you think I mean?" Marcia Kirkpatrick retorted.

"Oh my," Nora murmured smugly.

The other women, mothers and daughters, gaped in shock at the self-assured knockout in her neat blue dress and pearls. Her heels were low. Her makeup was pristine, so well applied it seemed nonexistent. She had a bit of the same polish and confidence Nora had. But she was younger than Nora, Cyndi, and Justine, and that got their backs up.

Arden broke the silence. "Uh-uh. Dad didn't like blondes."

"He liked *me*." Marcia's hands and voice were trembling but she held her head high. "In fact he *loved* me. That's why I'm here."

Justine gathered her wits and rose. Trying to gain control, she said, very lady-of-the-manor, "Marcia, we've met before, at a real estate party one year. I'm Justine, Rory's wife."

"I know who you are. I know who you all are." Staring at each woman as she spoke, the blonde woman pronounced their names: "Jenny. Cyndi. Meg. Arden. Nora. Rory talked about you so much."

"I'm sure he did," Justine agreed coolly, "because you both worked together for years. It would be odd if he hadn't spoken about his daughters."

"We did more than talk," Marcia insisted.

"That's ridiculous." Justine turned her back on the woman and returned to her seat. "Please. We're having a family conference. This isn't a good time for you to . . . to do whatever it is you think you're doing."

"Family conference? I suspected as much. I've been monitoring your activities—"

"You've been stalking us!" Jenny cried.

Marcia smirked. "So, this is the perfect time for me to be here." Reaching into her purse, she lifted out a pack of letters tied with ribbons. "I can pass these around. These are love letters Rory wrote *me*. As you can read, he promised me a house."

Justine froze in place. Only the pain in her eyes expressed her emotion—the ache deep in her gut said Marcia Kirkpatrick was telling the truth. Her chin trembled.

Seeing her mother's agony, Jenny stalked around to face the woman. "Stop it. You're lying. My father would never be untrue to my mother."

"Because, really," Nora interjected with a smirk, "Rory never cheated on his wives."

Jenny's head whipped around toward Nora. "He didn't cheat on my mother."

"Of course not," Arden said bitterly. "Not Rory Randall."

Meg rose and put her arm around Jenny's shoulders. Aiming her scarcely concealed disgust at Marcia, she asked, "Why have you come here? Whether you're lying or telling the truth, it seems needlessly unkind."

Marcia's mouth thinned. "As I said, I'm here because Rory promised me a house, and I want it."

"I see." Meg nodded. She scanned the faces of the other women. This had to be dealt with. "I think you'd better sit down."

"Thank you, Meg." Marcia gracefully sank into a chair, smoothing the skirt of her blue dress over her knees.

Impatiently, Arden cut in, "*When* were you our father's mistress?"

"For the past three or four years," Marcia answered. "Until he died."

Justine sank onto the sofa, hiding her face in her hands.

"That's just ridiculous," Meg blurted. "Dad was *sixty.*"

"Believe me," Marcia cooed coolly, "Rory was as virile as a thirty-year-old. He didn't even have to take Viagra. He could—"

"That's enough." Meg spoke with authority. "Let's stick to the matter at hand. You say that our father, Rory Randall, left you a house?"

Marcia shifted uncomfortably in her chair. "Yes. In a way." Before anyone else could speak, she hurriedly continued, "Rory and I were in love. Deeply, truly in love. We were business partners as well. Rory couldn't have run his agency down here without me. I did everything for him. He told me everything about his life." She glared at Jenny. "You, little miss, had a terrible time when your wisdom teeth were taken out. You had a dry socket and were in pain for a week, and he had to leave the island to help your mother take care of you."

Jenny put her hand to her mouth, as if protecting it from sight.

"And you, Meg, might be quite the smarty-pants but you couldn't have gotten your master's degree if Rory hadn't paid for your grad school."

Meg shook her head, baffled. "I was always grateful to Dad—"

"But you were the worst," Marcia said to Arden. "Running your TV show about simplifying houses, and did you ever once mention your father's real estate agency?"

Arden stared, stone-faced.

"You mentioned your *mother's* real estate agency. But not your father's, oh no, you wouldn't give him a break." Marcia's face flushed. "*I* was the only woman who cared for your father for himself."

Arden scoffed. "And that's why you're here trying to scam us for some money."

Marcia drew back as if slapped. "I'm not trying to *scam* anyone. I'm only asking for what I deserve. Rory promised he'd give me a house on Nantucket."

"Do you have any *proof* of this promise?" asked Meg.

"I have these letters." With a shaking hand, Marcia held up her packet. "Love letters. He says things to me—"

"Don't," Jenny cried. "I don't want to know the things he said to you."

"But if there is a promise in our father's handwriting that he will give you a house, I would like to see that," Meg clarified.

"Or any legal document," Arden added. "Hand it over."

Marcia looked down at her lap. She took a few deep breaths. When she spoke again, her tone was sweeter. "I was hoping it wouldn't have to come to this. I was hoping that Rory's daughters would honor his feelings for me. I didn't come here as an enemy. I came here as a friend. As—as, almost, a *relative.*"

Jenny muttered, "Ugh."

Marcia continued unfazed. "I've known about you girls for so long. You have no idea how many times I've advised Rory on the kind of birthday or Christmas presents he should give you."

"What you're trying to say," Arden interjected triumphantly, "is that you don't have any legal document."

Marcia drew herself up, shoulders straight, chin high. "Fine. I don't have a signed affidavit from your father stating that he will give me a house, but anyone who reads these letters will believe that was his intent." The slender blonde stood up. She laid a package on the coffee table. "These are copies of the letters. If I have to, I will sue, and it will cause a scandal. Think about it. Call me when you've reached your decision."

"Wait a minute," Meg said, holding out her hand. "Marcia, we don't have enough money to give you a house. If our father didn't leave you the money, then he simply went back on his promise."

"Sell this house," Marcia said coolly. "Then you'll have the money to give me." She looked around. "It's a historic old house on a prestigious street. I don't want it; I don't even want all the money you can get for it. I just want, let's say, half. You three could split the other half and we'll all be happy."

"You're not getting a penny!" Jenny's face was red, her hands clenched into fists. "Get out."

Marcia smiled. "It's too bad things didn't work out for you with Bjorn, Jenny. You made such a cute couple." She rose, chin high, shoulders back, haughty, bitter. "All Rory's women gathered together like this. How sweet. I wonder why? Well, now you have something serious to discuss." She sauntered toward the doorway. "Don't bother to see me out. I know which way to go. I know this house *very* well."

The front door slammed.

The room was silent. Then Justine burst into tears.

Nora said, "Oh, that Rory still has a lot to answer for." She made a stiff gin and tonic and put it in Justine's hand. Sitting next to her, she said, "Drink up. Believe me, I know the feeling. Here, take some tissues."

"Thank you." Justine blew her nose. "I can't believe Rory had an affair with *her*."

"For four years," Jenny stated baldly.

Justine's eyes and nose were red as she looked pitifully up at Jenny. "You must hate me to say such things."

"I don't hate you, Mother. I hate deception." Jenny poured herself more wine. "My entire life seems to have been built on deception. You lied to me about my biological father. You lied to all of us about the lost necklace. I missed all those summers of being with my sisters."

Justine bent her face into her tissues. "They weren't nice girls."

"*I* was!" Meg retorted.

"You're sorry for yourself because Dad had a mistress," Jenny continued. "Can't you spare a little pity for me? Because of you, I missed years with my real father and with Meg and Arden. I'll never get those years back."

"Easy there," Nora chided gently. "Give your mother a break, Jenny. She did what she thought was right. We've all made mistakes."

Cyndi looked up. "That's true," she admitted. "Especially if you've ever been alone."

Justine stifled her sobs at the surprise of Cyndi speaking at last.

"I know you never got on well with Tom," Cyndi said to Meg. "Don't think it hasn't troubled me at times. *Tortured* me at times. But, Meg, when you're right in the middle of life, it's like swimming: You have to keep splashing or you'll drown."

Justine sniffed. "I get that, completely."

Encouraged by Justine's support, Cyndi's voice grew stronger. "It was terrifically difficult when I was alone with you after Rory left me. You were a little girl, Meg. I was so lonely. I didn't know what to do. I was afraid, alone in the house at night. I know that's silly, I was an adult, but I was afraid someone would break into the house to steal things or rape me. I worried that you'd grow up weird, not knowing how to act around a man. That you might be afraid of men because you never saw any. When I married Tom, I believed I was doing a good thing for you, and I still believe that. He might not have been perfect, or loving—"

"You're right about that," Meg murmured.

"But he never abused you."

"Hey, there's the gold standard for stepfatherhood," said Arden cynically.

Cyndi went on, ignoring Arden. "He never hit you. He supported us all financially. He kept us safe at night. I could sleep. No one hurt you. You might not care for him, but you know what a man sounds like, talks like, acts like. . . . And something else." Her voice grew stronger, determined. "You know that *some* men can be faithful. You know that some men will take care of their families."

"Rory took care of all of us," Justine pointed out. "In his way."

Arden opened her mouth to object. Instead, she picked up a platter and passed it to Jenny. "Have an egg."

Surprised, Jenny obeyed. Arden passed the platter around. Every woman took a spicy, creamy deviled egg, ate it, and suddenly they were all starving. They reached for the rest of the food on the table. They practically inhaled the little sandwiches, the cheese and crackers, the olives. They wiped their mouths and their lipstick disappeared, and so did just a bit of their tension. Justine kicked off her jeweled sandals and curled up on the sofa with her bare feet beneath her. The rest of the women kicked off their sandals, too, and an aura of uneasy companionship spirited around the room like an incense. As if they were sitting in front of a campfire, in the dark, centuries ago. Just people trying to figure things out.

"Now," Arden said, after she'd placed all the bottles on the table in reach of anyone who wanted more to drink, "what to do about Marcia Kirkpatrick?"

"We should see a lawyer," Nora said sensibly.

"Right." Arden reached out to snap up the packet of letters. "I'll keep these with me. Unless anyone else wants them?"

Jenny shuddered.

"Fine. We'll show them to Dad's lawyer, Frank Boyd, tomorrow. We can't decide anything until we know whether or not Marcia has a legal leg to stand on."

Nora suddenly stretched and yawned. "I've eaten too much too fast and I've got too many words in my poor little brain. I've got to get out of here."

"You're leaving?" Arden's jaw dropped.

Nora aimed a sardonic snort at her daughter. "Yes. I'm leaving. Honey, I'm only going for a walk into town. It's a summer night, and I want to see the lights and move my ancient legs before the blood pools and I die of a blood clot."

"You're not that old, Mother," Arden said.

Justine stood up. "I'll go with you."

Cyndi said, "Me, too."

Arden said, "All right. We'll all go. My head could use some airing."

The six women put their sandals back on. They left the drinks and empty platters on the table, used the bathroom and fixed their makeup, swept up their purses, and went out into the Nantucket night.

It was dark. Stars speckled the sky and a salty breeze drifted past. They headed down Centre Street toward the lights of town. They strolled along, not talking, gazing in the windows at the four-inch heels with ribbon straps, the eight-hundred-dollar purses with opals on the clasp, the silk dresses, the cashmere sweaters. They wandered into Bookworks and spent a long time browsing. They headed to The Juice Bar and stood in the long line to buy cups and cones of decadently rich ice cream. They crossed South Water Street to avoid the crowd of people spilling out of the Dreamland Theater. They sauntered past the stately white Greek Revival library, past the brick post office, past The Hub, with its magazines and seashells for sale. On Main Street, several musicians performed, their instrument cases in front of them to catch coins. They perched on benches and leaned against trees and lampposts, listening to a Paul Simon wannabe sing and play guitar. They tossed him money and walked on.

All around them, others were doing the same, performing the much-loved ritual of rambling around a small town on a summer evening, enjoying the warm air, the laughter of strangers, the sight of honeymooners holding hands, or a baby asleep in a pack on his father's back. For this while, they were lifted out of their daily worries. They felt the satin air, the firm, enduring earth beneath their feet; they saw the luxuries offered up to them by merchants who had chosen the very best and arranged it for their pleasure. A pair of young boys on skateboards whizzed past, brushing their shoulders. A small woman with a large dog tugged on his leash, trying to prevent him from blocking the sidewalk. They skirted the dog and smiled at the woman. The cobblestones of the street had once been ballast in the hold of whaling ships, and thousands of feet had trod over the stones just as theirs did now. This was the past, and the present, and the windows gleamed with promises for tomorrow of dresses to wear, perfume to dab, books to read, and jewels to drape around their necks.

Finally they walked down to the dock to watch the last steamship of the day glide around Brant Point and, shuddering and swirling up foam, slide into its berth in the harbor. They sighed wearily with pleasure, and turned to walk back to the house.

TWENTY-FIVE

"I'm still hungry," Nora said as they all entered the house.

"Me, too," Justine agreed.

"We could order in," Arden suggested.

The three younger women exchanged glances. They'd thought the finger foods they'd set out would be sufficient. They'd assumed that someone, or perhaps all of them, would be too upset to eat. Hunger seemed like a good sign.

"Let me look in your refrigerator," Cyndi suggested.

Cyndi walked into the kitchen with the other five women following. She opened the refrigerator, scanned it, nodded, and smiled. "BLTs," she said, and reached for the skillet hanging from the rack near the stove.

"We usually microwave the bacon," Arden said.

Cyndi slanted her eyes at Arden. "Would you like to make the sandwiches?"

Arden waved her hands. "No, thanks. Sorry. As you were."

Nora carried in the bottles from the living room. Jenny followed with the ice bucket. The five women gathered at the kitchen table, watching Cyndi work with efficient, agile movements. Soon the seductive aroma of bacon filled the room. She found the cutting board and the large Bartlett's tomatoes and deftly sliced them.

"You cook like a pro," Justine noted.

"I cook for boys," Cyndi explained, adding, "although I suppose now they're old enough I should say I cook for men."

Jenny poured herself a glass of water and drank it down. "It must be strange having so many males about. It's funny how our dad always seemed to be surrounded by females."

Cyndi paused, a head of romaine in her hand, and contemplated the question. "That's right, the rest of you don't have sons or brothers." She washed the lettuce leaves, dried them gently with paper towels, and laid them on the bread. "Boys are slobs. I think it's kind of a missing-gene thing. They don't mean to be, they just are. They don't even think of doing their own laundry until they're down to the raggedest, holeiest pair of boxers. They love me and I know it, but they have no compunction about letting me do all the laundry, all the grocery shopping, all the cooking and cleaning." Turning, she looked at the others. "You know, I think there's an analogy here for the way men are in relationships."

"They let the woman do all the work," Nora supplied.

"Right," four others chimed in.

"Rory wasn't that way," Justine protested.

"Oh, come on," Nora snorted. "When did Rory Randall ever do a load of laundry?"

"Okay," Justine agreed. "But he did do a lot of the work in our relationship. He was always thoughtful. He remembered my birthday, our anniversary, he gave me great presents, he complimented me all the time. And when he came to sensual pleasures, he didn't just dive right in, he—"

"Stop." Meg waved her hands. "No talking about our father and sex."

Justine blushed. "I just mean that Rory was sensitive."

Nora clarified, "Rory was a salesman. He was a natural-born charmer. He was a prince among men, and that meant he never soiled his handsome hands with menial labor."

Cyndi drained the fat from the bacon and laid the meat on bread slathered with mayo. Arden jumped up to help her put the sandwiches on plates and bring them to the table. For a few moments, conversation stalled while everyone ate.

"To change the subject for just a sec," Nora said, wiping a bit of tomato seed from the side of her mouth, "I want the listing for this house."

Cyndi tilted her head sideways. "What do you mean?"

"I mean I want to handle the sale of this house. I'm a real estate agent, after all. I know how to show a house and how to read the contracts."

"So you want the commission," Justine said flatly.

"I do," Nora replied evenly. "I'm good at what I do. I can get the best price for this house. So the three girls will get the most money."

Cyndi shrugged. "I don't have any problem with that."

"Fine," Justine conceded. "It's okay with me, then, too. But, really, it's the girls who should be consulted."

Nora looked around the table. "Jenny? Any thoughts?"

Jenny made a little movement with her shoulders. "Only that I wish we didn't have to sell it. I have so many wonderful memories here."

Nora didn't allow a detour into the past. "It's a large house for just one person. It made sense for Jenny to live here when Rory and Justine came down for the summer and holidays. But Rory left it to all three daughters. Arden and Meg won't be living here full time. I think they'd rather have the money than a place to visit."

"Absolutely," Arden said.

"Me, too," Meg added.

"We can't forget that Marcia person," Jenny reminded them. "She says Dad promised he'd leave her a house."

Meg added, "And that Dad loved her. That she has letters from him attesting to that. *Attesting* is the wrong word in this case, though. I guess I mean—"

Arden cut her off. "Enough with the diction lesson, English major. The point is, I believe Dad told her he loved her and told her he'd leave her a house, but he didn't actually leave her a house."

"I wouldn't worry about her," Nora said. "If she'd had a binding legal document, she would have shown it to us today. We'll speak with a lawyer tomorrow, but I know something about the difference between legal wills and earnest promises. Any real estate agent knows."

"But if Dad promised her . . . ," Meg began, unsure of exactly what she meant.

"Do you want to give her something?" Nora asked.

"No!" Jenny cried. Then she looked confused. "But maybe we should?"

Justine said, "Why? You don't owe her anything. *I* certainly don't owe her anything."

"I think it's up to the girls," Nora decided.

Jenny, Arden, and Meg spent a few moments calculating their thoughts.

Meg spoke first. "If Dad really loved her, I think he would have given her something if he'd known he was going to die."

"He'd had a heart attack," Justine argued. "He was lying in the hospital, he asked his lawyer to come in, he made sure his will was in order."

"When you were home showering, Mom," Jenny interjected, "Dad added the stipulation about Meg, Arden, me, and the house. Why didn't he make a provision for Marcia then?"

"I don't think he truly believed he was going to die," Justine responded. "None of us did. It was a serious heart attack, sure, but he was recovering. He was sitting up in the hospital bed, talking, laughing, joking. His color was good. He was only *sixty*." She was tearing up as she spoke. "How could he have mentioned Marcia, anyway? You were always with him in the room, or I was. He never had a moment alone with Frank Boyd."

"So," Nora summed up, "we really can't be sure what Rory would have done for Marcia, legally, if he'd known he was going to die."

Very quietly, Arden said, "But we do know, because of the letters he sent her, that he loved her."

The others stared, confused.

"I read them," she confessed.

"What?" Meg asked. "When?"

"Just a few moments ago. I took them with me into the bathroom. I scanned them. I know his handwriting. Dad was wild for her. He—"

Jenny held out her hands. "Stop! I don't want the details!"

"Why wasn't I enough for him?" Justine wailed. "For God's sake, he wasn't a young man anymore! Couldn't he slow down?"

Justine's cry sent a wave of laughter around the room.

"It's not funny!" Justine protested.

Nora kept on track, even though she was grinning. "Anything about a house?" she asked her daughter.

"Nothing. It was all romantic stuff," Arden told her.

"Oh, ick." Jenny covered her face with her hands.

Coolly, Nora recalled, "Marcia worked in Rory's real estate office, right?"

"For fifteen years," Arden said.

"Okay, then. Give me the letters, Arden. I'll talk to the lawyer, and I'll handle Marcia. I'll work with her on the sale of the house, and she can take the seller's commission. That won't buy her a house, but it should give her a nice bunch of cash. I think Rory would like that."

"I think he would, too," Cyndi added.

"Fine," Justine acquiesced.

"Jenny, I'll help you find a house of your own on the island, and I won't charge you a commission when you buy it."

Justine raised an eyebrow at her daughter. "Sounds like a good deal, Jenny."

Jenny nodded. "Okay."

Meg and Arden nodded their agreement.

"Good. Now," Nora continued, crossing her arms on the table, "I think you three should get the house ready to be shown."

"What?" Jenny almost shrieked. "Not yet! We're still living in it. The summer isn't over."

"It's August. People with money are here. They'll be ripe to purchase a place on pleasure island. Plus, consider this, Jenny. Meg has to leave in September. She's got to get back to work. She's got a freshman English program to run. Arden will leave early in September, too, for Houston. Do you want to do all the work of getting the house ready to show by yourself?"

Jenny shrugged. "How much work can there be? The house is in great shape."

Justine said quietly, "All of Rory's Nantucket clothing is still in our bedroom closet here. I suppose I should box it up for The Seconds Shop."

"Brilliant," Nora said. "That's exactly the kind of thinking we need right now. Justine, you should box up your stuff, too, and ship it to your house in Belmont. Also, any of your artwork or vases, whatever is personally important to you. Go through the bathrooms, toss all the old prescriptions, Rory's shaving stuff, sunblock, and so on. First rule is to get rid of clutter."

"It's so sad," Jenny said. "What you call clutter is my life."

Nora smiled at Jenny. "Honey, you're young. You've

been living free off your father for too long. It's time to move on."

Jenny glanced at her mother, slightly hoping for some objection.

Justine smiled, too, gently. "Nora's right."

Nora continued, "We've all got to move on, really. The six of us. Here we are, the Rory Randall fan club—"

"—with the exception of Marcia Kirkpatrick," Arden reminded her.

Meg quipped, "The We Love Rory Randall Even Though He Was a Sneaky Shit Club. Very exclusive."

"No entrance fee," Arden joked.

"Because we've already paid it," Cyndi said.

Startled by Cyndi's addition to the conversation, everyone laughed, and the atmosphere lightened.

Jenny softly observed, "Dad not only married beautiful women, he married nice women."

Justine began to cry, quietly, averting her head from the others.

"Mom." Jenny reached out to touch her mother's arm.

Justine whimpered, "I don't know how to go on without him."

Nora said, not unkindly, "You can do it, Justine. Just like Cyndi and I did."

"Just like Marcia is doing." Arden drove the point home.

"Oh God," Justine wailed. "I think I've had too much to drink. I feel awful."

Jenny rose, fetched a glass of cool water, and handed it to her mother. "It's late. We should all go to bed."

"Have we covered everything?" Meg asked.

"Not yet." Nora held up her hand. "Where's Justine's necklace?"

"I put it in a safe-deposit box." Arden went to the rack by the back door and lifted a small key off the hook. She placed it on the table in front of Justine. "Here's the key. You can retrieve it whenever you want it."

Justine shuddered. "I don't want it. It's tainted."

"Really," Arden said flatly.

Justine wiped her eyes. "It's my fault, I know. I've admitted it. I'm sorry. I wish I hadn't done it. But we all have to move on, right? So why don't you three girls sell it and split the proceeds. Rory gave it to me, so in a way, it's from Rory."

"Kind of perverse, isn't it?" Arden wondered aloud. "I mean, to give me the jewelry you used to get rid of me?"

"Arden," her mother said, touching her arm lightly. "Get over it already. Sell it and buy something nice for yourself."

"Yes," Cyndi agreed. "Good idea, Nora."

"Fine," Arden said.

Nora stood up. "I'm going to bed. Tomorrow I'm going to talk to Marcia Kirkpatrick. The rest of you have work to do. You've got to get this house ready to sell."

The mothers pushed back their chairs and left the room, yawning, talking in low voices about how exhausted they were. Arden, Meg, and Jenny removed the dishes and glasses from the table, stacked the dishwasher, wiped the counters, prepared the coffeemaker for the morning.

"Your mother did really well," Meg told Jenny.

Jenny glanced at Arden.

Arden nodded. "She did, Jenny. It's hard to apologize."

Jenny let out a long sigh of relief. "God, it's like she's my child. I don't want her to embarrass herself."

"Come on. Let's go to bed," Arden said. "Tomorrow we'll all have fresh chances to embarrass ourselves."

Jenny headed out of the kitchen, down the hall, and up the stairs, turning off the lights as she went. Meg went into the den to sleep, too tired to open the fold-out bed, and collapsed on the sofa in her clothes.

Arden undressed in the living room with the lights off. Enough moonlight came through the windows for her to find her nightgown, which she'd brought down earlier in preparation for this moment. She slid it over her head, loving the sensation of silk against her skin. She settled onto one of the living room sofas, trying different pillows until she found one just the right softness for her head. She lay for a long time thinking about how she enjoyed sleeping in different places, like a cat she'd once had who sampled different places to nap: in Arden's lingerie drawer, under the sofa, in the laundry basket. She thought about Houston, how first she would sleep in a hotel, then perhaps in a rented apartment with a brand-new bed and mattress, and then, who knew, perhaps in bed with Palmer White. She closed her eyes and fell asleep.

TWENTY-SIX

Randall Real Estate was located in a small brick building on Easy Street, facing the harbor. The door was a handsome sea blue, the window trim white, and, of course, full of photos of houses for sale.

Nora had phoned ahead to make an appointment with Marcia at eleven o'clock, and exactly at that time, Nora strode up the brick walk and opened the door. Wanting to look businesslike but not forbidding, she wore her ecru skirt with a sleeveless white cotton shirt and all her gold jewelry.

It took her a moment to comprehend what she saw when she stepped inside the office. An expensive wooden desk held pride of place in the center of the room, but it was surrounded by cardboard boxes.

Marcia Kirkpatrick was working at the computer behind the desk. Today she wore a bright floral Lilly Pulitzer dress and a pink headband in her tumbling blond hair. When Nora entered, Marcia stood up. The two women eyed each other for a moment, then smiled nervously.

"Nora."

"Marcia." Nora looked around the office. "You're moving?"

Marcia nodded. "We only rent this space. Rory didn't want to buy it—he didn't much like the owner, but it's such a great location." She gestured to a comfortable chair. "Please. Sit. Would you like some coffee?"

"Not yet, thanks." Nora continued to scan the room, her brain clicking like a digital camera, summing up what she surveyed. Each opened cardboard box held color-coded files with marked tabs. The sides of the boxes were labeled clearly. More folders and piles of papers towered on Marcia's desk, but they were stacked neatly, edges aligned. The woman was busy, but unruffled.

"Who inherits all this?" Nora asked, gesturing with her arm to indicate the boxes, the files, the computer, the furniture.

"Rory didn't mention his office in his will." Marcia slid her hand over her skirt as she returned to her own chair. "For such an excellent businessman, he was remarkably lax when it came to certain details about his own business affairs. I think he believed he would never die. Or at least not for decades."

"Yes, that sounds like the Rory I knew," Nora agreed. "He probably thought he could charm even death."

Marcia looked down for a moment, then recovered her poise. "I've taken it upon myself—with Frank Boyd's knowledge and assent—to finalize the pending sales. I've stopped taking listings, although Rory handled most of that. I'm packing up the office, seeing that all bills are paid, and then I'll close it down. Our rent has been paid until October. I won't renew the lease."

"What will *you* do when the office is closed?" Nora inquired.

Marcia smiled. "I've had quite a few offers from other real estate firms for my services. I know the business, the houses, the people." She relaxed back against her chair and sighed. "I think I'll give myself a little vacation, first."

"I've got a proposition to make to you," Nora said. "Two, actually."

"Oh?" Marcia looked skeptical.

"You might know that I'm also a real estate broker."

Defensively, Marcia said, "Of course I know."

"My firm is based in Boston. The girls—my daughter, Arden, and her sisters, Meg and Jenny—have decided to give me the listing on the sale of the Lily Street house. The three of them will divide the proceeds from the sale."

Marcia waited.

Nora continued, "I stopped by the lawyer's office on my way here. Frank Boyd said your letters are called holographic wills, not enforceable by law unless witnessed properly. By *two* witnesses."

Marcia dropped her eyes.

"Did anyone witness those letters?"

"Of course not."

"So, as you said yesterday, you can make a scandal, if you'd like. But Frank also told me it's common knowledge that you and Rory were more than just boss and office manager." Nora paused. "I don't think your threat carries much power."

Marcia nodded in defeat.

"I have a proposal for you," Nora continued. "We'd like you to represent the seller and to take the commission when the sale goes through."

Marcia looked up. She picked up a pencil and twirled it in her fingers, thinking.

"The commission won't provide you enough money to buy a house on this island," Nora continued. "But it will be a good start."

"Justine agrees?" Marcia asked.

"She does, although legally that doesn't matter. The three girls agree. I'd better stop calling them girls, hadn't I? Legally, they're adults."

"That's kind of them. Kind of you, to let me be the seller's broker." She swiveled slightly back and forth in her desk chair, thinking. "Jenny lives and works in that house, so she won't be in a hurry to sell. That means we can price the house high and not negotiate."

"Do you have your broker's license?" Nora asked.

"Of course. Although Rory preferred to handle most of the listings and sales. He was so good at it. I'm better at the desk work, paperwork, that sort of thing. We were the perfect team." Her face fell. "Professionally, at least."

Nora had no patience left for grieving women. Almost brusquely, she continued, "I've never spent much time on this island, but I'm aware of the way it's boomed recently, with houses going for tens of millions of dollars. I've got a lot of clients in Boston who might be interested in a summer home here. I'd like to open a branch of my real estate agency here and hire you as the branch manager."

Marcia stared at Nora, speechless.

Nora took a pen and pad out of her purse and wrote a number on it. She slid it across the desk toward Marcia. "This is what I'd pay you to work for me full time. I also would offer health insurance. No retirement benefits. I assume you're savvy enough to work those out yourself."

Marcia looked at the number on the paper. She rose and walked across the room, crossing her arms beneath her breasts, staring out the window.

Nora kept on talking. "I would want a strictly business relationship. I don't need friends. I have friends. You have friends. I want a good office manager and someone who knows the real estate on this island from soup to nuts."

Marcia's voice was unsteady. "Rory never handled anything under a million."

"Nor do I. Also, no rentals. Strictly top-of-the-line." Nora paused. "I'm not doing this to be nice. You'll find many people in Boston who'll attest to the fact that *nice* is not my thing. I learned about real estate from Rory, and I've got to believe you've learned as much from him as I did. So I can trust your judgment and your capabilities. I think we could make a good deal of money with this collaboration."

After a moment, Marcia said, "Rory always did admire you."

"I've built up a successful real estate firm. Nothing to rival his own, but big enough. I've had a wonderful life with lots of friends and fabulous trips. I also have a first-rate staff. All seven people have worked under me for over fifteen years. I invite you to phone any of them and ask what it's like. I think you'll find the answers satisfactory."

"I'm sure I would." Marcia returned to the desk. Reaching into a drawer, she took out a tissue and blew her nose. "This is an amazing opportunity for me, Nora. As I said, I've had offers from real estate agents all over the island. Some are good friends. But this—well, this sounds like fun. Kind of adventurous. Connecting up with an office off-island. This will open our office up to a whole new crowd." She stood up and held out her hand. "Shall we shake on it?"

Nora smiled and looked at her watch. "Why don't I take you to lunch?"

After breakfast, all the other women were involved in tasks and errands, so Meg pocketed her cell phone and strolled down to the beach, settling by a dune out of the wind, where she could watch the blue water of Nantucket Sound.

"Hi," Liam said when he answered the phone.

"Hi," Meg said back.

For a moment they were quiet, just breathing together. Liam broke the silence. "How are you?"

"I miss you," Meg whispered.

"I miss you, too. A lot."

They were silent again. Meg closed her eyes and leaned into the warm shoulder of the sand dune.

"Okay," Liam said. "No more of this or I'll have to take a cold shower. Tell me about last night."

Meg opened her eyes and sat up. "Indescribable, really. Yet another one of Dad's women showed up." She recounted the evening, giving short shrift to Justine's admission of guilt for taking the necklace and focusing on the shock of Marcia's appearance and claims.

After a moment, Liam asked, "So what happens next?"

"We're getting the house ready to put on the market. Technically, legally, the three of us have to stay in the house until the last day of August, but there's no stipulation that we can't start showing it to prospective buyers."

"Are you ready for that?"

"Why wouldn't I be?" Meg kicked off her sandals and buried her feet in the warm sand. As she looked out at the horizon, a windsurfer sailed past in a blur of color.

"Oh, I don't know. A lot of people get connected to their summer homes. My parents won't move a shell or a cracked oar in our Maine house. Everything's still where their grandparents put it. It will be like that when it's excavated by Martians in the year 5013."

Meg laughed. "I have some good memories of summer here with Dad and Mom when I was about seven. That's when Dad bought the house. Mom took me to the beach and the library and the movies, and the swings by Children's Beach." She smiled. "I haven't thought about those days for a long time. They sort of got smushed into the back of my mind when Dad left Mom for Justine and everything was messy."

"So I'd say your feelings about the house must be mixed," Liam summed up.

"Pretty much," Meg agreed. She watched a naked toddler waddle past, shrieking with giggles. A moment later, his older sister ran after him, a diaper in her hand. "But the island's nice," she told Liam. "I'm on the beach right now. The temperature's perfect, not too hot, not too cold."

"Lucky you," Liam said. "We've got low nineties on the way with ninety percent humidity."

Meg suggested invitingly, "Why don't you come down here?"

"Could I?"

"I don't see why not. I have to stay till the end of August, but there's no reason I couldn't have a guest."

"I've got a lot of work to do to get ready for the fall semester."

"Bring it. We'll work together. You can stay as long as you'd like."

"Where would I sleep?"

"Who says you'd sleep?" Meg felt herself blushing. She'd never been so forward, so playful, with a man.

"Dude, I am *so* packing my bags right now."

Meg laughed, a low, intimate, satisfied laugh that came from deep in her belly.

"Seriously," Liam continued, "what would your sisters think? If I came down for, maybe, an entire week?"

"I'm sure they'd be fine with it. We know we're on the countdown stretch. Nora's getting ready to list the house. You and I would just have to keep our papers organized so the house doesn't look cluttered."

"Um, Meg. My papers? Don't have any. I'll just bring my laptop."

"Right. Of course." Meg spoke aloud. "I'll box up my Alcott books and notes and put the boxes back in the Volvo. That will free up space in my room."

"We can take our laptops to the library and work there." Liam suggested.

"So you'll come down?"

"As soon as I can."

Justine and Cyndi were on the second floor in the master bedroom, going through the drawers and closets.

"Really," Justine said, "Rory was such a dandy. Look at this! He's got more clothes in his closet than I have in mine."

Cyndi lifted out several hangers with trousers clipped on them. She picked through them. "Nantucket reds. Brooks Brothers yellow. Navy blue with embroidered green whales. Madras. White flannels. Pink. Pink? Jeez, was the man gay?"

Justine leveled a sardonic stare at Cyndi. "Really? You would ask?"

"Well, Tom would never be caught dead in any of these."

"I think it's fair to say your Tom could never fill Rory's trousers."

Cyndi opened her mouth to object. This was bordering on intimate territory. But it was all too much, surreal, going through her dead ex-husband's clothing with his widow after last night and the explosion of confessions.

She found herself admitting, "I'm sorry to say you're right."

Justine cooed, "Oooh, do tell."

Cyndi hugged the trousers to her protectively. "I don't want to criticize Tom."

"Please. Who am I going to tell?"

"It's just that—Rory was so skillful, wasn't he? He was so romantic."

"True." Justine hoisted an armful of long-sleeved shirts in her arms and dumped them on the bed. "He never let it get old."

"He never let it get *routine*. He liked having sex in different places in the house."

"Different places everywhere," Justine added.

"Where's the craziest place you ever had sex with Rory?" Cyndi asked.

Justine slid a shirt off the hanger and began to fold it. "I'd have to think about it. Wait. What size shirt does Tom wear? He might not like the trousers, but these are some nice shirts. There are more in the drawer, still freshly ironed from the laundry."

Cyndi's eyes lit up. "They might not fit Tom, but my sons are both big guys. Wow, they'd look wonderful in these shirts." She dropped the trousers on the other side of the bed and went around to help Justine fold the shirts in a pile. "Oh, this is fabulous."

"I'd have to say the craziest place we ever had sex was in the shower of Senator Mantori's house in Washington, D.C." Justine giggled, remembering. "Rory had helped Angelo get elected, and the Mantoris invited us to

stay for a night when we were in the area. It was just irresistible."

"Of course, for Rory, a mere bed in a senator's house
wouldn't be sexy enough," Cyndi said.

"Right. The shower raised the stakes, so to speak. At
least, the stake."

They laughed together and continued to remove shirts
from hangers and fold them in a neat pile.

"We did it on the beach at Cisco," Cyndi reminisced
dreamily. "The moon was out, we'd had champagne and
oysters, the surf was rolling in slowly. . . . Actually, it was
romantic but uncomfortable. I had scratches on my back
and bum for days. I was afraid they'd get infected and I'd
have to go to a doctor and they'd know what I'd done."

"I'm sure they've seen it before, and worse," Justine
said.

"Probably. Still . . . Still, I suppose I'm more content
with Tom. He's more my type."

"Yeah. I get that." Justine sat on the floor and began to
tape the sides of a cardboard box she'd found in the attic.
"Let's put all the shirts and stuff you want to take in here.
How about socks for your boys? Underwear?"

"Underwear, ugh. Who wears other men's underwear?"

Justine reached over and yanked a drawer open. "It's
Tommy Hilfiger. Look at the stack. Probably worn once
if at all. Wash it in hot water, who would know?"

Cyndi glanced in the drawer. "Rory had red boxer
shorts?"

Justine stared up from the floor, tilting her head as she
studied Cyndi. "Oh my gosh. I have such an idea." Jump-

ing up from the floor, she went to her own closet, shoved back the clothes hanging right in front, and lifted out a bunch from the back. "Cyndi. You should try these on. I bet they'd fit you and you'd look spectacular in them."

Cyndi eyed the rainbow of garments uneasily. "They're not really my style."

"Like you have a style," Justine joked. "Seriously, Cyndi, look in the mirror. How old is that dress? Where did you buy it? Goodwill?"

Cyndi bridled. "I have two sons. We're paying college tuition. We don't have the kind of money you and Rory had to throw around on clothing."

"Fine. So take some of these. Why not, for God's sake?"

"To start with, they belong to *you*."

"Honey, these are at least two years old."

"Gosh, how ghastly," Cyndi replied sarcastically.

"Now, look at me closely. How much weight have I lost since Rory died?"

"I don't know."

Justine made a face. "That's right. You don't. Well, trust me. I've lost over ten pounds since Rory died."

"I wish I could lose ten pounds."

"Try on one of these dresses. You'll look like you did. Better yet, you'll look like you don't need to lose ten pounds."

Cyndi's eyes were wistful as she fingered a simple blue linen shirtdress. "Well . . ."

She held it up to her and checked her image in the mirror. "It might fit."

Justine guessed at Cyndi's shyness. "Take all these into

the bathroom and try them on. If you think they work, keep them."

"You're sure you don't need them?"

"I'm sure."

Cyndi took the clothes into the en suite bathroom. Justine continued folding shirts. After a moment, she heard Cyndi exclaim, "Oh."

The bathroom door opened. Cyndi stepped out in the blue shirtdress. It fit her nicely.

"Doesn't it suit me?" Cyndi asked shyly.

Justine put her hands on her hips. "I want to cut your hair. Trim it. Trust me. I'm good at it. And I want to experiment on you with my lipstick and blusher."

"Oh, really, I . . ."

"Did you look in the basket on the bathroom counter? How many lipsticks do you see? How much blusher? How many eyeliner pencils? Please. Do me a favor. Or do you want me to just throw it all out?"

"You wouldn't."

"Of course I would. I have twice as much back at home in Belmont."

Cyndi was too stunned with hope to speak.

"Go sit on the toilet," Justine said. When Cyndi flinched, she clarified, "Put the lid down first. I'll come in where the light is good and put some makeup on you and trim your hair. When you get home tonight, Tom might find himself in a more *romantic* frame of mind."

TWENTY-SEVEN

At nine in the morning, Arden went for a walk around town by herself.

Arden's mother had left the house after breakfast, wearing one of her most casual power suits, on her way to visit Marcia Kirkpatrick. Justine and Cyndi were cleaning out the master bedroom. Meg had wandered off to the beach, and Jenny was deep in her closet, sorting through clutter.

Once Arden packed her bags, nothing of hers would be here.

Perhaps someday she'd have the money to purchase a small vacation cottage here. It would be hot in Houston. She'd be working hard, and she was all about working hard, but it would be nice to come here for a few weeks in the summer to beachcomb or laze in the sun.

She passed the library, the Catholic church, The Hub. She slipped inside The Hub, bought a few house and garden magazines, and wandered out again. She walked away from the water, up past Vineyard Vines, The Golden Basket, gazing in the windows at the straw hats with striped ribbons, the glittering jewelry, past the wide front window of Arno's restaurant, where Palmer and Zoey sat across the table from each other, talking intensely.

Palmer and Zoey?

She smiled, fluttering her fingers at them. They didn't notice her, so engrossed were they with each other as they leaned across the table, ignoring the food on their plates.

Arden's legs continued to move of their own accord, one step after the other, automatically. She was certain her expression didn't change from its pleasant, bland state. Certainly she didn't stop in the middle of the sidewalk, shrieking *Palmer and Zoey?*

What was Zoey doing down here on the island?

Why was she having breakfast with Palmer at nine o'clock in the morning?

Had Zoey spent the night with Palmer?

Shit, why did Arden even care? She didn't care! Really. She did. Not. Care.

She turned the corner onto Centre Street and collapsed on the first bench she came to. She would sit here for a moment and get her breath back. Then she would go home and make notes about tomorrow's filming session at Winkie's house.

After all, her relationship with Palmer was strictly work.

If Zoey wanted to fly all the way down here to be with the man, and she must have been with him all night long to be having breakfast with him, well, if that's what Zoey had done, yay for her. Arden was going to Houston.

People strolled past, holding hands, pushing baby carriages, swinging beach bags. They were chattering, linking arms, sipping beverages, giggling.

Arden gritted her teeth and started walking to Lily Street.

Deep in her closet, Jenny was filling a clear garbage bag with shoes, clothes, and miscellaneous—whatever had been hiding back here for years. Had she actually ever worn this purple jumpsuit with the pink trim? Frightening! What was this thing? A shell necklace glued to a ribbon, and not very neatly done. Wait, now she remembered. The year Arden and Meg were sent away, her mother had convinced her to create a little "project"— gathering shells, cleaning them, varnishing them with nail polish, and gluing them to ribbons. She'd sat out in front of her house with a table displaying them before a handmade sign offering them for sale for one dollar. One kind grandmotherly neighbor had bought three for her granddaughters, who were all about seven years old. Jenny had felt like such a dork. Such a lonely, miserable dork.

Her cell phone vibrated. She lifted it out of her pocket.

"Hey," said Tim. "What's up?"

"We're getting ready to sell the house. I'm packing up. Tossing out years of accumulated junk. It's like traveling through my past, which was not always a bed of roses."

"That must be difficult."

Jenny cleared her throat. "It is. Mother and Cyndi are in Mother's room, sorting through Dad's clothes, and Nora's getting ready to list this house for sale. I'm going to have to find someplace else to live and work."

Tim said, "Want me to come over?"

Jenny was shocked to realize she wanted nothing more.

"Jenny? Did you say something?"

She laughed again in slight hysteria. "I just nodded. Isn't that funny?"

"Nod as in yes?"

She continued nodding. "Yes. As in yes, please."

She crawled out of the closet, detached an old belt whose hook had caught on her shorts, and went to the mirror to comb her hair, which was adorned with a dust ball.

Tim was probably calling about work. They'd finished the arts coalition website, and Genevieve was so pleased she'd recommended them to a psychiatrist who was setting up a clinic with counselors who would be based on the Cape and make weekly trips to the island. Jenny looked around her room. Her bed was neatly made, but the rest of the room was chaotic. She'd awakened early, heart pounding, freaked at the thought of moving out of this house, out of this room, where she'd lived and worked for the past ten years since college. How was she going to get rid of this stuff? Would Nora expect her to move her computers, worktables, and printers out of the bedroom?

She'd gone into a bit of a fit, finding an old Staples box, tossing in her flash drives, her paper knife, a bunch of computer cords and power strips, several unopened

reams of recycled paper, a clipboard, her pen holder—
The pen holder had brought her to a halt. She'd made it
herself in sixth grade, when she'd considered it a work of
art, a ceramic mug dipped in whirling paints, very psy-
chedelic. Very stupid, sure, but she'd had it all these
years, and so what if it was unprofessional, it was part of
her life. It had always lived here in this room.

She heard Tim knocking downstairs. She raced to let
him in.

He was so tall, clean, and tidy, smelling of soap and
sunshine in his chinos and white polo shirt. He was so
together. His hair stuck up like a porcupine's, but it was
the style these days, she supposed, and around his blue
eyes, his dark lashes gleamed as if he'd put on mascara.
He was so handsome it wasn't fair.

"You look terrible," Tim greeted her.

"Thanks." She held the door open. "I suppose you
want to talk about the psychiatrist's website."

He came inside and shut the door behind him. "Does
that work for you?"

Thuds and laughter came from the second floor.

"You might as well come up," Jenny told him.

In the second-floor hallway, they saw Justine and
Cyndi hauling suitcases from the attic doorway. Cyndi
had on one of Justine's dresses and some makeup. She
looked like a different woman from the one who had arrived last night.

Jenny rolled her eyes and led Tim into her bedroom.
Plopping down on her bed, she gestured at the mess. "I
don't know how to do this. I don't know where to start.

I guess I knew we'd have to sell the house eventually, but I never expected it to happen so soon."

She noticed that one of her bras lay next to a computer keyboard. At least it was a lacy black one.

Tim pulled out her comfy typing chair, sat down, and swiveled to face her. "Okay. Let's break it into manageable parts. First, work. I can see that in order to sell this house, you'd need to get your computer workstations out of here. They take up a lot of room and make the bedroom look weird."

Jenny rolled her eyes. "Thank you again."

"I've got space in my office," Tim said.

Jenny gaped. "But you hate me."

Tim leaned his elbows on his knees and clasped his hands. "Bjorn told me you'd dumped him. Said you'd been a real witch about it."

"Bjorn? All this anger at me has been because of Bjorn?"

"Perhaps I wanted to believe him. Perhaps I needed to believe him. If you remember, Jenny, when I met you, it was at that party where you met Bjorn."

"Yes. I remember."

A flush stained Tim's neck. "We both talked with you that evening. Bjorn talked to you. And I talked to you."

"Right . . ."

"We both asked you out. You accepted Bjorn's invitation and not mine."

Jenny stared at him. He stared at her. She sensed so much going on between them, so much seriousness, intensity, and, suddenly she realized, sexual attraction.

"So that's why you've been . . . hostile . . . all this time?"

Tim shrugged. "First, you were Bjorn's girl. I was his best friend. Then, you shafted him."

Jenny struggled with her thoughts. "Bjorn is a really nice guy. Fun to be with. But he's not . . . my type. Plus, I didn't dump him. He wanted to live in California because the surf's better there."

"Yeah. I know now. I thought it was because you broke his heart. He was so cut up. He's in California now. He just e-mailed me to say he'd been a little *dramatic* about the way you broke up with him." Tim grinned. "Bjorn's kind of a yellow lab guy, you know? Likable, friendly, gets his feelings hurt easily."

"So maybe you don't hate me anymore?"

"I never did hate you, Jenny." Tim's gaze was almost tender.

"I never hated you," she replied.

They stared at each other for a long moment, unable to speak.

Tim straightened in his chair. "Okay. So here's what I propose: You and I should join forces. Go into business together. Robinson and Randall. Nice ring to it, don't you think?"

Jenny's jaw dropped. "Well, this is sudden."

"Hey, you've got to go somewhere, don't you? I know you're good at what you do. I think we balance each other out nicely." Restless, he rose from the chair and paced around her room. "You and I can dismantle all this and move it in a matter of hours."

"We need a pickup truck for the tables and chair."

"Gee, I don't know anyone who drives a pickup," Tim said sarcastically. More gently, he said, "I'll find someone. When do you want to do it?"

Tears welled in Jenny's eyes. "I don't know why I'm so emotional about this. I'm like some adolescent who can't grow up and get real."

Tim waited for a moment. Then he sat down on the bed next to her and put his arm around her shoulders in a comradely kind of way. He sort of rocked her toward him and away, patting her shoulder as if they'd just won a football game. "Let's take it one step at a time."

His touch almost obscured all thoughts of moving. Certainly it short-circuited her senses. "You're right, Tim. Thanks."

They sat together then, very still, with his arm around her shoulder. She put her hand on his knee.

"Oh God," he said.

She smiled.

Nora entered the house like a brisk summer breeze. "Hello, everyone!" she called.

"Up here," Justine yelled back.

Nora came up the stairs. "It's set," she told them as she entered Justine's room. "I've talked to Marcia. She'll represent the seller, and we've settled on the price. I just have to run it by the girls. I think they'll be pleased. Hey, Cyndi, you're looking fabulous."

"I know." Cyndi preened. "I can't wait to get home. And look, we're going to mail back all Rory's old things for my sons to wear."

Nora glanced at Justine, who said, "We're boxing up most of the stuff. Cyndi has a lot of my discards to take back in some of our old suitcases on the plane, but she can't fly it all back with her, so we'll have to tape up the boxes and take them out to UPS."

"I'll help," Nora told them. "It will be my bit toward getting the house ready to sell."

In her room, Jenny whispered to Tim, "You see? Listen to them. They're acting like friends."

"And that's a bad thing?"

"No, I guess not. It's just so—unexpected."

Looking pleased with himself, Tim remarked, "Unexpected can be good."

"I know. I'm just not used to things moving quite so fast." Removing her hand from Tim's knee, she hugged herself. "Where will I live when this house sells?"

"You'll have some money, right?" Tim reminded her. "You'll be able to find a place on the island. You do want to stay on the island?"

She nodded. "Of course," she said, meeting his eyes.

The front door opened and closed, and Meg came floating up the stairs, angelic with her strawberry-blonde hair and beaming smile.

She drifted into Jenny's room. "Hi, Jenny. Hi, Tim."

"Tim's helping me move my computer stuff," Jenny said.

"Great. I'll box up my books and papers and UPS

them back to the college." Meg came into Jenny's room and sank down into the desk chair. "I just spoke with Liam. He's going to come down for a few days. I hope that's okay. I mean, I can't leave until August is over, and he and I have some college stuff to do. We've got to prepare the fall semester." She smiled smugly. "Don't worry, though, we'll use our laptops. We won't have piles of papers or anything to mess up the house. He can stay in my room with me."

"Or in the front bedroom," Jenny suggested. "It's got a queen-sized bed."

"Oh, Tim!" Justine peered in from the doorway. "Just what we were hoping to find. Some nice, strong young man with muscles who could help us carry boxes to the car."

Jenny and Meg helped Justine and Cyndi pack more boxes, tape them shut, and address them. Tim went up and down the stairs, lugging them to the Jeep, which held a lot. Nora took the Volvo to Something Natural and bought several different kinds of takeout sandwiches for lunch. She set up a picnic area on the table in the backyard shade.

By the time she was through, the other mothers and Tim had returned from UPS. Meg and Jenny were in the attic, sorting through boxes of children's books (should they keep them for their own children or give them to the library?), shelves of board games, playing cards, jump ropes, and dress-up clothes—intending to get rid of them but instead lingering over them, as if gazing back into their childhood.

Nora called them down for lunch. She'd made a huge pitcher of iced tea with mint and another of lemonade. They all collapsed onto the lawn chairs, grateful for the cool drinks.

"We're all here but Arden," Meg noticed. "Where's she?"

"I'm here." Arden came around the side of the house, looking cross. "I went for a long walk in town."

"You look grumpy," Jenny noted.

"I'm just hot." Arden fell onto a lawn chair, kicked off her low-heeled sandals, and wiggled her toes in the cool grass. "Hi, everyone."

"Iced tea or lemonade?" Nora asked.

"Tea, please," Arden said.

"Is everything okay?" Meg inquired gently.

"I'm just hot," Arden repeated through gritted teeth. She noticed Tim. "Hi, Tim. What are you doing here?"

"Helping Jenny get organized to move her computer stuff to my shop."

"What a good idea!" Nora beamed. "That will make the bedroom so much larger, so much prettier!"

Arden sipped some tea. "Cyndi, hey. You're looking good."

Cyndi smiled. "Justine gave me some of her things. I can't wait to go home. My flight leaves at two."

"I'll drive you out," Meg told her mother.

"I'll stay another day," Justine told them. "I've got to go through the house and dig out anything I might want to keep. Paintings, silver, that sort of thing."

"Good." Nora straightened in her chair. "Because we're going to start showing the house next week. I've got to get the three girls to sign the listing, but that's a formality. I've talked to Marcia Kirkpatrick, and she's on the case."

"Marcia Kirkpatrick," Justine muttered.

"This way she'll get money from the seller's commission," Nora reminded her. "So she won't need to use any other means to try to get the money that Rory said he'd give her."

"Goody for her," Justine murmured.

"Mom," Jenny said.

"Furthermore," Nora continued, "I'm going to open a branch of my real estate office here on the island. Marcia's going to be my branch manager."

The news split Arden's face into a smile, lifting her away from her smoldering thoughts. "How awesome! Dad's first wife teaming up with his last liaison."

Justine's lips thinned in anger.

Jenny reached over and touched her mother's hand. "Come on, Mom. You've got to see how karmic this is. Kind of closing the circle? You know Dad's up there laughing his head off right now."

Justine looked at her daughter and her face was not completely bitter when she said, "I'm sure he is."

TWENTY-EIGHT

Arden had drawn up a rough script for the segment on Winkie Linden's summer house. After lunch she phoned Winkie to see if she could stop by to check out a few things. The senator's widow was gracious but terribly formal, and Arden wanted to make the process of having a cameraman in her house as painless as possible.

The Linden summer house was on Cliff Road, overlooking the sound. It sprawled in gray-shingled glory over the lawn, surrounded by hedges of privet and rhododendrons, the long porch railings smothered in climbing roses. Winkie sat here in a wicker rocking chair with a glass of what she called ice water at hand; Arden thought it probably wasn't water at all.

"It's nice to see a strange face," Winkie told Arden. "I've been in the midst of a contretemps with my family for days. I've got four living children, and each has passionate thoughts about what I should do with Harold's letters and papers. Of course several museums have asked me to donate the papers for safekeeping. I have the final say, but whatever I decide will make someone angry."

"I wonder whether I could video you talking about this," Arden said. "Most families have similar issues. Yours is exceptional, of course, because your husband was a senator. Most families don't have museums asking for memorabilia. But it's always hard to divide up family possessions. We're going through a similar process at our house right now."

"Oh dear." Winkie took a sip of her drink. She patted her crown of thinning white hair. "I look rather ragged today. Not at all the way I'd want Harold's former constituents to see me."

Arden thought fast. "What if I tape you talking? We could use your words as a voice-over while we showed shots of his papers, medals, books, and so on."

Winkie considered this for a moment, then agreed.

With the dinner hour approaching, Arden drove back to the Lily Street house in high spirits. Winkie, relaxed by her water, confided the complicated history of many of the objects in their summer house and the complex claims of her four children on those objects. Of course Arden would show the shooting script to Winkie and her children; she'd never want to reveal secrets or expose anything unsavory. Hers was not that kind of show. Perhaps she could get one of the children to work with her. . . .

Her mind tumbling with thoughts, Arden entered the house.

"Good, Arden, you're home!" Jenny called out from the living room.

Arden strolled in, slipping out of her low heels and pulling her silk shirt out of her skirt as she went. She stopped dead. Palmer White sat on the sofa facing Jenny.

"You have a guest," Jenny announced brightly.

"Hi, Arden," Palmer said.

Arden recovered her cool and continued to move casually to an armchair. "Hi, Palmer. I've just been working, talking with Winkie Linden. I've got lots of good stuff."

"Want a drink?" Jenny asked. Before Arden could answer, she offered, "How about a gin and tonic? With a slice of lime? Be right back." She left the room.

Arden unbuttoned the top two buttons of her shirt and lifted her shirt away from her, fanning herself to cool off. "You and I didn't discuss exactly when I'm going to Houston, so I wanted to get a few more segments done for Boston before I left." She was determined to be all business. If he was having an affair with Zoey, sweet for him. It didn't matter to her.

Palmer's mouth curved up in an irritatingly knowing grin, as if he could read her thoughts. "Right. Business. That's one reason I dropped in. I have yet another proposal to discuss with you."

"Oh yeah?" Arden crossed one leg over the other, slowly. She had great legs, and she let her skirt ride up her thighs.

Palmer kept his eyes on Arden's face. "Your colleague Zoey Anderson came to see me this morning."

"Lucky you."

Jenny entered the room with two drinks.

Arden said, "Thanks, Jenny. Just what the doctor or-dered."

"I'll let you two get on with your work." Jenny slipped away.

Palmer continued, "Zoey came all the way to see me because she wants something from me, and she wants it very badly."

"Oh, dear sweet blue-eyed saints in heaven, give it to her," Arden said.

"Wouldn't you like to know what it is she wants?" Palmer asked.

"Fine. What does she want?"

"She wants to go to Houston with you."

Arden almost spilled her drink down her shirt. "What?"

"Arden, Zoey is your biggest fan in, as she says, the whole wide world. She thinks you're totally awesome. She wants to be your apprentice."

"She wants my job."

"True, in a way. It might be more precise to say she wants to be you. She realizes she's got a lot to learn. She's smart, quick, and young. She envies your style, your class-iness, your finesse. At the same time, she doesn't want you to think she's only a stalker, a groupie. She's serious about what she wants to achieve in the television world."

Arden took a long, cool sip of her drink, letting her thoughts settle. "I'm pleased Zoey admires me," she ad-mitted, "but I'm not sure I like her."

"How could you know?" Palmer reasonably pointed out. "You haven't spent much time with her."

The small shot of gin gave Arden the courage to ask: "What about you and Zoey?"

"Me and Zoey? There's nothing about me and Zoey." Palmer's face cracked into a mischievous grin.

Arden eyed Palmer levelly and took another sip.

"You sophisticated, worldly wise, semifamous television personality," Palmer said, and the brown of his eyes took on the allure of melted chocolate. "Don't you have any clue yet about exactly which woman it is I want to be with?"

Something made Arden shiver. Perhaps the ice in her drink.

Palmer said, "Let me take you out to dinner."

"I need a shower," Arden told him.

Palmer said easily, "I can wait."

Arden slowly uncrossed her legs. She set her drink on the table. She stood up, smoothing her skirt down over her slender thighs, all the while keeping her eyes on Palmer. "Do me a favor first."

"Sure."

"Stand up."

His eyebrow quirked a question. He opened his mouth to speak, but instead rose from the chair, looking amused.

Arden ambled over to him, taking her time. She didn't stop until she was only an inch from touching his body with hers. Sexual heat exploded inside her, but she forced herself to act cool. She was playing this game for keeps. She was sure Palmer was, too.

Moving forward that one final inch, she brushed her breasts against his chest, teasing his face as she brought her lips close to his mouth, as if she were about to kiss him. Palmer no longer looked amused. His face was serious, his dark eyes as intense as a panther's. Slowly Arden tilted her head so her mouth came closer, past his jaw, his cheeks, settling near his ear.

She whispered, "You won't have to wait too long, I promise."

Palmer groaned.

She sidestepped around him, sauntering out of the room, unable to keep a satisfied smile from her face.

After driving Cyndi and her bulging suitcases to the airport, Justine, Meg, Nora, and Jenny decided to go out to dinner at Town.

"I'll treat," Nora told them. "It's a legitimate business expense. I've got the listing form in my bag, and after dinner I'll need the signatures of Jenny, Meg, and Arden."

"If Arden comes home tonight," Jenny said archly.

"I'm sure she and Palmer are discussing work," Nora said, eyebrows raised.

It was blissful to gather around a table out in the soft evening air, watching the other diners come and go in their cheery vacation togs. They ordered cocktails they'd never had before, martinis and margaritas with colorful liquors added, icy cold and delicious. They dined on Moroccan lamb sliders, grilled quail, mussels, and Korean short rib tacos, passing their plates around, sharing all the food. Tired from a day of packing, they talked only sporadically and shamelessly listened to nearby tables. Behind them, one couple was fighting. Next to them, a man was working on a seduction plan that seemed to be succeeding.

They strolled around town afterward, indulging in ice-cream cones for dessert, enjoying the twinkling lights from the masts on the boats moored in the harbor and the scent of flowers drifting through the air. Finally they went home, lazy and content.

They were getting ready for bed when Arden came in. She waved her hand and headed to her room.

But Jenny noticed that Arden's lipstick was smeared, and her lips were puffy, as if she'd been indulging in a lengthy kissing spree.

"All right," Nora said the next morning. Enough dilly-dallying; it was showtime.

They were gathered around the table: Nora and Justine, Jenny, Meg, and Arden. Breakfast was over and they sat with their coffee mugs nearby.

"This is the listing sheet. I made a copy for each of you. Read it over. It's a standard form. I'll want to go through the house and take some photos to put online, but before I can do anything, I need your three signatures."

Justine wanted to know how Nora had arrived at the price. "It seems high."

"Of course it's high. People love to negotiate. They want to feel they've knocked the price down, they've got a bargain, they've won. Or, if we're lucky, some wealthy couple will be captivated by this house and pay full price. More money for the girls."

Justine shrugged. "Understood."

Nora cast an unreadable glance at Justine. "How long are you planning to stay here?"

"Why?" asked Justine. "Does it matter?"

"Not to me. But Marcia Kirkpatrick might want to come through the house tomorrow—"

"Why?" Jenny demanded. "She told us she knows the house."

"She might," Nora agreed. "But she'll need to view it with selling it in mind. Describing it to potential buyers. We could arrange a time for her to be at the house, and you could take yourself off somewhere, Justine."

Justine shook her head. "No. No, I'll leave first thing in the morning. I'm done here, anyway." She glanced around the kitchen. "You can't pack up memories in a suitcase."

TWENTY-NINE

Justine and Nora left the next day. The girls had three weeks of August left to get through to legally fulfill the stipulation in Rory's will.

The first week, Liam came down, toting a laptop computer; a book bag of college directives, memos, and guidelines; and a duffel bag of clothing. Every morning he and Meg made the bed in the little back bedroom, organized their laptops and the book bag, and went off to the library to work on the fall course schedules and syllabus for freshman English.

Arden made coffee, dressed in professional clothes, arranged her voice recorder and iPad filled with notes for her show, and drove off to interview someone or to meet with someone else for lunch or to make notes as she sat on a bench in the restful corner park on Main Street and Fair.

Jenny pulled on shorts and a tank top, backpacked her Mac Air, and biked through town, stopping at Fast For-

ward to buy muffins and iced coffee. She carried these
into The Computer Guy shop on Airport Road, where
Tim was already at work. She set out breakfast for them
on a table at the back of the shop, and as they ate, they
discussed prospective projects and how to divide the
workload.

But by late afternoon, everything changed. Nantucket
summer evenings were the glitter hours. Wealthy patrons
threw lavish parties for their favorite charities: cocktail
parties, dances, sunset cruises on fabulous yachts, intimate dinners for two hundred beneath white tents sailing
upward, their posts rippling with banners like those of
medieval kings. These were the fantasy weeks, the fairy-
tale hours, the celebration of laughter, beauty, and camaraderie.

Arden, Meg, and Jenny would rush home at four or
five, slip into bathing suits and gauzy cover-ups in sherbet
colors, and hurry down to Jetties Beach for a quick swim
to cool off from the heat of the day. Back home, they'd
shower and dress, sharing jewelry and clothes, scarves,
shoes, shawls. Liam would don his navy blue blazer and
white flannels and drive the three women in the Volvo
to whatever party was on that night. There they'd meet
up with Palmer and Tim to sip champagne, slurp oysters
served up from the raw bars, help themselves to scallops
wrapped in bacon or deep-fried mussels. They danced.
If there was a band, they danced until the music ended
and their splendid clothes were completely soaked with
sweat, their hair plastered to their skulls, their legs weak.
If there was a band, Meg caressed the back of Liam's
neck during the slow dances, and Palmer whispered in

Arden's ear, and Tim, with each slow dance, drew Jenny closer against him, until finally she surrendered and wrapped both arms around his neck, allowing herself to hold on to this man.

But all the glitter was not at the parties.

Some nights the August meteor showers were in exceptionally showy moods. The six of them would take blankets out to Madaket at the farthest edge of the island, away from the lights of town. They'd lie on the sand gazing upward as the Perseids streamed above them, flashing in a display of heavenly fireworks, shooting stars falling toward them, streaking across the night sky, lavishing the darkness with silver-white light. Nearby, the ocean lapped at the shore, and occasionally something would splash in the water, as if a star had landed there.

Suddenly, there was only one more week left in August.

People were leaving the island in droves. Families had to get their children ready for school. Students had to get back to their dorms and buy college supplies. Clerks, salespeople, waitstaff, all took off for more permanent jobs, and the island emptied out. No more musicians played on Main Street. At night, the summer breezes sometimes brought a hint of chill.

The night before Liam left the island, he asked Meg if he could take her out to dinner. She understood—in the house with her sisters and sometimes Palmer and sometimes Tim, it was hard to find a private moment.

Even though it was still hot outside, Meg knew there would be air-conditioning, so she tossed a silk shawl around her shoulders, pleased at the way its swirling hues accented her strawberry-blonde hair. She was secretly proud of what she'd learned this summer on the island from her sisters, knowledge college textbooks couldn't give her: how to be feminine and adult without looking puritanical.

She was glad she'd worn the shawl when she discovered that Liam was taking her to the best restaurant on the island, one of the most famous in the country, Toppers at The Wauwinet hotel, and they were going there by water. They strolled down Easton Street to the dock behind the White Elephant hotel and boarded the *Wauwinet Lady*, a small launch that took them through the harbor to The Wauwinet hotel at the end of Polpis Harbor. The evening was calm, the water an impressionistic mirror of the deepening blue sky, the air heavy and still. They were served sparkling wine to sip as they observed the shoreline with its inlets, sandbars, marshes, and mansions. It was like being whisked away by magic carpet to another world, and as they were handed out of the boat onto the hotel's dock, Meg felt she was stepping into a fantasy world. All around on the beach were umbrellas, beach chairs, pots spilling with flowers, and then they were ushered into the bright restaurant with its sparkling crystal and crisp linen tablecloths.

After they were seated by a window, Meg asked, "What's the occasion?"

Liam shrugged. "The end of a remarkable summer?"

"And the beginning of a remarkable semester," Meg

agreed. "Liam, I've been getting positive e-mails from the other instructors about my freshman syllabus. I was afraid they'd balk at using someone else's organizational plan, but most people seem glad to have it."

"I'm sure they are. It's excellent. Plus, they're aware your students had the best scores last semester." He paused while the waiter poured them another glass of champagne and took their order. "How's the Alcott book?"

"I'm almost there." Meg sat back, sighing. "It's more difficult than I'd expected. I want to get it right. It would help to have someone else read what I've done so far and give me a critique. I wonder, Liam, would you have time to do it?"

"I was hoping you'd ask. I'd be very happy to. Which reminds me, I have a question for you."

"Yes?" She spread crab pâté on a cracker and munched it, savoring the taste of summer.

"Meg."

His voice was serious. She glanced up.

"I want to have children with you."

She swallowed her cracker, putting her hand to her throat, where her pulse suddenly fluttered like a bird taking wing.

"I want to have children with you right away." One side of his mouth quirked upward in a sexy smile. "Because you, Meg, are so very, very old."

She grinned helplessly at the way he'd turned the age difference around.

Terrified and courageous, she asked, "Liam—are you proposing?"

His voice trembled slightly. "I'll do it again, formally, on my knee, ring in hand."

Meg looked around the busy restaurant. "Perhaps not on your knee."

Liam sighed with relief. "Good call." Reaching into his pocket, he brought out a black velvet box. He handed it to Meg. Opening it, she saw a large diamond in an antique platinum setting.

"It was my grandmother's," Liam told her. "Shall I put it on your hand?"

Meg blinked back tears. "I feel like a Roman candle."

Liam smiled triumphantly. "I feel like a match."

"Oh," Meg said in a long blissful sigh.

Liam slid the ring onto her finger. It was slightly too large, but she kept it on, turning it this way and that, watching it flash flares of light.

Later that night, Meg and Liam returned to the Lily Street house, slightly giddy with happiness and hope. Meg showed her ring to Jenny and Arden. Jenny promptly burst into tears, and Arden discovered one last bottle of champagne for them to share in celebration.

So Liam was exhausted and a bit hungover the next day as Meg drove him out to the airport to catch his flight back to Boston. Meg would join him in a week, when the Nantucket house was closed. They both had heavy fall teaching schedules. Liam was putting together another book of poems. And they had a wedding to plan.

The week brought more change. Palmer flew back to Boston, promising he'd meet Arden's plane when she

arrived and sit down with her to hash out the details of
her Houston contract—and Arden would let him know
whether she'd decided to take Zoey with her or not. She
couldn't leave Ernest and Channel Six in the lurch; they
would all have to meet to strategize the next season of the
show. She'd filmed enough on the island to keep them
going for a few months. Arden could foresee a lot of
travel between Houston and Boston in her future.

Invitations to parties diminished, then disappeared as
families closed up their houses. Tim and Jenny rushed to
complete projects for their off-island clients. Time, which
had stretched in a golden dream during the summer, suddenly shook itself briskly, as hurricanes boiled and blus-
tered off the southern coasts. Fresh air gusted over the
island, carrying the electric energy of change.

The cupboards at the Lily Street house began to
empty. No more jars of capers, bluefish pâté, beach plum
jam. No more wine in the rack, no more champagne and
Prosecco in the refrigerator door. The bowl that had held
lemons and limes was washed and put away. The three
agreed to spend one day washing beach towels and bed-
sheets and going through the house choosing any objects
they might want to keep.

Three days before September first, Arden, Meg, and
Jenny lounged around the kitchen table, reluctant to finish their coffee and begin packing. They were all wearing
shorts, flip-flops, tank tops. The heat remained intense.

Arden had pulled her auburn hair back with clips so it

wouldn't get in her face. She wrapped an ice cube in a paper towel and dabbed it on her wrists as she talked.

"Jenny. Meg and I have been talking."

Jenny quirked an eyebrow. "Oh?"

"According to Marcia Kirkpatrick, there are several clients poised to make an offer on this house. So you're going to have to find another place to live."

"Wait," Jenny said sarcastically. "I didn't realize that."

Arden ignored Jenny's tone. "So here's what Meg and I thought: I'm going to be in Houston, and it's going to be damned hot there in the summer. Meg enjoys it here in the summer and would love to have a place to come with Liam. The three of us should each get a nice big pile of money from the sale of the house, at least six hundred thousand. So Meg and I think that we should buy another house with you, or part of another house. We've agreed on the sum of two hundred thousand each. That would add four hundred thousand to the amount you could put toward a house on the island. That means you'd be able to buy a bigger house—which you'd have to, because it would need to have at least two guest bedrooms, one for Meg and one for me, for when we come in the summer."

"Perhaps at Christmas, too," Meg added. "I've never been here for the Christmas Stroll."

Jenny had turned white. Softly, she said, "You two want to buy a house with me?"

"Um, yeah," Arden said. "I think that's what I just said."

Jenny began to cry.

Alarmed, Meg said, "Well, but you don't have to if

you don't want to. It was just an idea. We can always rent a place, or, gosh, we don't even have to come here—"

Arden said to Meg, "I think Jenny's happy."

Jenny nodded yes and made blubbering noises. After a moment, she repeated, "You guys want to buy a house with me."

Arden spoke with precision, as if to someone slightly deaf. "Yes, Jenny, Meg and I want to buy a house with you. Or at least part of a house. We'd also agree to help with taxes and upkeep. We can have a lawyer work out the details."

"This is wonderful," Jenny said, wiping her eyes. "I never dreamed . . . I always wanted . . . So we'll be spending time with each other, as if, as if, as if . . ." She stalled, unable to pronounce the words.

"As if we're part of a family," Meg articulated.

Jenny burbled, "I love you guys."

Arden sniffed. "Love you, too."

Meg had tears in her own eyes. Reaching over, she took Jenny's hand. "We're island girls," she said.

THIRTY

Drop a coin in the water as you leave the island, the saying goes, and you're sure to return. The first day of September was as sunny, hot, and bright as the last day of August, but on the island everything had already switched seasons. After her many years of living on Nantucket, Jenny was accustomed to this, but this day resonated deeply within her like the rings circling out from the pennies dropped into the water by the tourists leaving on the ferry.

She and Meg had driven Arden to the airport for her plane to Boston. Now Jenny stood on the dock at the Steamship Authority, watching as Meg drove the Volvo up the ramp into the great white ferry.

Meg paused at the top of the ramp, leaned out the window, and waved one last time at Jenny.

Jenny waved back.

Meg steered the car into the hold of the ship, and for Jenny the summer was over.

Still, she stayed until all the cars were loaded and the huge groaning boarding ramp was raised and locked to the stern. Meg came out onto the upper deck, peered over, spotted Jenny among the others, and waved to her. Jenny waved back. Meg blew Jenny a kiss. Jenny blew a kiss back and cried a bit, but the tears were more sweet than bitter.

The vessel churned, hummed, and pulled away from the dock. Slowly it made its way toward Brant Point and around that significant landmark, and soon it was out of sight.

Jenny slowly walked home. The morning was too enchanting for weeping. Birds chirped and swooped from tree to bush. Honeysuckle spilled sweetness as it frothed over white picket fences. The low mutter of lawn mowers drifted through the air, carrying the fragrance of cut green grass. The sun was hot on her shoulders. She let her thoughts float free. When she got home, she would sit down with a fresh cup of coffee and consider the day ahead.

She was going to live in the house until it sold. Until papers were passed and checks cut and the closing carried out at the bank. She dreaded entering the house again. It would seem so empty—it would *be* so empty. Meg and Arden had left, and so had her mother. So had her father. Her father, who had, in his own way, given Jenny her sisters.

Perhaps it was thinking about her father that made her hallucinate a man sitting on the front porch of the house. She stopped dead at the end of the sidewalk, lifting her sunglasses to get a clearer view.

A man. Wearing a suit. But not her father, because he didn't have Rory's thick silver hair—

But her father, after all. William Chivers rose from the wicker chair and stiffly waved at Jenny.

"Hello," she called, hurrying up the walk. "What a surprise."

"I intended it to be." His smile made him look almost handsome, in spite of his white-fringed chrome dome and wrinkled forehead.

He held out his hand, but Jenny bypassed it and gave him a quick, light hug. "I'm so glad to see you. Come in. Would you like some coffee? The door was unlocked, by the way. We seldom lock our doors here. I could make iced coffee. We could sit out in the backyard, it's very shady with all the trees—" She laughed out loud. "I know I'm babbling, but I can't believe you're here!"

William Chivers followed her into the kitchen, where he told her he'd prefer lemonade. Jenny filled two glasses and carried them out the back and down the steps to the wooden lawn chairs.

"Look," she whispered, pointing to a birdbath at the far end of the garden. "Meg suggested we get it. I don't know why I never bought one before. It's such a pleasure to watch the birds drinking and bathing. Look at the fellow—what is it? I think it's a house finch—splashing away so happily."

"Do I make you nervous?" Chivers asked in a gentle voice.

"What? No, no. It's just so surprising to see you. And I'm all over the place emotionally. We've got the house up for sale, and I'm going to have to move out, and the summer has been one bombshell after another. . . ." She put her hand on her chest and inhaled. "I'm sorry if I seem nervous. I'm glad to see you. I guess I'm just so surprised."

"Take another deep breath," Chivers told her. "I speak in my professional capacity as a physician."

Jenny cocked her head quizzically. "Um, okay."

"Jenny," Chivers said, "I bought the house. I bought this house." Reaching into his pocket, he brought out a stiff piece of paper and held it out to her. "For you."

Jenny stared.

"This is the deed," Chivers continued, still holding the paper out for her to take. "The house is now in your name."

Jenny took the paper, unfolded it, and read it. She raised her eyes to William Chivers's face. "I don't understand. Why would you do this?"

"Because I can." Leaning back, Chivers crossed one slim, elegant leg over the other. He couldn't stop smiling. He seemed pleased with himself.

Jenny said, "But this house cost so much!"

"True. But if, for example, I'd known about you when you were born, I would have supported you financially your whole life. In a way, I'm making up for all the lost time."

"Won't your"—Jenny stumbled over her words; she almost said "your *real* children" but caught herself in time—"other children be upset that you've given away so much money? Two million dollars?"

"They have plenty of money," William Chivers assured her. "And, Jenny, they know about you now. They'd like to meet you."

"This is overwhelming," Jenny gasped. "I don't know what to say."

"It's only money," William Chivers told her quietly. "It's only, after all, a house. I would trade all my money to get back the years I missed when you were growing up. You are my first child. I would have liked to have held you when you were born. Look at you, how fetching you are, like your mother, and I can tell you have a superior mind. Your college graduation—I've missed it all."

Jenny bit her lip to stop it quivering. "I'm slightly on overload."

"This money, this house, isn't meant to be a bribe," William Chivers continued. "I mean, I'm not trying to buy my way into your life. But I would like to see you in the future. I'd like to introduce you to my son and my daughter. I'd like to meet Meg and Arden."

Jenny nodded, robotically, still stunned.

"Drink your lemonade, Jenny," William Chivers told her.

She picked up her glass and drank. The tart, sugary cold braced her, revitalized her.

"I'm acting like an idiot," she said. "I want to say thank you—but it's almost unbelievable."

"You're perhaps a bit in shock, yes," he agreed. "Drink more lemonade."

She drank more lemonade. They sat together in silence for a few minutes.

"You know," she said, "Meg and Arden have offered

to help me buy a new house. With part of their share of the money they'll get from the sale of this house."

"Which you arranged for them to inherit," William Chivers reminded her.

"But they don't *know* that." Jenny leaned toward William Chivers. "That's the important thing, don't you see, the essential thing. They have no idea I was involved with the stipulation. All on their own, because we did get along so well this summer, they decided they want to buy a house with me, so they can come here in the summer. So we can all be together."

"Do you think they'll be jealous when they find out I've bought the house for you?" William Chivers asked. "Do you think they'll be angry?"

Jenny slid lower into her seat and let her eyes travel around the yard, taking in the birdbath, the privet hedge, the cheerful petunias and hardy phlox still blooming away in spite of the heat.

Jenny smiled. "They'll be happy for me. For all of us. We'll use their money to put an addition on the house, so they'll have bigger rooms, for when they're married and have children."

William Chivers nodded. "Yes. You now have a world of possibilities."

Jenny inhaled deeply. She smiled gratefully at William Chivers. "Thanks to you."

"Yes," he agreed. "In many ways, thanks to me. But also, thanks to Rory Randall."

THIRTY-ONE

Justine was watering her houseplants after her short time away when someone knocked on the door. Surprised, she looked at her watch. It was late afternoon, almost time for a relaxing drink. Carrying her watering can to the door, she went down the hall. She opened the door.

William Chivers stood there, in a seersucker summer suit and a snowy white shirt. His head was bald except for a fringe of white hair, but his brown eyes were as warm as they had been so long ago.

He said, "*Justine.*"

ONE

Alison had no trouble spotting her younger daughter in the crowd milling around the ferry's blue luggage racks. Felicity was the one who looked like an 1890s Irish peasant. She wore a flowing skirt undoubtedly made from an Indian bedspread, a lace blouse, a brightly colored shawl, and Birkenstock sandals. And dangling beaded earrings and maybe a dozen multicolored bracelets. And a backpack made out of what looked like corn husks.

Even so, she was lovely. Her dark blond hair tumbled down her back and her sweet face was heartbreakingly beautiful.

"Mom!" Felicity embraced Alison tightly, swiftly, then drew back and did a little dance. "Can you believe it? Look, Ma, no kids!" Felicity laughed. "I'm awful, aren't I, but you know I've never been away from them for three days. I'm not sure I can walk without holding someone's hand."

"Hold my hand," Alison suggested and led her daughter to her SUV. "Do you have luggage on the rack?"

"No, I've got everything in my backpack. Clean underpants, a toothbrush, and a bathing suit."

Alison opened the hatch so Felicity could stow her backpack, and then they buckled themselves in and headed for David's house. "How was the trip?"

"Oh, Mom, it was divine."

Alison had worried when Felicity said she was taking the slow ferry, which took two and a quarter hours to cross Nantucket Sound. The fast ferries took only an hour but cost more. Alison assumed it was a matter of expense. Noah kept Felicity on a limited budget, which was why Felicity's clothes were all from thrift stores, which Alison knew was her daughter's preferred way to shop. Felicity was a great believer in resisting the powerful draw of consumerism. If Felicity's half-sister, Jane, ever had children, she'd probably dress them in Chanel, but Jane swore she was never having children.

In the passenger seat beside her, Felicity was in full flood. ". . . so I bought a beer—a beer! In the middle of the day! And took it to the upper deck, outside, and settled in one of the seats looking out to sea. I leaned my head back and soaked in the sun. It was so heavenly, so peaceful." Felicity burst into laughter. "And, Mom, a guy tried to pick me up! Seriously—and I think he was just out of college. I couldn't tell him I'm an old married woman with two kids, I was afraid it would embarrass him."

Alison glanced over at her daughter. "Well, Felicity, you are only twenty-eight. And with your gorgeous hair, and, um, the way you dress, you look like a college student yourself."

"Mom, you're crazy. I have bags under my eyes and I've gotten all pudgy. Still, it was so sweet, talking to this guy. Okay, flirting with this guy. He wants to get together for a drink tonight, but I said I was here to visit my sick mother. I'm sorry, I don't want you to be sick, but I needed to pretend this visit was a real crisis so I couldn't possibly get away." Felicity laughed again. "How's Jane? Is she here yet? Did she come by private jet?"

"Stop it. Jane is flying but not by private jet. She said she'll rent a car and drive to David's house."

"Oh, good. I didn't bring my laptop or even a pad of paper, because I'm sure Jane brought hers, so when we plan your wedding, she'll keep a list of what we have to do."

"It won't be all wedding talk. It's going to be such a treat, having both of you together again."

"Yes, because it was always a pleasure before," Felicity muttered and automatically apologized. "Sorry, I don't mean to be snarky. But it's strange, don't you think, how different I am from Jane? Maybe it's nurture, but I blame it on nature. I mean, Alice is seven now, and actually? She's so much like Jane. She needs a lot of private space. I think it's hard on her, having to share a room with Luke—"

"But, Felicity," Alison protested, "your house is enormous. You have four bedrooms."

"I know, but Noah thinks the kids will bond better if they sleep in the same room. Also, he doesn't want them to be spoiled when so many children in the world hardly even have houses."

Alison wanted to ask why it was, then, that Noah had purchased such a huge house. The cathedral ceiling in the living room held a fourteen-foot evergreen at Christmas; Noah had to climb a ladder to decorate it. But she bit her tongue. She didn't want to be disapproving before they even arrived home.

"Alice is bossy," Felicity was saying, "and Luke, well, Luke is a maniac. So much energy!" She sagged, fake-pouting. "I miss those little guys already." Immediately she rallied, smiling at Alison. "But this is going to be so much fun! The three of us together again. Oh, my gosh!"

Alison laughed at her daughter's enthusiasm. She steered the Jeep between tall rose of Sharon bushes and up David's white shell driveway, and there, in front of the house, stood Jane, leaning against her rented dark green Mini Cooper convertible. She wore a lightweight gray silk pantsuit and Manolo Blahnik stilettos. On the ground next to her were a small Hermès suitcase, her purse, and her briefcase. Her briefcase? For two nights and a day and a half on Nantucket?

"Jane! You're here!" Felicity jumped out of the Jeep, raced over to Jane, and clutched her in a rib-breaking bear hug. Jane wrapped her arms around her sister and rolled her eyes at Alison over Felicity's shoulder.

"It's real. The three of us are really here together!" Felicity crowed. "And look at this house! Wow, Mom."

"Yes, it's wonderful, isn't it? Wait till you see the view." Alison held the door open. "Come in. Look around.

Go upstairs and choose any bedroom you want—except the master bedroom, of course. I'll pour some iced tea."

"Do we need snacks?" Felicity asked, talking more to herself than to the others. "Probably not, we don't want to spoil dinner and I did have that bag of Fritos on the boat. Oh, man, it is *outrageously* satisfying to eat Fritos without the children fighting for them or Noah acting like I'm eating toxic chemicals."

"I'll bring out a bowl of grapes," Alison said.

She leaned against the refrigerator, eyes closed, just listening to her two daughters chatting away as they went up the stairs. It had been a long time since the three of them had been together like this, and she wondered if they could make it through this weekend without some spat or disagreement and hurt feelings. When Alison looked at her grown, capable daughters, it was as if she were seeing living Russian matryoshka dolls, the façade holding a memory of each stage of their development, down to the smallest, youngest infant, still residing within.

Her girls had never been close, and Alison felt responsible for that. True, they did have different fathers. Alison was married to Flint when she had Jane—she'd married Flint *because* she was pregnant with Jane.

Jane had always been a loner, a reader, a prickly little perfectionist with her straight brown hair held back with a headband. Her arguing abilities were astonishing; no wonder she became a lawyer. She was always a level-headed, straight-A student, never once crashing the car when she learned to drive (Felicity had dented it a few times), and—as far as Alison had ever known—never once falling into the depths of a tumultuous adolescent love affair. It wasn't that guys didn't pursue Jane. She was attractive, but aloof. *Elegant*. She was tall, lean, with naturally arched black velvet eyebrows over her hazel eyes. She was smart, no genius, but ambitious and hardworking enough to make all As and get accepted to Harvard and then Harvard Law.

Four years younger than Jane, Felicity was the adored daughter of Alison's second husband, Mark. Mark had tried not to show any preference in his treatment of the girls, and he'd succeeded. If anything, he let Jane have her way far too often. But he couldn't help the way his eyes softened when he looked at Felicity, who had the blue eyes and blond hair of the LaCosta family.

Felicity, Alison had to admit, *was* adorable. From the moment she'd toddled across the floor, babbling with glee, Felicity was happy and friendly and girly and sweet. As she entered her teens, she chose lace and ruffles, pale pink and baby blue, short flippy skirts, and multicolored friendship bracelets (which she and her friends made themselves, of course). In high school, she'd had lots of friends. And boyfriends. Felicity had been the drum majorette for her high school's marching band. She'd been prom queen her senior year. She'd attended the University of Vermont, married Noah right after graduation, had two babies, and become what Jane sometimes called "the little wifey."

Now Jane was a lawyer in New York, and so was her husband, Scott, although they worked for separate firms. They rented an upscale apartment on West Sixty-Fifth and went backpacking in Costa Rica and river rafting in Utah. Their lives were crazy busy and stressful and completely adult. Alison wasn't sure how she felt about Scott. He was so quiet, restrained, locked up. He was probably perfect for Jane.

Alison wasn't sure how she felt about Felicity's husband, Noah, either. Noah was an idealistic man, brilliant and ambitious. Straight out of college, he'd started a company selling organic drinks with catchy, healthy names. Now, Noah was trying to make "green food," alternative protein foods made, as far as Alison could tell, basically from kale and beet juice. Alison wished him well, although she worried about the stress he carried with him and how exhausted he always seemed.

Noah and Felicity's two gorgeous, funny, good children were the lights of Alison's life. The children adored their father—when they saw him, which wasn't often, since he worked at the office late into the night and on weekends. Alison did her best to feel fond of him and to smooth Felicity's life in little ways—buying her a nice new SUV for driving around with her children, or taking them on a Disney vacation.

But she couldn't wave a wand and make things perfect for Felicity; and, as David reminded her, Alison had her own life to live.

And she was living a wonderful life.

She'd never dreamed, after Mark's death six years ago, that she would love again. Of course her love for David was quite different from her love for Mark. Mark had been the love of her life. They'd been married for nearly twenty-five years, and after his sudden death, after the shock and the bitterness of grief, and the support of her friends and the days of mourning with her daughters, after the tedious legal work of life insurance and the will, after the months spent with other widows joining together to relearn the movements of normal existence, Alison had finally settled down like a swan without her mate, understanding that even with his loss, the nest that was her life was a lovely creation. She took a job as a receptionist for a dental group and became friends with the staff. She was busy, helpful, and grateful for each daily pleasure. She had her two daughters, her beloved grandchildren, her comfortable house, happy memories. Many friends. Many pleasures. She could go on.

And on she went, if not happily, at least gratefully, for almost six years. She hadn't been prepared last June, when she visited a friend on Nantucket, to meet David Gladstone. The love of his life, Emma, had died after a long illness four years ago, and David had never planned to marry again. Like Alison, he had a busy, if lonely, life.

When Alison and David met, at a simple summer cocktail party, it was as if the moment they stepped out onto the patio, they boarded a train that would speed them into lives they'd never anticipated. For one thing, the first miraculous, surprising, joy-making thing, there was the *chemistry*. Right from the moment their eyes met, a physical attraction reawakened them to the joys of the body. Who knew that a woman could experience adolescent sexual hunger in her fifties? Right there, in the midst of perhaps two dozen other people, men and women in light summer colors, wineglasses in hand, canapés floating by on the caterer's trays, right there, right then, *Boom!* David introduced himself. Alison shook his hand. They couldn't stop smiling at each other. Alison heard herself laughing softly in a feminine way she'd thought she'd forgotten. She practically cooed like a dove at the man.

"Would you like to leave this party and join me for dinner?" David had asked.

"Oh," Alison had said. "Yes. Yes, I would."

They'd departed without saying goodbye, like a pair of teenagers sneaking away from their parents. David took her to Topper's, the poshest restaurant on an island blessed with posh restaurants, and while they feasted on lobster washed down with an icy champagne, they talked. Their conversation told them much about each other, but the hours they spent together told them more.

Alison quickly learned that David was a man of action, not of contemplation. He was a man of hearty appetites. He was only a few inches taller than her, but he had a wrestler's shoulders and arms, so the extra weight he carried looked good on him. He was more enthusiastic than elegant—when he laughed, his entire body shook and others around him, overhearing that wholehearted laugh, found themselves smiling. David loved to eat and drink and travel. He loved to dance and make puns and tell jokes and swim in the ocean no matter how cold it was. He was a successful, well-educated man who over the course of his life had worked for and then become the CEO of a popular skin-care line called English Garden Creams. At sixty-three, he was wealthy and planning to retire, even though he still enjoyed the complicated responsibilities essential to manufacturing and selling a fine product. He liked his employees, the challenges, the rivals, the achievements. He enjoyed the work.

His hands were big and elegant. Alison was mesmerized by his hands—how would they feel on her body? She imagined he'd be an enthusiastic lover. And he was.

They both lived in the Boston area, and for three months they spent every free moment together. They attended art gallery openings and concerts. They sat in front of the fire on rainy days reading books. They went dancing and spent the next morning in bed with the Sunday papers. They made each other laugh. They reminisced about their spouses and consoled each other for their losses. They fit each other like two halves of a Fabergé egg.

They met each other's children. First, David took Alison to Boston's Top of the Hub to meet his daughter, Poppy, and his son, Ethan, both in their late thirties, both with all of David's charm. Ethan, who lived an easygoing life as a gentleman farmer in Vermont, had been delighted to see his father with a new love interest. Poppy, not so much. She was married with two children and was in line to take over English Garden Creams when her father retired. And Poppy was ambitious. Alison could almost read her practical thoughts like a ticker tape running across Poppy's sapphire blue eyes: *New woman, marriage, retirement, the business will finally be mine!*

That encounter had been cordial if not delightful, so Alison and David considered it a success. Soon after that, Christmas arrived, held that year in Alison's house in a Boston suburb. Her oldest daughter, Jane, and her husband, Scott, traveled up to stay with Alison for the holidays. Felicity lived in the Boston suburb of Arlington with her two small children and her husband, Noah, so of course they came for Christmas. David stopped by for a drink that Christmas evening and met Alison's small clan. He brought presents for Jane and Felicity—beautifully wrapped gift packages of English Garden Creams products—toys for Alice and Luke, and handsome bottles of Scotch for the men. He also brought champagne for them to share. That evening was great fun.

In January, David asked Alison to marry him and live with him in Boston and wherever else he was. And really, since they were together every morning and night and weekend, it was silly for Alison to retain a house that she scarcely even saw. Alison had sold the home she'd lived in for years, with Mark and the girls, and then with Mark when the girls grew up and got married, and finally alone, in the years after Mark died. She put some family furniture and china into storage and placed the money from the sale of the house into money market accounts and wrote a will dividing all her assets between her two daughters in the event of her death. She was surprised at how free she felt when she said goodbye to the house. It had become for her a place of mourning and loneliness. She happily moved into David's large apartment on Marlborough Street in Boston, and now here she was, hostess and chatelaine of his gorgeous Nantucket summer house and about to marry David in the most fabulous party of her life.

Today, Alison reminded herself, she had her daughters with her for the weekend in David's beach house. She wanted to savor each moment.

"MOM!" Felicity burst into the kitchen. "This house!"

Jane followed more quietly. "It's stunning, Mom."

"I know," Alison agreed. "Let's go out on the deck so you can enjoy the view."

They sat at the round wooden table on wooden chairs softened by cushions—another David touch, this comfort. Steps led down the deck to the tangled mass of wild beach roses and razor-edged beach grass. A well-trodden sandy path wound through the shrubbery down to the golden beach and the deep blue ocean, today rolling calmly toward shore.

"This is heaven," Felicity cooed, resting her feet on another chair and pulling her skirt up to her hips to allow the sun to tan her legs. "Are you so thrilled, Mom?"

"I'm thrilled to be with David. The beach house is wonderful, but it's David who makes me happy."

Felicity eyed Jane. "You look fabulous, Jane. How are you?"

"I'm good. Scott's good. And you look great, too, Filly."

"I do?" Felicity glowed at her sister's compliment. "I don't feel like I look great. I'm so exhausted from the children, I never get enough sleep, I haven't lost my baby weight, and my breasts are all saggy from nursing."

Alison laughed. "Oh, darling! You look beautiful."

"So, Mom," Jane said, "when do we get to hear about your plans for the wedding?"

"After dinner. I've got quite a special show organized." She wanted her daughters to have some time alone together to talk, so she said, "But first, I need to go buy a few groceries. I thought you two might like to take a long walk on the beach."

Jane looked at her watch. "Sure, yes, if we have time."

"We've got all the time in the world. David is in Boston, so it's just the three of us, and I've already made an enormous salad and I thought I'd grill some salmon—"

"Oh, Mom? Um . . ." Felicity blushed. "Instead of salmon, could we have, maybe, steak?"

"But, Filly," Jane said, "you're a vegetarian!"

Felicity was bright red. "Actually, it's Noah who's the vegetarian. He doesn't want me to cook beef or pork or lamb in our kitchen. And of course, he's absolutely right, we do need to think of the animals. But sometimes . . ."

"I'll go to Annye's," Alison suggested. "Their meat is from cattle that drink champagne while they lie there listening to the *Pachelbel's Canon*. They never know a thing."

"Oh, Mom! You act as if I'm demented! And I'm not," Felicity protested. "It's just that—only for the time I'm here—I'd really enjoy eating some meat."

Alison kissed the top of her daughter's head. "Good. I'm off. You girls have a walk on the beach." She rose, biting back a laugh. "And I'll pick up some bacon for breakfast tomorrow."